DAR
WITH
DAY

A book by Mark Vernon

For
Carolina, Lily and Mazy
with all my love.

Back on the street I saw a great big smiling sun
It was a good day and an evil day and all was bright and
new
And it seemed to me that most destruction was being done
By those who could not choose between the two

Amateurs, dilettantes, hacks, cowboys, clones
The streets groan with little Caesars, Napoleons and cunts
With their building blocks and their tiny plastic phones
Counting on their fingers, with crumbs down their fronts

Nick Cave (Darker with the day)

As the 21st Century slowly picks up pace in a blur of meaningless dullness around me I truly feel cut adrift. This modern world where I find myself is way too fake for someone like me as it's driven along with this sickness of social media and self-importance. I find it troubling that everyone tries way too hard to fit in to what are, after all, their own little self-obsessed, media friendly pigeon-holes. It is sad really why so many feel they must live their pitiful lives craving to be accepted or liked over actually being themselves.

I won't do that, I refuse. You can take your faceless celebrity-filled world and stick it up your arse. Myself, I have never felt the need to be popular or even liked and could never get my head around why a person would crave acceptance. Why is it so important to fish for compliments? I actually think the nicest thing ever said to me was "you are such an oddball" and maybe that moment was the first time I was genuinely happy. Well I say that but there was that time when as a sexually confused minor I found a copy of my mother's Cosmopolitan magazine, now that did open a door and why wouldn't it?

So, who am I? I don't fucking know and even if I could explain you wouldn't believe me. One thing for sure is I refuse to accept my role in this reality. I just can't, life has to have more meaning! Saying that there is an egotistical part of me which feels like I have some sort of "calling." Now when I say calling I don't mean a "God asked me to murder all the black folk" type calling but definitely something; I just haven't worked out what yet. As my life approaches its 26th year I guess I am feeling slightly lost and maybe in need of answers. A more weak-minded soul may have found solace in the good book or religion but I will never believe in any sort of God as he, she or it has never given me any reason to. Yes the drugs help and always have, same with the alcohol but still that void, there is always that void.

"You need a good woman!!" I hear you cry. I have heard it

all before and way too many times so "fuck off!" Anyway, what the fuck is a good woman? Sex is sex; I don't need all the bullshit baggage that comes with it. Trust me, you don't want to be telling me about "how your mother didn't hold you," or asking me to be your date for your brother's wedding, fuck off. The last thing I need is some middle-of-the-road token girlfriend changing her status on Facebook to "Attached" accompanied by a selfie of the two of us in a loving embrace. It just isn't going to happen. The long and short of it is that I am more likely to take that selfie stick and use it as a sex toy than play happy families which on the upside, would at least lead to more entertaining status updates.

Don't get me wrong, recently I have been questioning both myself and my life choices a lot. I have even tried to ride the road to happiness or normality but have always ended up feeling the same which is: "Where's the fucking detour?" I can assure you I really have made an effort to change my ways because after all maybe it was me that was wrong and therefore missing out on something special. I mean let's face it you shouldn't knock anything unless you've tried it and I may be a lot of things but a hypocrite I'm not.

So first up there was Kelly, an Aussie temp from work, now she was a fun girl. Although she was very hairy I have to say the sex was great but that was all we had, sex. She loved an afternoon fuckfest, that one, after a few lunchtime pints which was all good apart from her Aussie flat mates. Now like most of these cunts from that part of the world they all seemed to be caveman types with ten of them living under one roof. All they would do was sit in the room next door while we fucked, drinking their beer and watching their sports. I am still convinced to this day they were jacking off as Kelly screamed the roof down as her orgasms were often accompanied with chants of "Aussie Aussie Aussie!" It wasn't long until things came to an inevitable end which wasn't the greatest of surprises to be honest. Of course, it is always sad to say goodbye to great sex but that's life and she was never going to be good enough to invite back to mine. My parting gift was a simple one as running my knife into their inflatable kangaroo that sat so annoyingly on their front porch gave me both peace and closure.

2

Then there was Irish Sara who I met on a bus, now she was a nice girl with beautiful brown eyes and the bonus of her own flat. However, all early potential soon disappeared on our first visit to her bedroom which was like a toy shop bedroom hybrid filled exclusively with cuddly toys. It all started to fall apart when one night she got upset after I shot my load on Paddington Bear. But come on, throw me a fucking bone, this good little Catholic girl didn't want to use a condom and refused to swallow. At times during sex there seemed to be so many limbs it actually felt like I was in the midst of some deranged Roman orgy. Orgies are great just not with a bunch of Ewoks or half the cast of Toy Story. After a few weeks the excitement of sex with a different body was wearing off for me but it was her who finished it after she tried to surprise me with tickets to see IL Divo. I guess she never did see the humour in my "I would prefer to eat my own shit than watch those cunts" comment.

So there you have it, I have tried but normality is just not for me. However you do get what you deserve in this life and now I have become my worst fear, a phony. It has been well over two years now since I sold my soul and started working in the huge corporate world. Just like the other suited lemmings I slotted straight in to become part of the human work cycle. Of course I may have wanted to believe I was different but was I really any different to the masses of people I followed into work every day? OK, so my degree opened the door but it was still me who decided to step through it, which meant I had a choice. So for all those who I criticise or secretly mock I am here working amongst their masses at their sides. My life fucking sucks.

Another Monday morning and life was once again bullying me seemingly crushing me under the heel of some sort of imaginary shit-covered boot. The darkness of my mood hasn't been helped by my lack of sleep whose fault once again lay directly at my door. My weekends now tended to be spent engulfed in solitude losing myself in a world of drink and drugs behind the safety of a locked front door. My only companion was my music which completed my escape from reality but it was turning into a problem. At first it seemed all under control but now these lost weekends had started becoming the norm and a road I felt dangerously at ease upon. Without fail a sort of peace would fall across me in the moments of debauchery. The lyrics and music of the many songs I played would flow through me filling my mind with a roller-coaster of emotions.

I was lost but alive at the same time yet no matter how hard I tried I could feel the corner I had pushed myself into now closing in upon me. As Sunday would draw to a close I would watch the tranquillity slip through my fingers as the week ahead raised its ugly head once again. I had tried to convince myself that I felt happy being isolated, that it suited me, but deep down I knew that wasn't true. In reality I was becoming more estranged from the world around me and this just wasn't healthy.

You often hear a change of scenery is a good thing but the blunt truth was I had found the whole moving to the big city a difficult one. Once I had become settled I had truly become the recluse I had always threatened to be during my student days.

In many ways the University life had prepared me for the move as I would hardly have been described by my fellow students as a social butterfly. The lure of the student bar or social life never appealed to me as I just preferred the company of a good book but for the most part, my free time was taken up by listening to music.

For large chunks of my free time I would find myself spending hours with my new friends: Bowie, Iggy, Bolan and

Reed. It wasn't like there weren't interesting people at the University it was just that I was scared they wouldn't match up to my new-found friends that span around in my room at 33 1/3 RPM. Let's face it, there was no way the faceless fucks from my economics class with their "Meat is murder" or "Amnesty International" badges were ever going to match up with the joy I felt when I was consumed by "Life on Mars" or "Rock'n'Roll Suicide".

On fleeing the family nest my father hadn't so much given me but more like presented me with his record player and a case of old LPs. I am sure he looked upon this moment as some sort of musical rite of passage. I can still remember how he handed them over stating that they would change the way I would look at the world forever. Of course hindsight can be a wonderful thing but now all these years later I know how right he was.

I could never claim or even say I really knew my father but for the most part I think he had been a good man. During my first year at University he had died at the hands of a sudden heart attack. At the time I hadn't been filled so much with grief, rather it had more of a strange numbing effect on me. I would never have described our relationship as close but in the little time we had spent together it did seem like he had understood me albeit without ever expressing it. This now seemed even more apparent by the way the music he had given me was shaping my way of thinking, often leaving me cursing myself that I hadn't played those records earlier. It saddened me knowing that I would never have the chance to sit down with him to discuss the greatness of the music but there was something else.

The first of many I found was tucked inside a copy of Bowie's "Hunky Dory" and like the others was just a simple hand-written note:

Bowie was Bowie and was never afraid to be himself, always be yourself

My father always had problems in expressing himself when

he was alive so finding his note came as quite a shock. I guess this was his attempt at communication as it suddenly became apparent that he had been trying to speak to me or even guide me in his own way. It left me with a curious feeling to think of him writing these notes with an expectancy that I might find them. I was left to wonder what he had been hoping to achieve knowing he would never be able to answer that question. As I delved deep into the records more and more notes started to appear and the plot thickened as it wasn't just messages but also random lyrics; Inside The Smiths´ "The Queen is Dead":

It's easy to laugh, it's easy to hate, it takes guts to be gentle and kind

Inside Pink Floyd´s ""Dark Side of the Moon":

The lunatic is in my head, you raise the blade, you make the change

Then back to messages inside The Stooges´ "Funhouse":

For some what is perceived as strange is normal to the more open minded, express yourself

It just went on and on, with every record revealing its own secret. However, the unearthing of every new note just seemed to cut away at me that little bit more each time. Of course this would never have been my father's intention not that I would ever know that for sure. But the one thing it did achieve was that I felt closer to him now than I had at any time when he'd been alive and for that I was grateful.

Shortly after my father's funeral my mother made the decision to take her own life in a hot bath with a razor blade. The usual "she just couldn't cope being alone" reasoning followed which maybe brought her the dignity she never found when she'd been alive. I knew differently; she had been a weak person and the death of her husband had now given her the excuse to do something which in all honesty had always only been a matter of time in coming.

I knew very little about my parents and how they had met but recognized the fact that they shouldn't ever have been together. Guessing by the close proximity of their wedding anniversary to the date of my birth it would be safe to say that I was unplanned for. My mother spent much of my early childhood in and out of what I now know were mental hospitals or rehab centres. She had an all too familiar tendency for self-destruction with both legal and illegal drugs complimented by a heavy consumption of alcohol. Her mood swings or state of mind would depend a lot on how sober she was but as the years passed being sober occurred less and less which told me one thing and that was that it was never going to end well.

My father's well-timed entry into the computer industry meant we were not a poor family and he had bought a huge ten-bedroom mansion in the countryside. The garden and house were huge but in truth it was a soulless place that for 90% of the time was empty due to my father being away for work and my mother's often unscheduled holidays. As for me I was shipped off to an expensive boarding school where I was left to fend for myself and then raised by an ever-changing number of nannies during the school holidays.

Before I had reached my teens, I had been exposed to more fucked-up shit than the average adult experiences in a whole lifetime. The house where we lived would often be used for crazy sex and swinger parties, not that I knew what that was at the time. As the first guests arrived I would be shuffled into my room with a family bag of crisps and a bottle of Coke and then told not to leave until morning. I would peer out of my bedroom window watching as hordes of people would come and go, once even counting as many as thirty cars parked outside. On occasion boredom would take hold so I would slip out of my room to gawk through the cracks of unclosed doors. The sights of all number of naked bodies tangled in knots raised a curiosity in me although that didn't mean much at the time. Their laughter and joyous moans could only mean one thing and that was that they were having a good time so I didn't really care and left them to it.

My nights at the family home during these occasions came to an abrupt halt after a random act of violence by my father. I think I must have been 11 or 12 when one of his many guests found his way into my room sitting himself on the end of my bed. I still remember it as if it was yesterday, he had pulled back the sheets where I laid naked then had started to stroke my leg all with a charming and calming smile.

Who knows how far that would have gone but for my naked father to come bursting through the bedroom door knocking the man off my bed with a huge right hook. The power of the punch shocked me as the blood sprayed halfway across the room leaving fresh red droplets running down my bedroom mirror. As I sat there from my ringside seat he then proceeded to beat this man while pinning him to the floor. I just watched as if in slow motion as his body quickly went limp leaving both my carpet and his face a bloody mess.

It all happened so fast and I soon found myself being dragged out of bed then from the room. I still had time to catch sight of my father standing up coated in blood and remember how he looked at me as I disappeared around the door giving me a reassuring nod. The events of that evening were never raised or discussed and I still don't know if that man even survived, not that I cared to be honest. My dad was my hero that day, he was great and although the sight of his erection as he had beaten that man may have puzzled me, the look of pure joy in his eye never left me.

3

I remember as a child being fascinated by the word "soul". What was this mystical thing that people talked of and how did it work, what did it even look like? My understanding of the subject grew even more puzzling when I once overheard a visitor to our house talking of how "the eyes were the window to the soul." As a young boy of no more than maybe ten years this just added to the confusion as I would sit sometimes for hours just staring at my eyes in the mirror.

Of course my parents laughed at me thinking no doubt I was being vain or just going through some silly childhood phase but this was different. Apart from the peace I found in my own eyes it was an early life lesson. Hope is a word thrown around a lot these days but that's what I had sitting there for hours, however I soon learnt that hope was a dangerous thing.

I never did see my soul but it did teach me the eyes are powerful things and not to be underestimated. The thing is you can learn a lot about someone just through their eyes, those little moments of indecision, treachery, confidence or my personal favourite, longing.

There is nothing better than longing eyes in my book with all the stories they tell or secrets they hide. Most of the time they are expressing unspoken doubts, maybe something simple like: "what is worse: the heartache or the heartbreak?" That one is easy, a bit of both maybe. But saying that, what's the point of the ache if you are scared of the break? "Throw those dice baby," because there is one thing worse than that ache and that's regret. It's best to know "he or she just didn't want to" rather than think "maybe they would have". Most people don't see this as they don't see at all but I do, I see everything. The saddest thing of it all has to be that 90% of people avoid direct eye contact. It is almost as if they are eyeing some sort of diseased leper and feel it is almost rude to look, but they couldn't be more wrong.

OK this is where I come in as I love the power of the eyes, to make someone squirm, smile, to place some warranted or unwarranted hope or even suggest a possible moment of intimacy. The eyes may not be the windows to our souls but they are weapons and damn good ones at that. I would actually go as far as saying I judge 95% of people I meet on how they look at me during that first contact, fuck all that body language shit, it's all in the eyes.

Now as I sit here I can see why this guy in front of me is struggling and, notwithstanding his numerous other faults, there is just no eye contact. When I refer to "this guy" I mean this big, fat piece of shit standing in front of me trying to lecture a bunch of people who unlike him deserve to be there rather than just are. I would quite happily state for the record with great confidence that the wholesome, bran friendly shit I took this morning had a higher IQ than this fuck. Yes, this fuck, my boss, the one and only William Dilly.

Cock-sucking, Phil-Collins-listening, Daily-Mail-reading, Clarkson-loving, right-wing voting, overweight, sweating, patronising baboon of a man. I guess you may have got the impression I don't like my boss and you would be right. This is the kind of man that enjoys looking at soft porn sites on his office computer yet doesn't have the balls to beat one off and definitely doesn't know how to wipe the history. Maybe I should go scan my cock and balls and then install them as his screen saver, but that wouldn't offend a man like this. He has too many unanswered questions in his private thoughts so surely such an image would only lead to his first in-house orgasm, no sir I will not give you that pleasure.

"OK Lee, would you do us all the pleasure of summarising what we have discussed so far."

Now this is the moment that Mr Dilly thinks he's got me, you see he doesn't like me very much and he presumes that I am not listening as:

1. I haven't been giving him my full attention and

2. He just caught me trying to look up Maria from accounts skirt as she crossed her legs.

Just for the record Maria from accounts is not wearing knickers and her garden needs some tending.

"Yes captain of course."

He won't like the captain reference as it will bring back some painful memories of last month's team bonding paintballing weekend. He smiles politely before continuing.

"OK Lee, we are not on the battlefield now so no need to refer to me as the captain."

Jesus, people actually laughed at that, bunch of sheep. I bet they would laugh even more if Captain Bully Boy and I were to share our secret of my sharp shooting. He won't have forgotten, wait for it, there he goes a little shuffle in his seat and an awkward smile in my direction, I bet those plums are still purple. I knew the Captain reference would lead to a painful flashback but now time to get the crowd back on my side.

"Sorry sir, but may I please take this opportunity to thank you on behalf of all the team here today for a great day out paintballing."

A bunch of faceless cunts applauding, there you go right on cue. Of course, I should have been enjoying that particular weekend in a rather more, shall we say, X-rated manner, but instead found myself stuck with my co-workers in a small field in the middle of nowhere. I guess getting to double barrel "Captain Billy" in his bits and pieces was a plus point though, so it could have been worse.

"Thank you Lee, very kind words and thank you everyone else, but back to the task at hand. Lee, I believe you were about to talk us through the financial forecast."

Of course he still thinks I wasn't listening, but face it, my economics classes at school were more advanced than this shit, except they didn't contain as many mistakes, but still time to turn on the charm.

"Yes of course, first off excellent presentation sir and I believe you are right when you refer to the growth already seen in the first 2 quarters of this year. Indeed, as you say, the future does look bright."

People in power always love having their ego stroked, a little bit of cock-sucking never fails but sometimes a little teeth action, spices things up; I will continue but not so much in the same vein.

"However, as much as I applaud you for your optimism for the remaining part of the year I feel that your figures are way off."

He doesn't like that and he thinks he's going to speak, but this is a roller-coaster he can't get off and this unprepared, non-university graduating, only-got-the-job-as daddy-owns-the firm mother-fucker is about to feel like he brought a knife to a gun fight. Of course, he won't know of today's financial news, how is the hangover boss, I guess the 5 bottles of Chardonnay you drank last night with that large-handed and big-breasted woman from recruitment aren't helping you now. Yes, no doubt you got a grope in the back of the taxi but should have gone with champagne and should have gone with Maria from accounts, she wears no knickers. It was time to go for the knockout.

"Sorry sir, let me stop you, don't get me wrong with the proposed merger with the Anderson Group the future is very bright. However, I do feel today's news that they have won a major contract with the American Government to supply software for the next four years means that this firm are likely to see a huge boost meaning your figures for the next two quarters are way off."

"Of course, you have seen today's news?"

Bang bang you're dead.

4

I tend to think a lot about different things but one thing I am sure of is that life is a truly dull affair. I haven't rushed to this conclusion and feel my opinion is both objective and logical. There is a possibility that I have been wrong all along but up to this point in my life I am still waiting for it to be proven otherwise. It could always be a case of not mixing with the right type of person or even not trying to broaden my horizons but whatever it is, for me it just doesn't really stack up.

Take those thrill-seeker types for example, maybe their lifestyle choice has led them to some sort of utopia and it could be possible they have found something that I have managed to miss all along. Saying that I never could quite understand the appeal of wanting to jump off a mountain with a pair of plastic wings or off a bridge attached to a rubber band, it makes absolutely no sense and I have zero interest in following suit. I find it hard to pinpoint exactly what it is but find it inconceivable how life has become, or maybe always has been, just so structured. Who decided this? And why are we all following this blueprint? We are born, we go to school, we work, we meet someone, have babies, buy a house, raise children, watch those children leave and then we die. In all that time we eat, drink, shit, sleep and fuck, is that really it?

For these reasons of late I have been questioning life a lot. But to be fair most of these questions tend to raise themselves when I am off my face on something. There has always been a beauty in the escape I find in drugs or alcohol that seems to give me a kind of clarity that I never find when sober. It is just that I feel more focused it's as if these substances are able to channel my overactive mind leading me to places that not everyone would understand or want to. I don't like to hide from the voices in my head and if I did my world would be worse for it, for that reason alone I will always fuel them.

It would be fair to say that my experiences so far in this relatively short life have probably given me a slightly different outlook than your average man on the street. A family history with substance abuse and death has no doubt darkened me somewhat, almost certainly leading to me having my own issues.

I remember a few years back now a worrying time occurred during the months after my mother had taken her own life. I had questioned my biological make-up, my genes, as I found a lot of similar thoughts that had no doubt aided in my mother's demise swimming around in my own head.

It had all started with insomnia and my tendency to spend hours watching mindless late-night TV. Sometimes the drivel would have its chosen effect quickly sending me to sleep, whereas on other occasions something silly like a nature show about lions mating habits or an old Frank Sinatra movie would keep me up until morning. Amazing to think back now but this one time a small snippet on a music show awoke me from what I thought at the time was a lifetime of sleep; ironically pushing me towards a more permanent one.

Normally when a rock star chooses to engage with the media these days it is all about publicity, sometimes it's a new record or tour or it's just promoting their self-indulged ego but this time it was different. It may have only been a 5-minute segment and to be honest the band's music had never done it for me so normally I wouldn't have paid much attention. I actually remember reaching for the remote control but then stopping on hearing the words "authenticity" and "values" being mentioned. Suddenly I was engrossed as he continued to talk of intellect in such a manner and with such passion it was refreshing and inspirational.

As the piece rolled on it became almost spellbinding as he launched into a rant about how difficult he had found living in this modern world. For him it seemed to come down to one thing, his superior intelligence and how because of it he found people in general disappointing. I was lapping it up but the part that struck a chord with me more than anything else was how he described the way he found his own company far better than that of others.

14

A kind of sadness entered into his voice as he continued explaining how these feelings had led to a loneliness that at times had him looking for an escape route. I suddenly felt not so alone in the world knowing there were others like me. I could understand him completely as if it was my own voice coming from that screen. What I hadn't realised at the time was that these words had planted a dark seed which was to grow over the following months.

After University broke up for the summer I returned to the family home, which was due to go under the auctioneer's hammer in order to cover my parent's debts. I had always thought my father was a wealthy man but now unfortunately for me it appeared he had been living way above his station. Neither of my parents had bothered with any sort of life insurance so now what remained of their legacy was to be sold meaning my days here would be limited.

The house had a lonely but calming feel to it with 90% of the furniture now under white blankets giving it a kind of purity which seemed ironic seeing as how the place had entertained so decadently. My fondness of being alone had become all-consuming meaning I did very little except sleep, read and take long walks in the surrounding countryside. Sometimes whole days could pass me by without seeing a single soul which with my current mindset suited me just fine. I felt my actions at the time were justified and often I would find myself drifting back to that 5-minute TV interview comparing his issues of high intelligence to those of mine.

It wasn't long before myself self-imposed exile from the world came to an end as the house and all its belongings were sold. The actual day of the auction I had decided to watch from afar as what had been a large chapter of my life ended with one final fall of the auctioneer's hammer. It had been a strange day and I had felt the pity of those who knew who I was follow me wherever I went that morning but in general I did a good job avoiding contact.

As proceedings finally came to a close a representative from the auction house had found me sitting in the garden under a large apple tree. It appeared I would be permitted to stay until the end of the weekend then allowed to remove only my personal items which had been rather coldly tagged. He then handed me a list of things that were no longer legally mine and with a smile informed me I would be able to collect all funds due to me the following Monday morning from their local office.

The money in the end wasn't a lot but would ensure that I enjoyed the rest of my summer break. It didn't take long to disappear and soon I was holed up in one of the dirtiest hotels that Eastern Europe could find spending three weeks strung out on a steady diet of prostitutes, drugs and alcohol. I thought of some of my literary heroes: Thompson, Burroughs, Kerouac and how they would have approved of my behaviour but I knew I was slipping.

Sometimes three or four days would go past without sleep as I wandered the city for some sort of rush. Nobody really spoke English which added to the drama but everything was readily available and cheap. One night I was jumped on the outskirts of the red-light district ending up with a bloody nose and split lip. They got away with no more than thirty Euros but it had been well worth it as the high I had felt when tasting my blood trickle into my mouth was priceless.

By the beginning of my fourth week away the brakes suddenly seemed to be stuck as the drugs were no longer having the same effect as before. I hadn't been able to cum for at least a week now and had started using the girls as drug camels rather than for sex. What I didn't realise was that the night of the 16th of August would long live in the memory and was about to snap me out of this sleepwalk that had consumed me. The date had always had significance to me as when my mum had been alive she would light a candle without fail as it was the anniversary of the death of Elvis. For some reason this memory came flooding back to me as I drove the needle into my vein while watching the strung-out prostitute I was sharing it with lie comatose on the bed.

I wasn't exactly sure how long I had been out but awoke in a bad place with the sweat burning in my eyes. It couldn't have been long as I remembered how the prostitute had still been there, high and out for the count. As I sat up I started to cry as thoughts of my mother, the candle and then Elvis flooded my mind.

Dragging myself from the floor I stumbled across the room towards the door as a sudden desperate urge for some fresh air devoured me. I just had to get out as suddenly it seemed Room 29 had been my home for far too long, it felt small, claustrophobic, more a box than a room.

Pushing the door open I headed out onto the landing and up the stairs. I climbed and climbed until finally reaching the roof kicking open the fire exit with all my strength. As the door swung back the wind instantly hit my face almost like an after tremor from my previous hit.

A moment of serenity washed over me as the lights of the city combined with the cold breeze stopped me in my tracks. I was high up, very high up, and once again my mother's face filled my thoughts as another tear rolled down my face. I slowly edged to the side of the building and onto the ledge. Was this to be it? I dared not look down, the wind was blowing like some sort of big bad wolf trying to push me back. I opened my arms Christ like almost waiting to embrace its cold touch. Once again, I asked the question: was this to be it? At that moment as I faced the moon its light seemed to awaken me, my tears seemed to dry almost instantly and I started to howl.

"Fuck you mother fuck you!"

I must have shouted that ten times before finally stepping back but knew at that second this just wasn't me. My world was never destined to end this way as I was special, I had a calling. Tomorrow I would go home to start on a new path vowing this would be the last time I touched heroin. I should have known better really as it was in my genes, I had been foolish but from now on I would stick to drugs that didn't alter my state of mind so dramatically. My thoughts needed to express themselves not to be polluted with the wrong fuel. This was a wakeup call that I needed and a reminder that my mind was a fragile playground where I would always need to play with care.

5

This Tuesday morning's journey to work on the city's underground system seemed to sum up life in this concrete jungle. Like every other morning or evening there I would sit or stand surrounded by so many unfamiliar yet familiar faces with no one daring to make eye contact or conversation. It was almost as if some unwritten rule punishable by death was being strictly followed. On occasion I would catch the bars of a familiar song escape from an earphone or the flash of a familiar book but like everyone else never broke ranks to engage in conversation.

It had now been four months since IL-Divo-loving Sarah who had been my last sort of relationship and I was strangely starting to feel hollow. I had been alone, or what folk would no doubt classify as a loner, for the best part of my life but had now started feeling for the first time an actual sense of being lonely. I tried to rationalise these feelings but could only come to the conclusion that it was maybe the physical contact I missed more than the sex.

I needed to try harder as my loneliness was now in truth not only guiding me but controlling me. It was hard to really know what to think any more as in reality I only had myself to blame. I guess it was hard to pinpoint what was wrong; I was popular, not bad looking and people found me funny so being lonely shouldn't really be a problem but it was. What was I thinking as there was no way I would shed this fake persona within which I had trapped myself, nobody would like the real me, I just did fit in.

I frequently spent the best part of my work day mentally undressing the female staff. I remember the young blonde temp who had sat across the office from me for a week. To relieve my boredom I had tried to imagine the two of us in the throngs of passion as I took her from behind or came in her face. She had always worn tight short skirts and had a firm set of breasts with her body language giving away a feeling of insecurity so she had been there for the taking. I tried to convince myself I just need to get back on the bike, find my mojo again but a voice inside my head would question everything, in this case "Why would you want to spend time with a woman who had a One Direction poster above her desk?" I just couldn't let it go as it was just so offensive on so many levels. Maybe I was destined to climb into an empty bed forever but how happy I would be doing that now started to worry me.

I continued to beat myself up as I wandered through the office towards the lift. As I pressed the button the doors parted and in front of me stood a young short-haired attractive woman.

"Is it just me or is Sofia a complete cunt?!"

Tuesdays had never seemed so interesting as those lift doors shut tight locking me inside with this lovely creature whose use of the "c" word had given me an instant erection. My feelings of despair seemed to disappear for a second as I was almost lost for words but what came out of my mouth next shocked even me.

"I think I may have just cum."

Her laughter was a thing of beauty that felt more pleasing than insulting. However just as quickly as this short interlude began it was over as once again the lift stopped and she went to leave. I knew we had made a connection which was confirmed when she briefly paused then turned back looking straight at me. Our eyes met as the lift doors slowly slid towards each other, allowing her a split second to once again speak.

"Fuck me, a real person."

As the lift started heading down my mind was awash with all sorts of wonder. My body felt invigorated and I could feel my juices once again starting to flow. Who was this vision and what was she doing in this mainstream world, my mainstream hell? Was this another trapped soul? My morning work was ruined as her words of "Is Sofia a complete cunt" rang through my head like some sort of demonic version of many a faceless 80's chart topper. I need to find this thing, this enchanting-creature, could this be my salvation?

My morning encounter with that dirty mouthed harlot quickly became a distant memory as my afternoon became overloaded with work. It seemed William was trying to punish me for my previous day's smugness or inflict some sort of revenge for "paintball gate." As the clock ticked around towards the end of the day I couldn't wait to escape both this fucking building and this fucking job. A long day of "number monkey" numbness at my desk meant one thing and that was that I needed a drink followed by several more.

I had heard rumours of a new basement bar called Bar Geld that had opened around the corner and was keen to check it out. What made this establishment just so appealing was how it had managed to offend 99% of the office with its no-tie policy which boded well. The stupid bitch on reception did nothing to dismiss the stereotype of blonde dumbness by referring to this new establishment as "racist" until someone explained it was neck ties and not actually Thai people. Maybe here I would find my Nirvana amongst all these faceless, overly lit wine bars; a secret hideaway, maybe a glimmer of hope on my door step? Who was I kidding? Hope, please, hope is a dangerous thing that will never trap me in its web.

6.

I had always felt a sort of comfort in a dimly lit room so Bar Geld had my heart before she even let me see her breasts. Let me see:

1. Music? Check: blues, solid, John Lee Hooker.

2. Beer? Check: a couple of Spanish lagers, Peroni but more importantly no Fosters or "wife beater."

3. Clientele? A few cool cats, no ties and no one from the office, perfect.

4. Personal space? Check: plenty of room, dark corners and wait, the girl from the lift sitting alone reading a book, maybe God does exist after all.

I go with the Spanish "Estrella" and then make a beeline for a dark corner with a certain optimism that my day will end better than it started. I confidently approach her table knowing my first impression is crucial.

"So is Sophie still a complete cunt?"

Maybe this is the greatest chat-up line of all time and I can already tell she is impressed. As I peer at her through the dim light she looks so radiant and I pause allowing her time to speak.

"You do know that some women find the C word very offensive? But for the record let it be noted that I am not one of them and that yes, Sophie is still a complete cunt."

My heart races as she, as before, doesn't break eye contact, waiting for my reply. Jesus, she is reading "The Wasp Factory" by Iain Banks, I fucking love that book. I wonder if she likes to torture insects, now that would be a turn on. I feel a movement in my lower regions, fuck these fucking work chinos are going to leave me exposed.

"Hello, anyone there? Or have you just cum again?"

Her directness is such a turn-on and after my great start my form is suddenly dipping.

"No, I mean... not yet."

Bollocks. I am stalling. This is a very different sort of beast I am faced with and I am feeling tense yet at the same time her dirty smile is somewhat comforting. I know I can't let this moment slip through my fingers, I have to strike, the next five minutes could shape my life forever, damn you hope there you go again. But no, this feels different I have that kind of feeling. I glance down at her book which now lies face down on the table, then begins to speak.

"The Wasp Factory´, I fucking love that book, I think I must have read it at least 30 times it's had quite the influence. I can't speak for you but as a kid I would sit around for hours and torture insects, I found a kind of peace in those moments. But saying that nothing was quite like the day I discovered I could burn them with a magnifying glass, it was quite liberating you know, sexually arousing even."

And that is where it started, that night I think I may have had real sex for the first time. Our bodies connected like I had never experienced before and my mind felt free of all its fears. A strange type of tranquillity washed over me as I felt her alcohol fuelled body spasm as she climaxed. In a strange way the manner in which her vagina locked and tensed against my cock during those rushes of passion reminded me of my lonely youth. It was as if she was the spider and I was the first beam of sunlight passing through the magnifying glass, curling it up while cutting it apart. This was beauty, pure joy, glory, hallelujah.

I felt strange for a few days as I actually started to feel more joy than anger for the first time, maybe ever. It wasn't only the fact that we were fucking and fucking a lot which maybe would fulfil a simpler soul, it was just something else. I always knew I had been different but now it dawned on me how alone I had always felt and suddenly that wasn't a place I wanted to return to. Here it seemed I had found someone, albeit in the most unusual of places who could maybe understand me. Could I finally let my mask slip?

The questioning of myself began once again and for a few moments panic filled my mind as I started to maybe feel hope. I was scared to be happy as I didn't know that as a reality, it felt good but I wasn't certain if it was real. The worse thing was there was nothing I could do about it; I was just being swept along. Who would be there when it all came crashing down? I thought of my mother and her suicide; had she ever felt a non-chemical or non-alcohol induced happiness? I knew I had my own issues but would the current world be prepared for the real me? Was she prepared? Was even I?

One thing for certain was that I couldn't depend solely on hope and had to try to shape my or our destinies. To do that I had to believe that she was like me and that we had been cut from the same sort of cloth. One thing for certain was we were not following the other lemmings on their long walk to the cliff, we were different.

7

I wouldn't say that I changed but the arrival of Nellie Brown in my life had certainly made me feel more complete and for two full weeks now we had been inseparable. Everything had seemed to click as we spent just as many hours discussing books, films, lyrics, music and life as we did fucking. I wondered how many others there must be moving through the world never connecting with one another and I felt a moment of pity for them, obviously not for too long as surely pity is a weakness.

Our whirlwind two weeks suddenly hit the brakes as Nellie found out her grandfather had died and she was summoned to take part in the expected family grieving process. After a rather spectacular blow job in the photocopying room she had headed back upstairs and on returning to my desk I found a vinyl copy of Frank Zappa's "Hot Rats" and a simple note:

My Grandfather died, no worries, I had been waiting for that call, see you in a couple of days:

HOT MEAT HOT RATS
HOT ZITS
HOT CHEST HOT RITZ
HOT ROOTS
HOT SOOTS

Willie the Pimp will rock your world

The whole grieving process is something I never got my head around and no doubt it will always puzzle me until I finally cash in my own chips. All those family members or so-called friends who come out of the woodwork as it's the "right thing to do." If you don't like a person and he or she dies then why make the fucking effort to grieve or to say "you're sorry for the loss" when you're obviously not, they wouldn't have wanted you there anyway. Then there is the religious bollocks and just like a wedding why do people need to get those fuckers involved. I have news for you: you don't. Just tell those tax-dodging, kiddie-fiddling, wannabe do-gooders to FUCK OFF!!

On my way home that night I sat in silence as normal on the train thinking about Nellie. It was funny how she had referred her mother as a "fucking freak." I had never told anyone about my parents but saying that I had never been close enough to anyone to do so.

I gave a little laugh out loud as I recalled how she had explained to me why she had been called Nellie.

"Yeah my mother was a drugged-up hippy weirdo and named me Petronilla after some Saint. That's right a fucking saint who in this case was a 1st century Virgin Martyr, go figure that shit. You would think she was someone special but no, this silly bitch died after a hunger strike, some shit about refusing to marry a pagan king. I mean come on, I am not having that fucking bollocks following me around all my life so I shortened it to Nellie."

My father had named me Lee after Lee Marvin the actor as he had loved his song "Wandering Star." I knew even less about Lee Marvin than I knew about my father which was saying something. I had however read about something called "The Sons of Lee Marvin," which was some sort of secret society created by the film director Jim Jarmusch.

I had loved his movie "Broken Flowers," and once read an interview where he talked about this very society. Basically it was a fictional club of people who all had to have a physical resemblance to Lee Marvin to be included, so we got: Tom Waits, Neil Young, Josh Brolin, Nick Cave, Iggy Pop and Jarmusch himself. I guess that was kind of cool as all the members were people I loved and it kind of gave my name its own personal seal of approval.

8.

For me the gym has always been an important part of my weekly routine as I look for alternative ways to kill the pain the stress of my daily life brings me. Apart from my alcohol or drug-fuelled moments this is perhaps the only thing I have that allows me to escape normality. There is a certain type of joy I find in those moments of pain as I push my body to its limits. Also it was apparent that if I was to continue my high standard of fucking it would be best not to neglect this part of life; plus a new toy had arrived in the post for me that day that I was dying to try out.

At times I draw from Bret Easton Ellis' lead character in "American Psycho" as like Mr Bateman I believe the importance of appearance shouldn't be underestimated. Clichés are clichés but it is true when people say that "a healthy body leads to a healthy mind". It's funny really as for me American Psycho is maybe the greatest book ever written so it makes me laugh when I hear that kids at school are still studying Shakespeare or Chaucer. Not only is Easton Ellis' work far superior in all departments it would also surely better prepare them for the demands of this flawed modern world. With the exception of Mr Bateman's taste in music which in truth should lead to him turning the chainsaw on himself, I believe that this book could, with a few touches here and there, be marketed as a life guide.

The gym I am forced to attend could be used as a metaphor for all I hate about life. Overloaded with faceless fucks in Lycra and designer sportswear, working out to loud generic dance music on space-age machines you need a degree to operate. I don't mind a bit of camel toe and there is plenty of that on display but the place has a weird kind of dark meat-market sexual energy vibe going on. It's as though everyone is window shopping while hoping to be noticed as they fill their wank banks.

It's a pain in the arse sharing the place with my co-workers but to be honest it can be quite amusing. It always tickles me to see John from accounts drooling at Sofia from marketing´s extremely well-shaped, sweat-covered torso as he battles not to get

27

an erection in his cycling shorts. That's fine, they all deserve each other but then there are all the white-teethed, hyperactive personal trainers. Why is it that they all have names like Andy, Johnny and Crystal? Why are they always so happy? Is there like a hidden opium den next to the spinning room that I don't know about?

To say I am forced to attend this place would be pushing it as I go there under on my own free will and receive a nice corporate discount. However, I feel my days at this particular establishment may be numbered as it can only be a matter of time before my bitterness and resentment for my fellow gym rats boils over.

I guess I just can't help it but I have come to see myself as some sort of vigilante for gym justice. It had only been a month since my first chance to act but the peace and solace I had gained from that moment still coursed through my veins. It's quite simple really if you are coming to the gym leave your fucking phone in the locker. There is nothing worse than a bunch of fat fucks walking on the running machines as they yap into their fucking phones. For starters, it's called a running machine so why the fuck are you walking and secondly, we don't want to hear your mundane conversation especially about how you are at the gym.

Well, one day enough was enough and I knew for the sake of common decency I would be forced to act in some shape or form against these despicable creatures. I had already set the punishable mark and referred to it as "running machine bingo." The bingo was quite simple; At least three of the running machines had to be occupied by three fat people all walking and all using their mobile phones, and that day the line had been crossed.

It didn't take much really just a small squeeze of my water bottle in the direction of an uncovered power socket and BANG! I didn't even have to turn back to look as I headed to the changing rooms with a smile on my face letting the trip switch and gravity take care of business, TIMBER! Maybe a few innocent gym users were hurt but that was just collateral damage and the ambulance parked outside as I left that day made me feel good. But that was nothing compared to the satisfaction I got over the following days as I learnt how the "mysterious power cut" at the gym had led to: one broken nose, a broken arm, some severe grazing and a couple of broken IPhones, nice, BINGO!

Today punishment was once again on my mind and I just hoped my attended target wasn't going to let me down. Of course they weren't, these types of people are just as predictable as they are vile and then there it was; That white Audi parked in the disabled spot again which by my counting made three days in a row and three times in my book means you're out.

I reached into my gym bag for what bartenders or chefs refer to as a "channel knife." OK, so this was not the type of equipment you'd expect your normal office worker to carry but then there was nothing normal about me. I had been fascinated by this strange blade since seeing a barman in New York use it so artfully to peel a lemon while preparing a cocktail called a "Horse's Neck." That night I actually had the chance to steal it but felt that it was wrong to deny a master a tool of his trade. So shortly after my return from the Big Apple I picked up my own, courtesy of EBay, and was now on the verge of giving it a test drive. The knife is designed for cutting channels as its name suggests but those channels are normally cut in fruit and veg, tonight it was time to see how it worked on an Audi.

The first run took off a metre strip of sheet steel and white paint as the knife sang with joy as it cut into the surface almost bringing a tear to my eye. Within minutes my work was almost done, it was hardly a Picasso but with every separate panel now showing its own battle scar it was, in its own small way a beautiful piece of art. Once again I reached into my bag but this time I pulled out a disabled sticker which I stuck in the middle of the windscreen, I think they would get the message.

The whole concept of right or wrong wasn't mine to decide, who was I to hand out punishment or commit random acts of revenge? But for me the modern world had lost its moral core and some balance needed to be restored. The ability to respect your fellow human beings was being lost in this world of social media, status updates, plastic lives and self-importance, but I refused to let it consume me. For me it came down to one basic human flaw and that was the inability to understand and adhere to the concept of respect. I now saw myself as a kind of "punisher" to those who had lost their way and when time permitted I intended to judge them and then sentence them in my own inevitable way.

I had always drawn strength and inspiration from a heart-warming story I had once come across online. It was a tale about a young Australian man called Drew who had decided to find himself by travelling the world. Of course tales of travel are often inspiring yarns but this one had a twist. During Drew's time passing through India he had been visiting a sacred temple where his moment of karma had been stolen from him by what can only be described as a selfish act. On reaching the top of the highest tower his moment of joy was ruined as he was confronted with, carved into one of the scared walls, the words:

"Thomas and Anita, Maysville, Kentucky were here."

Now this is the part I like because he didn't just shake his head in despair at the human race, he actually decided to do something about it. As his around-the-world trip reached Stateside, with a little help from the internet he managed to track down those dumb fucks and so took a little detour. Luckily for him and unfortunately for Thomas & Anita, Maysville was a small town so it didn't take him long to locate their house. During that night he carved away maybe 250 times into their various cars, walls, doors, in fact anything he could get his hands on the words:

"Drew from Australia was here."

He was eventually arrested early the following morning when the police spotted him on their neighbourhood rounds as he was trying to burn his message into the front lawn. I am not sure of the aftermath of this tale or even what happened to the young man but one thing I am sure of is that the world would be a better place with more people like Drew.

30

9.

She was back and launched into a rant even before we had a chance to light our first cigarette after the good-to-see-you again sex.

"My half-sister for a start, where the fuck has she been for the last 6 years of his fucking life? Well judging by her triple chin and XXXL Funeral outfit I would guess eating. This fucking cunt lived no more than 3 miles down the road from our Grandfather yet had visited him twice in the last 4 years. Fuck you and your fucking tears, what a stupid fake bitch, she even tried to hug me and her limp-dick husband shake my hand all very inappropriate."

I had felt the anger in the way she had fucked me that afternoon and then experienced a certain relief in the fact that I had no close family or siblings. Both my parents' funerals had been attended by no more than half a dozen people. You had to ask yourself where were all their so-called friends? These people that I had seen in various states of undress over the years had disappeared just as quickly as they'd arrived.

The need for friends is something I have never subscribed to. I understand the concept of a sexual partner as there is a certain need for human contact in the physical sense but friends no; it's just that humans are so flawed. For this reason alone, why take the risk of letting someone in? Chances are they will only let you down, which is just pure and simple human nature. I have never been unpopular or aloof but also have never had a true friend, yes, many an acquaintance but never what the general consensus would refer to as a pal or a mate. That had always been my stance up until now as Nellie had me rethinking my whole approach to letting someone in.

I had always been honest with myself, it was just that I had never clicked with anyone before and now I was finding it all a bit confusing. Normally in the past even with my regular and more compatible sexual partners I had felt no need to stick around once our sexual transaction was finished. On occasion I had been known to linger if the hour dictated so but without fail it would lead to mundane conversation about nothing which would leave me questioning why I had fucked them in the first place.

I am far from ugly and have never struggled to find sex when needed. My quiet and sometimes mysterious approach to life must have given off some sort of vibe to the ladies as I never had to chase it. Quite often I would find strange women of all shapes, sizes, nationalities and ages starting conversations with me on the bus or even the "Mecca of silence", the train. I had been asked out more times than I could remember and had become something of an expert in the "meet a stranger in some random place" one-night stand. I had discovered quite quickly that a large city could be a lonely place at times and even more so for the single female. Besides, we all needed a bit of human contact now and again so for me it was just a case of providing a service with benefits.

Nellie was different; I had known this since our first encounter in that lift and then later that day in the bar. It wasn't just her body language or the way she talked, it was that she never broke eye contact. I had looked into those dark brown eyes and she had never looked away, there was an instant connection. But where did we go from here? I may have had feelings for a fellow human being for the first time in my life and was not sure what my next move would be as I was scared of the responsibility of actually caring about someone.

My thought process was broken as Nellie continued with her rant.

"This fucking funeral, my grandfather was just like me you know, nobody understood him. For the most part my fucking family just left him alone to rot in that old people's home hoping every time the phone rang it carried the news he had finally passed. I bet they were all secretly happy he died knowing that they wouldn't have to fork out any more for his care."

She was sharing. I guess this is what people did. They offloaded their anger. There wasn't much to do but sit there and listen so that's exactly what I did.

"But you know what, I embraced his final years. At least once a month I would make that long shitty train journey just to pass a few hours with him. For fuck´s sake, this was the man who brought Johnny Cash into my life, it was the least I could fucking do!!!"

The ranting stopped and there was a sudden pause. Should I say something? Was I meant to hold her? She had turned her head to the ceiling then back again, her eyes once more connecting with mine. In that split second the anger seemed to have left to be replaced by a glazed but almost focused look as her voice regained its normal tone.

"It was just so fake; these so-called precious moments of family unity and togetherness after he died just filled me with hatred and resentment. I hate everything, I actually wished they all had died and I had been there alone, now that would have made me happy. But life doesn't work like that, does it, and like always I find myself pointing an all too familiar finger at everything that is wrong with mankind. I know you would have felt the same, I can feel it in you and I could see it in your eyes the first moment we met."

Her openness had taken me aback as I wasn't used to hearing someone be so honest. My heart had started to race as I had drunk in her anger but then this, could we be kindred spirits? I felt compelled to suddenly open up.

"I hate everything, my dad died, my mum killed herself and 99% of people I meet I instantly detest. I constantly question this shallow world we live in and feel extremely uncomfortable living amongst people who will never be my intellectual equal."

"Disappointment doesn't even come close to describing how I feel about life, I want to change it and most of all I want to

33

punish those who fail to understand common moral decency. I recently allowed my thoughts to come to practice in the form of revenge. I have taken great pleasure from the fact I have hurt people and although I am yet to kill I feel it is an act I am well capable of. For me it's not a question of if it will happen, just a question of time until it does. The first time I looked into your eyes I saw something and it was something that was new to me, something more than hope, I saw someone to believe in."

She reached forward taking my hand in hers then started to stroke it softly as we looked silently into each other's eyes. As she smiled I found myself unexpectedly lost yet smiled back which I guess instinctively lead to her pulling me close. It felt good; a true moment of affection and something I had never experienced before. I couldn't remember my mother or father ever hugging me and was actually surprised at the warmth of the moment. I guess I was no longer alone.

The following morning the bright sun awoke me through the open curtains as it swept through the room. I felt its heat run across my skin, which felt good but then a sudden sense of loss filled me: Nellie had gone. My whole world seemed to crash in upon me in that split second as I now realised I was alone.

My emotions were hijacking my thought process as a panic started to fill me. I calmed myself with a few deep breaths and my more logical approach to life seemed to return. I had never been close to anyone or even considered it, so this was something where I had no previous experience. Maybe letting someone into my world or even giving them a glimpse of it had been too much. I had let my mask slip for a moment so last night's honesty and words had been a mistake, hence the empty bed. I was obviously being irrational but life just had a way of lifting you up before bringing back down to down earth with a crash. I had always had a problem of opening up to anyone so what had made this girl so different? I tried to recall my exact words but couldn't as my mind could only focus on the closeness I had felt when she had stroked my hand, then held me in her arms.

I guess I'd always known in the back of my head the importance of having some sort of human contact but it wasn't until last night that it dawned on me how important that actually was. I had felt something that had been new and now a realisation that human contact was more than just physical was a reality. It was strange but now as I laid there I actually felt scared of being alone which in itself was ironic. Throughout my whole life I had basically rejected anyone who tried to get close to me, sometimes quite deliberately, and I guess at other times just out of habit. My parents had never shown any sort of affection towards me so I just imagined that was how it was meant to be. Growing up there had never been a reason to question this as it had always felt comfortable. Of course, as a young boy there had been times when I had made friends at school but my fondest and happiest memories of that time were of playing alone. It was silly really thinking that far back as at that age you're not really discussing anything of great value, well not until you discover masturbation.

The closest I got to knowing anyone properly would have been Brenda. I was about 13 at the time and that summer she came to live with us as my Nanny for maybe a month. This had been the year of the Party incident involving my father and his naked moment of great violence. So it seemed strange at 13 I would have needed a nanny as I was almost a man and maybe more wise to the world than poor old Brenda. Puberty had come early to me at 12 so nights of masturbation had become common practice and the small collection of pornography I obtained at the previous term at school was being well used. First it was the pictures that got me going but then I found the beauty in the stories or letters, giving my masturbation time a more imaginative edge. That was until Brenda.

She couldn't have been more than 17 which even questioned the legality of her being allowed to look after me in the first place. I was not complaining as suddenly the images of reader's wives and shaven pussies on printed pages gave way to Brenda being the subject of my nightly orgasms. During her first week I sneaked into her room in the middle of the night to find her sleeping naked which progressed into me stealing a pair of her used knickers and on one occasion actually smelling her hair.

That summer had seemed more joyful with Brenda around; she would take me on long walks and talk to me about life. In the most part the conversation was pure crap but I just pretended to listen while surveying the curves of her body which were far more interesting than her dreams of backpacking around Europe. Her breasts, although small, were so shapely pushing out against her tight T-shirts, her legs long and that ass, wow. She knew I liked her and would smile at me when she caught me staring at her body. This led to her beginning to tease me with her short skirts and even tighter t-shirts obviously trying to boost her ego but also meaning I would count the seconds until my nightly pilgrimage.

I could hear the groaning before I had even reached her bedroom door. Like usual I hoped she would have been sleeping naked and had brought a pair of scissors with me to claim a locket of her hair. But as she came into view I found her spread eagled on the bed her hand firmly lodged between her legs. The light was poor on the landing which allowed me to watch and enjoy as she reached her climax. The show had been so spectacular that I had almost cum myself without even having to touch my penis.

I returned to my room hot and flustered then reached under my pillow for Brenda's knickers. Lying myself on the bed I kicked off my shorts and went at it, I never even heard her arrive.

"I guess it's my turn to watch this time."

The sound of Brenda's voice froze me for a second but then I turned my head to the door where our eyes met. There she was standing in the half-light wearing just her underwear. I made no effort to remove my hand from my penis or her panties from my face, I wanted to say something but she beat me to it.

"Well don't stop on my behalf."

I don't know what came over me but I did just that and shutting my eyes went back to my business. It didn't take long to finish as the previous show Brenda had put on had already left me on the verge. Opening my eyes I turned to the door expecting to meet her eyes again but she was gone, I don't know how long she had waited but it didn't matter, tomorrow would prove to be an interesting day.

The following morning I ate breakfast alone like most days as my parents had both been away. I awaited the arrival of Brenda not knowing what to expect but just the thought of last night's events were turning me a shade of red. Then there she was greeting me like she did every morning before excusing herself to take care of the washing. Just her appearance in the kitchen had been enough to arouse me but now she was gone almost as quickly as she'd arrived making me think that maybe I had dreamt the whole thing.

That afternoon we walked through the woods once again with Brenda outlining her plans for the Italian leg of her trip. We often stopped at a small brook and today was no different so as I sat I reached into my backpack to pull out my water bottle. Taking a long drink I turned to hand it to Brenda but as I looked up she was stood over me with her shirt open. It was heavenly, she was wearing no bra and the breasts I had envisioned on many an occasion were now a 3D reality. She smiled and then broke the silence.

"Someone has been a bad boy, a peeping Tom, a panty sniffer."

My face not for the first time today turned a shade of red and I looked away in embarrassment as I now knew it hadn't been a dream after all. Before I had a chance to even go fully red I felt her hand reach under my chin, lifting my head. Then pressing her lips against mine she forced her tongue inside my mouth, guiding my hand up to cradle one of her breasts. I became instantly hard which she instinctively knew, unbuttoning my trousers, then reaching inside and clasping my cock with her soft hand. It wouldn't have taken long maybe 5 strokes and as I gave out a small groan she started to laugh, then spoke.

"It looks like you and I have a dirty secret to share now, a secret I am sure your father would just love to hear?"

She obviously didn't know my father or had attended one of his famous parties so to be honest she would have had no idea what he would have thought. Anyway, the empty threat somehow tickled her as she gave out what could only be described as a callous-sounding laugh before leaning forward once again giving me a soft kiss on the check before whispering in my ear.

"To be continued."

A funny feeling once again filled me as I tried to digest her words while being treated to a full frontal of her breasts. Before I could get a handle on anything or even speak she was gone, disappearing into the woods in front of me. I was just left there on that tree stump to contemplate what had just occurred still with my trousers unbuttoned and my cock out. I still remember how I had just sat there with a huge grin across my face as I relived my first non-self-performed orgasm. As I walked slowly back through the woods I knew I wanted more but this time I desired to be the hunter not the prey.

I didn't see much of Brenda for the rest of the day as she was preparing my parent's room for their return at the weekend. My mind however wasn't so much focused on seeing my family for a few days but more on what sort of continuation Brenda had in mind.

Even in this day and age some people still like to save their virginity to the day of their wedding night guarding it like a precious family jewel. Away from this fairy tale the majority will either take part in the normal courting process until the deed is done or just lose it in a drunken one-night stand. The whole sex thing with Nellie had been confusing me somewhat as fucking for me had always been nothing more than a release, yet with her I felt more.

The short time I spent with Brenda that summer   taught me a lot, especially cunnilingus. We had both taken advantage of our youthful energy as we had fucked and fucked. There was nothing loving about it, it was just two people fucking, albeit one a minor. For me it was a crash course in sex and Brenda would guide me where my tongue, fingers or penis should be, often chastising me if she missed her orgasm. This introduction to sex was a dream but maybe something that shaped me in the wrong way as sex was just that, sex, well it was until now. My thoughts of Brenda and that summer were lost as I heard someone at the front door and as it shut Nellie's voice.

"Hello."

Picking myself up off the bed I headed into the living room where Nellie stood with 2 large suitcases. A type of euphoria raced through my body as if it knew that from that instant my world was going to be a better place. I could never have said that I had been waiting for this kind of moment all of my life as I never knew such moments even existed, but it felt right. Happiness was something I had only ever experienced through substances or in the ecstasy I found in music and perhaps more recently revenge. But here I was standing naked in front of this girl only feeling one thing: that she completed me. Putting down her cases she raised her head slowly, first nervously looking away and then straight at me. She paused to take a breath, then licking her lips began to speak.

"I know this may seem a bit rash or even mad, but it just feels so right Lee, I am a cold calculating bitch but this is different, maybe two negatives do make a positive, there is no other way to say it: you complete me."

Without doubt, this was the single most joyous moment of my life, but suddenly my head was filled with flashing images of the past trying to gatecrash the party. There was my father's face as he beat that man on my bedroom floor, my mother's sullen eyes as she passed out in front of me, then Brenda's pussy as she pushed my head towards it, and that ledge on top of that building. Jesus, how close had I been to ending it? Why was I thinking of these things? This was meant to be happiness.

"Lee, for fuck´s sake! Will you say something if only to tell me to fuck off!"

The sound of her voice brought me back to the present. I didn't care anymore; the past was the past and I was in the moment. I rushed forward taking her in my arms, lifting her from her feet and it felt joyous. I was alive.

11

Life, it seemed was full of surprises, but to think that I was now cohabiting with someone had truly come out of the blue. I needed to believe this would work as I was well aware that it was something that just a few weeks previously I would have dismissed as fucking preposterous. The living together would no doubt bring many highs and lows, but the idea of sharing intimate thoughts or desires scared me as much as it excited me. Just where these kinds of conversations could lead it was hard to say, as for the both of us it would be a step into the unknown. Guidelines would need to be set but then neither of us had a good track record when it came to following rules. The best course of action was to keep it simple, so for starters, the use of the "L" word was out, prohibited, confined to fairy tales. We both agreed that the foundations for a successful relationship was to be open with each other when it came to needs, wants and desires. Then last but not least it was essential that honesty was always the key no matter how much it may hurt, and we promised to abide by this.

It was strange but it was as if we were on the same page from the very first moment our lips and bodies had connected. I thought back to my childhood obsession with the soul but peering into her eyes I sensed hers. She would often ask jokingly "if her voodoo was working" and I believed it was as she certainly had me under her spell. It was all in those beautiful dark brown eyes, there was something there. I couldn't see it but I knew it was there, I just felt it and it was making me stronger.

Nellie in her own words had been living under a different skin for far too long but seemed more than at ease to shed it in my presence. It was no surprise really that the both of us had our own work skins or camouflage, which had become almost comfortable lies in our day-to-day struggles around the office. Away from that stale, stagnant place we were very different people, yes, we blended into that mundane world and hated ourselves for it, but we knew it was a necessary evil. The question was how to turn our perceived office blandness to our advantage; plans and strategies would have to be formulated.

One of the greatest things about Nellie was her bluntness; there was no fishing around a subject for her as she just came out with exactly what she was thinking. It had now been two nights since she had arrived and half way through a litre of vodka led to one such moment.

"Remember when you said you were capable of killing someone, did you really mean it?"

I had wondered when this subject would be raised again and after recent developments knew it was going to be sooner rather than later. My words still rang in my ears and a slight chill ran through my body as I recalled the sadness I had felt that morning when confronted by an empty bed. I had regretted being so honest at the time but now realised that moment had been key to the position where I found myself today. I went to speak but with a raise of one of her hands she stopped me.

"Look, this is going to sound cheesy but just hear me out."

She paused, looking at me for some sort of reassurance. I obliged with a nod, then a smile, which I could see pleased her as she reached across and took my hand before continuing.

"OK, when I said the other morning that you complete me I meant that in every possible sense. I've never believed in fate but that day in the lift, then later in the bar, was just that. I am not some stupid schoolgirl with a silly crush so this shouldn't feel right to me, but it just does. It's as if I have brought some sort of ticket for this ride and as long as we are riding it together I ain't looking to get off. For far too long I have been this fucking rudderless boat on a sea to nowhere which in truth has led to some dark places. I won't lie to you because there have been times I have come close to ending it, very close in fact, but every time a voice inside me tells me no, and I am starting to think that it's all been for this. I see the same in you, the pain, it's hidden in those eyes, I feel it in you when you fuck me, so don't even try to disagree. This world has become a vile place and I feel constantly surrounded by these types of creatures that need to be punished or eradicated. Jesus, just the sight of these worthless shits makes me want to vomit. So go ahead Lee and tell me I'm wrong because I'm not, we are cut from the same type of cloth."

It was interesting and refreshing to hear such powerful honesty delivered with so much calm and poise.

"No problem Nellie I'm in. Who are we killing first?"

I wouldn't have said that there had been an air of tension to lift, but I felt our openness had filled us both with a kind of reassurance we had obviously craved. What path this might lead us down only time would tell, but I could already feel a sort of anticipation tinkling inside of me. Nellie looked radiant in the morning light.

"I bet like me you've always kept a shitlist? Because if we are looking for a starting point I think I can come up with some names that could really do with some overdue attention."

Just the thought of Nellie having such a list excited me. It just seemed so simple, yet made complete sense. While this may have worked for her, I had never really had my own "shitlist", as I had always been more impulsive than structured. Although the concept tickled my interest, I wasn't sure there would be a big enough piece of paper if I put my mind to compiling such a thing.

The word "shitlist", however, had stayed with me since the first time I heard The L7 song of the same name. The grunge movement had been yet another great era of music I had missed out on due to my age. While this short lived musical period had been remembered for Pearl Jam, Soundgarden and Nirvana, I much preferred the female bands of the time. Both Hole and L7 had made great strides for feminism with an attitude which was maybe more punk than grunge. I had once read a piece about the lead singer of L7, who had removed her tampon while on stage throwing it into the crowd with the immortal words: "Eat my used tampon, fuckers." This was what music was all about, rebellion, and it was hard to imagine one of today's so-called stars like Adele or Taylor Swift doing the same.

Her words of us being "cut from the same cloth" had never rang truer as it now was becoming apparent we were one person living in two separate bodies. My mind had always been a ticking clock of revenge "tick-tocking" away in my head, waiting for the alarm to sound. All my doubts that maybe I was just fucked up and on the verge of going crazy had now been put to rest as I had someone else to share this burden I carried. We would walk through this door together and I was pretty sure the world would be a better place for it. Plans would need to be forged, which I had no doubt would lead to the kind of results that up to now I had only secretly lusted after, tick tock.

All "shitlists" apart, it was very important we talked through our goals and established a set of rules otherwise there was a potential for it to all go horribly wrong. Our actions needed to be cold and calculated but without repercussions for ourselves. As appealing as wiping out a whole train carriage of faceless fucks on their way to work one morning seemed, I now knew that just wouldn't be right. Not everyone was as they appeared on the surface, we were an example of that, and so we would have to be sure that whatever actions were taken were completely justifiable.

The troubling question for me was: how does one make such a set of rules? I had come to detest this modern world so much I felt I could perhaps justify a culling on biblical levels. I often wondered if I had been born in the wrong decade and for me, my musical tastes, with a few exceptions, had more or less confirmed this. I wish I had been there as punk exploded to fight against the establishment or to see the blood of Altamont as the Stones singled handed killed off flower power. Unfortunately it was the here and now that I had been dealt, so I just needed to grin and bear it and soldier on. This was easier said than done, as trying to ignore the commercially driven masses that marched to a soulless, manufactured soundtrack was difficult. I knew it wasn't their fault, so maybe the man on the street shouldn't be blamed, but the meaningless dullness of their lives just summed up this lost generation, so they had to be held at least somewhat responsible.

44

The rules were proving to be a lot more difficult to compile than we originally thought so we decided to head out in hope of clarity or even inspiration. The neighbourhood I or now we lived in summed up this city almost perfectly as it was neither good nor bad. It was a fair mix of professional and working-class people sprinkled with asylum seekers and various groups of immigrants. Yes, the streets were tree-lined but you still had your alcoholic bums drinking from brown paper bags at the bus stop, and as we passed one such "down and out", Nellie gave me a mischievous look before speaking.

"Let's kill one of these smelly motherfuckers just to get the feel for it. Come on, it's not like they will be missed."

As much as I was keen to get started the thought of killing one of these lost souls filled me with sadness. I had always had a fascination with these homeless street wanderers as at times they seemed far more at peace than the working sheep that queued for the bus at my side on a daily basis. The thing was there was nothing fake about them, they were just what they were, and I for one felt no need to do them any sort of harm. I couldn't be sure if Nellie was joking or not so merely laughed off her comment and anyway it felt like a good time to grab a drink.

I don't think I had actually gone out in my neighbourhood or felt the need to in all the time I had lived here. I was never one for socialising, so if I did go out, it tended to be closer to work with the aim of killing the pain of the day as quickly as possible rather than to talk bollocks with strangers. True, I liked a drink, but I also preferred to drink alone as the answers to life for me were often found at the bottom of an empty glass. To the best of my knowledge I was a good drunk, but just one who wanted to be left the fuck alone, so the idea of going out with Nellie to a public place suddenly felt strange. Like me, Nellie liked to drink but apart from that first time we met, our drunkenness had always been contained in a controllable environment that was the comfort of my place and to our own soundtrack.

I had to remember it was Saturday and that was the day

that most of the world felt the need to go out. Saturday for me was like a mini New Year´s Eve, where nearly everyone was dressed to the nines, proudly showing off the fact they were a couple or were selling themselves to become one. During the week I would see all these kinds of fucks in the gym gearing up for this very moment as they tried to hone their bodies into what the media had decided was a desirable form. Now here they were in front of me: drunk, squeezed into a new pair of jeans or a figure-hugging skirt while entertaining the hope of not leaving alone. I wanted no part of this with the exception of the getting drunk bit which had always worked for me. It was just the feeling in the air of a Saturday night and maybe there was some kind of energy bringing these faceless fucks together but in all honesty, it only filled me with despair.

After passing several bland-looking establishments, I started to believe maybe all the pubs had been cloned. Every one of them was the same, all flashing disco lights, god-awful music and wannabe gangster doorman, which was kind of depressing. As we turned another corner, Nellie stopped outside a non-imaginatively named pub called the "Hole in the Wall." For some reason she instantly liked it, but fuck knows why, as to me it seemed no different to the previous four pubs we had passed. I couldn't see things getting any better, so just went with her impulse, plus seeing the outside world in all its Saturday glory meant I really needed some alcohol.

As we made our way through the front door it all suddenly hit me, as I was confronted by a scene of tribal-like urban warriors bumping and grinding to some abortion of a song amongst a mass of neon colours. This really wasn't my kind of place, and as my eyes quickly adjusted to the multicoloured light show I began to recognise a few faces from the weekday bus stop. What a bunch of cunts, look at them and how they had cast away the shackles of their working clothes to replace them with equally uninspiring forms of street-wear, pathetic.

One thing was for sure: I would need a very quick fix of alcohol if I was going to remain here any longer. Nellie turned and shouted in my ear, trying to make herself heard over the music.

46

"I know you hate this place and so do I, but come on, let us channel this anger and tomorrow we will detest the world a little bit more, but tonight let's get fucked up in the world of our enemy."

I guess I could understand her logic and so that's exactly what we did. The first 2 pints were followed swiftly by two more and a mixture of shots. We found a kind of quiet corner, which was somehow a blind spot for the speakers. I was amazed at how these people were seemingly having a good time, Nellie just laughed at the primitive way they courted each other with a subtle touch here or a suggestive dance move there; it really was mankind in its purest form, almost caveman-like.

The ever-increasing flow of alcohol we were consuming combined with the flashing lights and monotone beats started having an almost hypnotic effect on me. Jesus, this girl could drink, and I was in desperate need of a pick-me-up. I still had some cocaine in my wallet from a past lost weekend, so excused myself and headed to the toilets.

If I had hoped for any sort of respite the toilets were not it. What is it with pub toilets? Why are they so fucking grim? I queued with the other coke heads and thought bad thoughts while being subjected to the troglodyte conversation of the modern man which did nothing to convince me that these people were anything other than worthless pieces of shit. The sight of one guy throwing up in a urinal was a much-needed distraction becoming especially enjoyable as his pink shirt and beige chinos became stained by a mix of vomit and piss.

Finally the freak show ended as my turn arrived and I found a moment of peace behind the safety of the cubicle door. I could still hear the voices and distant music but they became secondary as I consumed my much-needed pick-me-up. Instantly I could feel the effect of the drugs as they entered my system, so with a final gulp of urine-scented air I headed back out into the madness of swirling lights and noise with a swagger.

I first caught sight of him through the ever-maddening crowd as he slid down next to Nellie; I stopped and observed from a distance, wondering how long he had been there. She seemed uninterested in his advances yet had made no effort to stop him taking my seat. I knew his type, he was your stereotypical weekender, Saturday-night wide boy, and he actually thought he had a chance with my girl. I headed towards them.

Nellie spotted me cutting my way through the dance floor as he leant into her, whispering something into her ear. Our eyes never broke contact and now I could see the size of my prey all dressed up in his white jeans and checked shirt, completed by a boy-band haircut. As I reached the table, he looked up at me as if he had been waiting for me and then spoke.

"Hello darling, can I help you with something?"

His accent instantly ground on me as a list of options ran through my head. The cocaine was kicking in and my head was clear. I wouldn't take the bait, and this piece of shit wouldn't drag me into the gutter, I needed to remain calm.

"Sorry, I think there must be some sort of mistake as you are in my fucking seat!"

That was kind of calm enough, which would have at least got his attention but now a wave of very dark feelings started to wash over me. Nellie notices how tense I am and catches my eye, giving me a wink which has me hitting pause as I now realise I am part of some sort of game. I have no problem with a threesome but really hope this isn't what she has in mind. To his credit his eyes never leave mine and it is only when Nellie whispers in his ear he finally stops clocking me.

My mind goes into overdrive as I survey the situation before me looking for weaknesses and going over options but this train of thought is broken as my potential foe stands. Briefly he crouches down as once again Nellie whispers something in his ear. This raises a smile on his face which he holds as he makes his way around to my side of the table briefly stopping in front of me. Nellie calms me with another wink which is a good thing as all I want to do is break this guy's jaw. I know it's the coke talking as he must have at least 20 kilos on me but I will take my chance. Like boxers before a big fight neither of us is willing to break eye contact then after a few seconds that seemed like an eternity the posturing ends. With a wry smile he finally turns away making his way past me and is gone.

Turning I watch him rejoin his fellow Saturday-night lookalikes, then lose sight of him completely as he is swallowed up amongst the sea of dancing bodies. I battle within myself trying to hold it together, struggling not to readdress our size difference by getting in a sucker punch. The moment quickly passes, however, and I feel at my most primal yet calm as the different emotions inside of me fight for my lust. I am impressed I have actually held it together so now turn my attention back to Nellie.

"What the fuck was all that about and who the fuck is that cunt?"

She starts to laugh, which may or may not be trying to get a rise out of me. Surprisingly it doesn't sting and actually feels right but wrong at the same time, which makes no sense at all. Eventually her laughter stops and composing herself she speaks.

"That was Joe, quite the little charmer to be honest, even reckons he's been watching me since we first came in, all very flattering. You know the first thing said was he thought I was your sister or some sort of fag hag. Basically the long and the short of it is, he wanted to know what a girl like me is doing with a loser like you."

Once again I am hit with a mixture of confusion, then anger as I feel a part of Nellie's fucked-up game. The veins on the side of my head start to throb in a less than calming fashion as a craving for violence starts to take over. I instantly regret letting this smug fucker off the hook, how could I have let him even look at me like that, belittle me, fuck, how dare he. All I wanted to do now was

49

find him and hurt him bad. I raise my finger and point it at Nellie but before I have a chance to voice my anger she smiles then lifts her hand to stop me. I notice a subtle change in her demeanour as her eyes narrow suddenly becoming focused.

"Channel that anger babe, because this is where it starts, Lee, you have to trust me. Look, I am pretty sure this moron thinks he is going to fuck me, but that won't be happening. This is the kind of scum we talk about, for Christ's sake he was showing off about his 12-inch penis, it's pathetic. In two minutes I am going to meet him round the back of the pub, you know what to do."

I am left standing in silence as Nellie rises then steps towards me before taking my face with both hands and peering deep into my eyes. Tenderly she kisses me on the lips, then holding me close whispers in my ear.

"So it begins, you know where to find me, give me 5 minutes."

With another kiss followed by a wink she is gone. My pint is still on the table and what remains I down in one as I try to balance my thoughts. The next four and a half minutes are maybe the longest of my life as I sit there peering at the empty glass in front of me. All sorts of craziness are racing through my mind, I knew this was a test and one I would not fail I just needed to, like she'd said, channel my anger. Momentarily I lose myself in the hypnotic beat of the music while watching the second hand on my watch eating away the time. Finally it arrives, and without hesitation I lift myself from my seat, heading for the exit.

The horrors of the pub's sound system soon disappear behind the closing doors as I am greeted by a serene outside world. The crisp cold night air feels good against my face, giving me a sobering jolt as I turn to survey my surroundings. There isn't much happening as the night is at its peak with the majority still inside continuing their Saturday night ritual. The doorman is away from his post talking to what can only be described as two very loose looking girls. He doesn't even notice me leaving as no doubt his animal desires outstrip his work ethic, which sums up everything about this shithole.

I don't stop to discuss job satisfaction with this troglodyte idiot as I need to move. Walking slowly to the corner of the building I find a passageway which I presume must lead to the back of the pub. Pausing for a second I peer into the darkness seeing nothing, which fails to deter me and why would it. My girl is down there somewhere so nothing is going to stop me. As I make my way forward weaving through the highly stacked crates and empty beer barrels, the alleyway's darkness is gradually replaced by the glow of the disco lights. They filter through the smoked windows giving it an almost eerie, alien like feel. The stink of piss and vomit is overwhelming making me gag, but I know I am coming to the back area, so slow down not to be seen, I need every advantage I can get.

I don't like the feeling of walking into the unknown and still am not sure exactly what I am going to encounter. As I finally reach the back of the building I spot two figures in the shadows. I can see it is Nellie as I recognise her beautiful curves that my hands had so often explored so was pretty sure the big lump was Joe. I squat down behind a stack of beer barrels to get a better view but could hear nothing as even out here the music was still quite loud. They seemed to be just talking with Nellie leant back against the fence in what could only be described as a "come and fuck me" manner. I edged forward, treading carefully between fallen crates and broken bottles that laid there carelessly discarded and then I could see them. Joe had his cock out, beckoning Nellie forward, who seemed to be teasing him.

What happened next will forever go down as my first official kill, and I was angry as it had been a reckless act. The alcohol and drugs in my system had no doubt played their part, but I knew it was Nellie's provocations that had been the catalyst for this irrational moment. Although as I had picked up the broken bottle off the floor I had only one intention for it so I wasn't entirely blameless. It had all been so easy, almost too easy, I didn't even have to creep up on my victim as the sea of lights and music had hidden my approach until it was far too late for Joe.

I am not sure how much pain he had actually felt as it was all over surprisingly quickly. I had delivered the broken bottle into his neck with some force then had ripped it out with a sickening twist which had seemed to have done the job. He had never even seen me coming which in a way was a shame, but the one deadly blow had been enough to see his body slump to the ground in a matter of seconds.

I looked coldly into his eyes, anticipating his recognition, but as he struggled for breath I sadly knew this wasn't to be the case. He just lay there with his hand gripped to the wound, unable to speak, almost frozen in an orgasm of shock as the blood spurted over his Ralph Lauren shirt. It didn't take long for the life to drain from his face, then a stillness fell over his body, bringing calm to the whole situation. It was almost anticlimactic in a way, the two of us left standing there bathed in a rainbow of multicoloured lights with a soundtrack not befitting the moment. I had a sudden desire to urinate over this fallen piece of shit but Nellie brought me back to earth.

"Let's go home, I want to fuck."

12

I don't often smoke but find the occasional cancer stick clears my mind, especially when laced with cocaine. The first hit is always the best but by the halfway point my world would always seem a lighter shade of grey. Of course these days my world was far different from the dark place I had too often inhabited in the past. My relationship with Nellie had revitalised me in a way I never knew was possible and now tonight's events had taken that to another level.

We sat in near silence enjoying the moment as the room filled with large clouds of smoke. I pushed myself back into the soft sofa, allowing the drugs to overcome me somewhat, and began to reflect. It had only been a couple of hours since I had killed, and I was starting to ponder the effect tonight's event might have in reshaping our lives forever. Finally I broke the silence.

"Something's been troubling me babe and I just have to know, did he really have a 12-inch cock?"

We both laughed, as I recalled Joe's blood-stained body on the floor and now regretted having missed the opportunity to remove his prized asset. Killing him hadn't really affected us, it seemed, and Nellie in particular had remained dead calm in the aftermath of the bloodshed. There was no doubt that we had rushed into things but saying that, it was good to get off the mark, and I was looking forward to what would happen next.

I was already convinced we would get away with it as murder was not that uncommon in this part of town. Several groups had been fighting a turf war over the local drug control with a murder occurring at least once, sometimes twice a month. On top of all that we had both been careful to walk out of that alley without being seen. We had hovered in the shadows waiting for the right moment to exit, then had done so quickly, blending into the crowds of another drunken Saturday night. I remembered looking over to the pub entrance making sure we hadn't been spotted, then laughing as I'd seen the doorman. He had still been doing an excellent job and hadn't even moved away from the girls I had previously seen him chatting up.

I doubted anyone would find the body until the morning if not until even later as the alley had a feel of abandonment about it. The far end where Joe's body now lay was a mass of empty crates and barrels that looked like it hadn't been touched in months. Nellie at the time had the state of mind to stop me throwing away the broken bottle which now of course was much more than that as it was a murder weapon. We had wrapped it in a plastic bag and disposed of it up the road in one of the many glass recycling bins, it's good to recycle so I've been told. There had been a moment of glory as we heard the remains of the bottle smash on impact, it was almost as if we were launching a ship. The sound of broken glass felt symbolic or official, giving us closure to our first act of what I hoped would be many.

The thing that surprised me most was how easy it had been to kill. I was going to be a natural. Maybe this was my calling and I knew repeating the act wouldn't be a problem. Human flesh had been no match for a broken bottle, and the way it had torn away the skin when I removed it from Joe's neck had been impressive. The fact still remained that we had been rash and we both agreed we had also got lucky. Things could have gone so differently with maybe the worse scenario being Joe penetrating Nellie with that giant penis of his. We needed to go back to the rules we had been so keen to establish before our Saturday night drinking session at the Hole in the Wall pub. Whatever happened from now on we would plan and then execute without the reckless nature of our first kill.

That night we went to bed and fucked without a care in the world, our bodies once again connecting as one, yet this time the bond feeling even stronger as we had now spilled blood together. As Nellie reached her orgasm, she clamped her hands to the sides of my head and staring me hard in the eyes called me my killer. Jesus, what a turn-on, I really was the luckiest man alive. I returned the compliment as I reached my climax, this time clamping my hands to side of her head, then staring her deep in the eyes called her my fucking whore. Life was good.

Over the next week life went on as it had done before Joe's date with destiny. The weather had turned truly shit and it wasn't until the Thursday that I first read news of our crime. It appeared that Joseph Williams had been a bit of a local piece of scum and that the police were treating the crime as gang related. I would be lying if I said I wasn't relieved because I was but felt a touch of disappointment the crime had received such little coverage. These days the police were generally underpaid, overworked and were not going to waste much needed resources on someone like Joe Williams, that was for sure. However, a few paragraphs in the local rag I felt to be a little underwhelming, even insulting.

It wasn't that I wanted to be a star or famous, but I now realised how day to day murder had become in the modern age. Fear is a powerful thing and if people are scared they tend to tread more carefully or think more about their actions. This was true, I had even proved it with the way the Audi I had vandalised at the gym had never parked again in the disabled spot, people could change, they just needed a wake-up call.

I refused to think of the whole world as a completely lost cause but examples needed to be made so that people would sit up and take notice. I looked forward to discussing the matter with Nellie over large amounts of alcohol that evening and knew she would agree. We may have rid the world of Mr Joseph "12-inch cock" Williams but his death wouldn't be in vain as it had taught me something about life and now I just needed to put my plans into action.

I found Nellie already on her second bottle of wine as I arrived home from work. She was stretched out on the sofa wearing one of my old Smiths T-shirts while listening to a copy of the Velvet Underground's "White Light/White Heat" that was obviously having an effect on her as I was greeted with the pearls of wisdom.

"This is one fucked up LP! These guys were so fucking avant-garde."

We often talked music and early in the week I had been telling her about the Velvets. I loved both Lou Reed and the Velvet Underground and was so happy that she now got them too. One of her favourite songs was "There she goes" by the La's and she hadn't even been aware of the connection to The Velvets, in fact she hadn't even listened to them.

I started her off slowly with the famous Banana cover LP: The Velvet Underground and Nico, which she had adored. But by the look on her face as I told her about the tales of fellatio, drag queen orgies, a transsexual's botched lobotomy and the heavy drug influence of "White Light/White Heat" I knew I would have my revenge for her springing Zappa's "Hot Rats" on me. She had been right though as "Willie the Pimp" had rocked my world but I knew her mind was elsewhere. Maybe it had been the music that was triggering this, I mean I remember this record doing funny things to me as well, just the seventeen-minute-three-cord drone of "Sister Ray" can push the best of us to our limits.

It is amazing how music can have such an effect on the human state of mind. I remember a boy in my boarding school who pierced his ear with a safety pin and then stuck his head through a glass table after listening to the Sex Pistols "Never Mind the Bollocks." I am sure he must have felt very punk that day and I can still picture him showing off those six stitches of his. However, his fame came at a price and his new-found popularity soon vanished as our out-of-touch headmaster banned all music from the school in a Footloose-esque moment. My mind slipped back to the present and Nellie as she confirmed that her mind was not completely on the music.

"You know I am jealous as hell?"

I guess I could understand her frustrations and where she was coming from. After all it had ended up with me delivering that killer blow despite all her groundwork. We had both been on a high for a couple days after the events of Saturday night yet still hadn't really talked them through. Although we were in agreement about how reckless we had been I still felt that the way in which Nellie had instigated our first kill still needed addressing. Now it became clear she was suffering as she viewed Joe's demise as my kill and not ours I needed to give her some reinsurance, to put her at ease.

"Hey, no problem the next time is your turn, just don't beat yourself up over it, remember we are a team."

I instantly felt that same feeling of unease as she started to laugh; it was deep and evil and a side of her I'd yet to see. I guess it was more surprise than unease as the laughter was almost coy, yet at the same time extremely sexy.

"No darling, the next time will be yours, what I should have said was that I was jealous as hell, I've been busy."

The unease I had felt before suddenly returned like a punch in the gut. She was now no longer laughing and was peering at the floor in what appeared to be a dramatic attempt to build tension. Slowly she raised her head and smiled.

"You remember that old homeless guy from the bus stop?"

Before she even finished I knew she had killed him, but why the homeless guy? I couldn't understand it, this man did no one any harm and he was just some drunken bum who slept rough in our neighbourhood. I thought we were going to set rules and our victims would deserve it but he was an innocent. I instantly felt a mixture of annoyance and inner turmoil but wasn't allowed to dwell on it or even express my disappointment as she continued her explanation.

"Don't worry, it was all very simple and clean, an easy kill. Come on! We should celebrate, this means we have now both popped our cherries, onwards and upwards I say!"

I guess "Stinky Pete" as he was locally known had been more offensive than I had originally thought. For as long as I could remember and had lived here he had always been there by that

57

bus stop. Of course there had always been the rumours, one that he had been a banker that lost it after a bad batch of drugs while others said he had been a teacher who had been struck off after being caught touching kids. Whoever he had been he was a shell of a man who never said anything as he consumed can after can of industrial-strength beer. When he wasn't to be found at the bus stop he would be passed out in his bedroom which was the alley next to the kebab shop. Yes he would often piss his pants where he stood, hence the nickname, but he was hardly public enemy number one. She went on.

"I think I may have actually done him a favour, let's face it this world offered him nothing. Anyway, why the fuck are you so upset? He was a despicable excuse for a human, more an eyesore than a man. You've heard the stories he was a teacher that liked a bit of kiddie fiddling."

The way the words left her mouth gave no sign of remorse. She was trying to get me to believe her actions were justified although I knew it really was a smoke screen. She had a lust to kill and this was her way of starting on the nursery slopes, still I refused to let it go.

"Come on Nell, he was harmless, you know all those stories are just local gossip. When I first moved here I he was a banker who lost it after a bad batch of drugs."

She suddenly burst into laughter as if I had just told her the funniest joke ever. I looked at her almost in shock, more than anything else as the source for the humour was crass to say the least. When she saw I wasn't participating in her joyous moment she stopped and began to speak.

"What the fuck, come on, lighten up will you, this is good news if you're right because there's nothing people hate more than a fucking banker."

Now we both started to laugh, which may have been a bit inappropriate seeing how we were discussing the demise of a fellow human being. She had ended up suffocating poor Stinky Pete with a dirty rag as he had laid peacefully passed out on his bed of dirty cardboard. It seemed he hadn't moved a muscle no doubt due to his intoxicated state yet as he took his final breath had briefly opened his eyes before shutting them forever. As the moment calmed she took a breath as if she'd now had time to reflect and collect her thoughts.

"OK, I guess you're right, I do feel a slight regret. Maybe I should have jacked him off or something before killing him, he couldn't have been all bad so giving him one last moment of happiness that didn't originate from a can might have been a nice gesture. But Jesus he stunk, you know I actually think he may have even shit himself as he took his last breath. I thought that only happened when you hung someone but perhaps in this case his arse muscle was the last part of him capable of showing any form of resistance."

We both burst out laughing and any anger I had for this angel or perhaps more appropriately, this "angel of death" now disappeared. I felt truly blessed that I had found someone like me, I was one fortunate soul. I got up and headed into the kitchen for another bottle of wine.

13

We had taken to keeping our relationship a secret at work
and apart from the odd relapse it remained that way, very discreet.
Even though we both worked for the same company and in the
same building our daily work lives never seemed to collide which
was strange really, seeing as how close we were on a daily basis.
All that separated us for 8 hours a day was a floor/ceiling of
concrete with Nellie working up on the eighth floor and me on the
seventh. She tended to start an hour before me so we only really
saw each other at home, which was at times both frustrating and
curious. Often I found myself peering up at the ceiling above me
wondering if her day was as frustrating as mine, longing to run my
hand up the inside of her leg.

Like most work love affairs we had a period of fucking on
the job but the initial excitement of that had already worn off. Our
sex life had evolved into marathons at home with the quick fumble
in the office toilet or various other dark corners just not cutting it
any more This may have been a good thing seeing that the subject
of inter-staff relationships was a hot one at the moment after a
string of scandals had rocked the firm.

A local temp agency that supplied many of our staff had
now been labelled in house as "Aussie whores" after a few high-
profile affairs. It did seem harsh to blame the temps as ninety
percent of these cases involved married members of our higher
management who were obviously abusing their power. One
occasion had even made the papers after the wife of the Vice
President had stormed into the building to confront her husband's
lover. When the whole episode went viral after being caught on
camera phone the firm decided enough was enough vowing to
clamp down on any future misdemeanour's.

Even though the images of the two women cat-fighting in
the lobby brought endless amusement to us workers it meant we
needed to watch our backs. The lowly status of us worker ants in
the food chain meant our pay grades were seen as easily
disposable. This high-profile scandal had already put an end to the

Vice President's future and although I was pretty sure work relationships weren't illegal a carefully worded memo had already appeared basically stating work romances would be frowned upon.

Of course, we couldn't give a fuck, but with our new-found agenda we agreed it would be best to remain as low profile as possible and so curtailed our workplace rendezvous'. As the rules came down hard and fast the idea of fucking on the job became more appealing and we did have our enjoyable slips. However, the thought of being used as an example as the hierarchy tried to appease its shareholders sickened me, so we vowed to remain strong. My sex drive was at times demanding but I managed to confine my urges to masturbation, which actually turned into a quite enjoyable part of my mid-morning routine.

I had never planned this type of work and to say I resented it would be a huge understatement. A working life never appealed to me but any future plans of travelling and seeing the world required money so here I was. After struggling to adjust to a life without family and then my own demise I had felt a need to bring my life down a few gears. Maybe my demons had been well and truly washed or blown away but more than likely they were just hiding or waiting for the perfect moment to mount a comeback. Unfortunately for me a place I was likely to face these demons again was the big bad city. I guess it was a bit of a catch-22 as it was also the only place I could expect to make serious coin.

I had left university with excellent grades so even my starting salary would be a fair bit higher than the average citizen's in this fair land. The whole interview process for me had been like a TV game show, I loved the smell of arrogance, fear and hope that only a room full of potential candidates could bring. Everyone just looking each other up and down while trying to hide any last-minute nerves or self-doubts.

I breezed the interview and was practically offered the job on the spot. No matter how charming the others were I knew my grades would be hard to beat. Let's face it a job as a financial analyst where 90% of the job would be sat behind a fucking computer didn't require great wit or an outgoing sense of humour, they just wanted a number monkey.

Well, for what now had seemed an eternity, I had been working in front of that fucking screen. Yes, my bank account was healthier but those demons had all been reappearing in various shapes and forms. It was funny as that in my darkest recent moments the hatred I had for my work, my work colleagues and my life had seemed overwhelming. Yet it was still this place that had somehow managed to conjure up true happiness. Many believe paths are chosen that shape our lives but if that was the case I had constantly taken the wrong turn or walked through the wrong door. I didn't believe in fate but somehow Nellie had ended up in my arms so if fate truly existed, meeting her would be just that.

The financial year was coming to an end, meaning both of us had been overloaded with work with twelve-hour days becoming the norm. The extra money was a bonus but the extra working hours were putting a hold on our personal project at great frustration to the two of us. I hated spending so much time in such an enclosed space with these vile people in what could be described as a stale atmosphere at best. On several occasions, a "being at work too long" madness would overwhelm me, leading to visions or dreams of drawing out a large machine gun, Scarface style, and gunning down the whole accounts department. I laughed to myself as I imagined the bullets cutting through the room, tearing flesh and furniture apart.

You had to wonder how far this game that Nellie and I had started would take us. I always knew I had the capacity to take a human life, but could never have predicted that my first murder would be such a violent one. No matter how sloppy the start of this adventure had been a kill was a kill and now we were both following a path. I knew we would kill again but was pretty sure Rambo or Scarface acts of violence would only ever appear in our lives through the silver screen. A more conservative approach would lead to longevity and what I dearly hoped would be a long-running project.

My moment of bliss is ended as my screen bleeps to tell me I have more data incoming, all of which would need to be crunched, talk about pissing on my parade. Visions of great acts of violence were surely only my mind trying to amuse itself as my brain was forced into a type of slave labour. As much as my mind drifted, it also had the amazing capacity to focus when needed, which was a Godsend as Jesus this work was boring.

One good thing about finishing so late was that the trains were a lot quieter for the trip home. This meant actually being able to sit rather than having my face pressed up against the glass or at worse somebody's armpit. I sat in peace while watching a young Italian couple who had obviously been enjoying a Friday night on the town sucking each other's faces off. I had no doubt these kisses would soon be replaced with a long night of passion as these young lovers expressed their feelings more physically.

Just the thought of sex had my mind slipping back to Nellie and I hoped she'd still be up when I finally got in. Unlike myself she had got lucky today escaping a full four hours early, meaning she was certainly already home and more than likely on her second bottle of wine. I chuckled to myself imagining her trying to unzip stinky Pete's trousers, wondering if she actually would have given him a hand job. Even though she had murdered him just the idea of doing such a kind act proved she had more layers that I had yet to see, which was intriguing.

The unmistakable sounds of the Velvet Underground greeted me as I closed the front door behind me. The music of course was great but for me taken to a higher level by the sight of Nellie wrapped up on the sofa enjoying it so much. I already knew she was listening to "Loaded" before she even picked up the cover to speak.

"I think this one may be my favourite."

It was definitely the easiest of their albums to listen to but I still preferred the tales of a botched transsexual´s lobotomy that "White light/White Heat" brought to the table. The bad vibe of sitting in the office now disappears as her happiness fills the room with a backing track of Lou Reed singing "Sweet Jane", making the moment almost perfect. I think back to the kissing couple on the train and know Nellie can sense my attentions.

"Oh, is my Voodoo working?"

She pulls back the duvet to reveal she is wearing no clothes, then pushes her body back hard into the sofa resting her arms behind her head.

"You can call me Sweet Jane if that's what you want sweetheart."

As the words leave her mouth she ever so slightly opens her legs to tease me with her freshly shaven vagina. She knows what she is doing and I don't need a second invitation. Besides, tomorrow is Saturday.

14

It had been easy to forget some of the simpler things life could offer as the years had shaped me into what I guess could only be described as an intense individual. Although in general I had always hidden behind a smiling face, something deep within me had always been raging and telling me my life would eventually spiral out of control. On a plus side it was a testament to my mental strength that my demons were kept in check. However, at times it was as if the different parts of me made up by mother's and father's genes were involved in a power struggle to guide me. I too had my say in this constant battle but at times I had honestly believed that I would never experience happiness.

As I lay there watching Nellie sleep, I remembered her words "is my voodoo working?" There was no doubt in my mind they would have been stolen from some feminist singer but she did however have a point. I truly had fallen under her spell and my ability to kill for her had proved that she already had a dangerous hold over me. I had to confess I had found some sort of inner peace and believed it was the same for her. It was strange really as I was starting to enjoy this new experience of feeling good, maybe even happy as all of a sudden being angry just seemed so unproductive.

"What you thinking about, babe?"

Her words instantly startled me as I hadn't noticed she'd awoken. Just to think that she may have been lying there studying me should have made me feel uncomfortable but for some reason didn't. I rolled on to my side to look at her then answered.

"Life, I guess."

I could see in her eyes she didn't believe me but ironically I was telling the truth. I had the impression, however, that she was more interested in continuing last night's sexual encounter than discussing my deeper thoughts. I laughed to myself as I hardly recognized all these new feelings coursing through my body but forgot them as her hand sank beneath the sheets to find my erect penis. She already knew it was hard before she even touched it; she just did, back to the voodoo again. A tingling of happiness filled me as she took me in her mouth and I knew it was more than sexual: this was joy, pure joy.

Only a month ago my Saturdays had consisted of being the second act of the weekend's path to self-destruction. In recent times I had rarely spent a weekend outside the four walls that were my flat, only on occasion leaving if my supplies ran low. I had found the numbing process through drink and drugs a satisfying one but chose to never remember the times I had been brought to tears, always somehow managing to shut those moments out the day after.

I now knew that there was a different way and my pondering of life continued as I stepped out of the shower. I couldn't recall a time when I had felt the need to listen or was even compelled to do so. The female form for me was always nothing more than a vessel for my sexual releases and now it was hard to believe I had been so naive. It disappointed then saddened me now to think back to all those girls I had just dismissed, never giving them a chance to grow with me. Always I'd played it safe, never taking risks as all my sexual conquests had been a one-way street and under my rules. It was now quite apparent that was wrong as I had feasted upon the more fragile of soul, easy pickings. Although I had no doubt physical satisfaction had been delivered they had never got much change out of me emotionally.

Guilt was maybe the wrong word as after all these moments had been consenting adults exchanging fluids in the name of pleasure, but for the first time in my life I felt some regret. I was determined not to make the same mistake with Nellie, she was my soul mate, Jesus did I actually think that? I cast my mind back to my youth and my obsession with this thing we called a soul had me almost laughing out loud as I stepped onto the bathroom mat.

The brakes suddenly hit my strange chain of thought as through the bathroom door I caught sight of Nellie. She was sitting, naked, cross-legged on the bed crying. Fuck, what had I done?

"I am so sorry Lee, it's just me, I don't know what it is? I guess, I just feel a little lost."

I had to confess this was the last thing I was expecting to find as I left the bathroom that morning. Nellie had come across as steel-willed and in complete control of everything yet here she was looking so fragile. I was now venturing into new territory as I sat down next to her on the bed and cradled her head in my arms. I said nothing as her sobs continued but as I stroked her hair they seemed to ease so I guess I was doing something right. She sat herself up and drying her eyes on our sex-stained sheets continued.

"I don't know what came over me, I just......"

I stopped her mid-sentence but wasn't sure if this was for my benefit or hers. I guess my previous thoughts of getting to know someone were about to get a lot more real and would certainly now be tested. I hoped I was ready to walk through this door because now actually I wanted to. This relationship was evolving before my eyes and I couldn't say what was going to come next but had to try.

"I'm sorry I didn't mean to stop you, I am not really sure why I did to be honest."

Was this the best I could come up with? I was pathetic and now she would see through me, I needed to try again.

"Nell, it's all good I'm not going anywhere. I have been honest with you since the day we met and that won't change, but there is something you need to know, I am a complete emotional spastic."

I took solace that at least my clumsy choice of the word "Spastic" had lightened the mood as she began to laugh. I guess

67

this kind of broke the ice but at the same time I did feel a bit silly at its particular choice and Nellie didn't let me off the hook.

"Spastic, who the fuck uses that word any more, what, is this 1985?"

Her laughter like always lit up the room and I reached over to take her hand, then stroked it gently like she had once done to me. Once again a serious look fell across her face.

"Lee, I don't really know what to say, I'm the one who should be sorry as you didn't sign up for this."

I felt instant relief that she was taking the blame and I had somehow not blown it. I wasn't sure why I had suddenly become so self-conscious because in reality I had played this situation perfectly, it just needed a final touch.

"If someone had told me a month ago what I am about to say I wouldn't have believed them, but........."

She stopped me by shaking her head as this time here her look of sadness was replaced by pure horror. I paused, allowing her to speak.

"Please oh God, don't tell you are going to use the L word?"

Of course I wasn't going to use the L word, she knew that just as much as me. Neither of us actually believed in love but we did believe in a human connection, which was what we very much had. I had looked at Nellie as untouchable, even Goddess-like up to this moment and to see her cry had made her seem even more perfect in my book. Like me now she also appeared to have been hiding behind some sort of mask and although the two of us had let them slip somewhat recently the time had now arrived to reveal our true selves to each other.

The whole idea of the outpouring of emotion in front of another human being was a concept I never understood or could even get my head around. I would actually go as far as to say that I couldn't think of anything worse, yet here I was about to cross that line, yes, this was happening. It was amazing really at this point that I had never put any importance into getting to know anyone or even considered such a thing, for Christ's sake I hadn't known my parents or even wanted to. Maybe the closest thing I ever had that resembled a friend was Brenda, but classifying that as friendship would have been stretching its meaning to its limits.

I am not sure how long we lay there on the bed together but was pretty sure it was the longest I spent on a bed without fucking or sleeping. Every second we talked and every emotional layer we peeled off revealed more scars than secrets. We both opened ourselves up completely, with Nellie at times almost breaking down to what seemed to a point beyond return. I could feel the negative energy escaping her body and sucked it in before it would have a chance to return to hers. My indestructible girl wasn't so indestructible after all, especially from this darkness she had never let go.

This mask she had worn had never slipped but finally it was coming off, allowing for her to start some sort of almost religious-like cleansing or healing process. As a complete amateur in these situations I held up well and drawing from her lead quickly learnt when to hold and when to speak, with the whole process becoming quite natural. I hadn't held back either telling her everything, which I'd found surprisingly easy. For her it was so different with every emotionally weighed-down word hitting her hard as it left her mouth.

Nellie was a far more complex creature than I could ever have imagined. I could now see where her bitterness for this world came from. Let's face facts a life spent growing up in various foster homes never ended with a "happily ever after." Tales of her single mother's violent partners were quite shocking but then the low end of the food chain mixed with drugs and alcohol rarely produced positive results.

She credited her intellect to her gifted but flawed hippy

69

mother as she had never known her father, or even who he was. Her whole family was a mess, from a grandfather being in and out of jail to her half-sister she hadn't even known had existed until three years ago when she came around begging for money. My childhood seemed so much more open and closed than hers, for which in a way I was now grateful. These tales of broken childhoods were familiar in this modern age as acts of procreation were often committed with no thought of consequence. The only benefactor it seemed were crass TV shows that dotted the morning TV landscape which people still for some unexplainable reason chose to watch as a form of entertainment, scum.

As time passed we both started to feel the benefits of sharing. I wouldn't say the mood exactly lightened but tensions certainly did ease. I was under no illusions that Nellie had been suffering deeply for years, with her ability to hide such sadness being quite astonishing and admirable. Not at one moment did I pity her, as that wasn't what she was looking for. Her baggage was a heavy load and seemed to pain her far more than anything I had ever experienced or been through.

I had only really fallen into a kind of dark funk over the last few years, whereas her scars were far older and deeper than mine. The loss of my parents hadn't really hurt me, just diverted me down another path. Yes, I had my dark moments but to be honest these tended to be self-inflicted, so I really deserved no sympathy, especially after hearing the tales of Nellie's struggles.

It must have been early afternoon by the time we finally paused for a silence that hadn't been punctuated by Nellie's tears. This time a sort of peacefulness covered her face as she smiled, obviously feeling a weight had been lifted. I reached over pulling the hair from her eyes and gently kissed her, allowing my lips to linger in a non-sexual manner. I was starting to like this sort of vibe and affection as it was making me feel happy and wanted, but it was time to break the silence.

"Hey, what doesn't kill us makes us stronger, right?"

I hadn't meant for it to sound like a self-help slogan but for some reason it had. Nellie, although amused rolled her eyes before once again leaning in to hug me. I could feel a strength returning to her body as suddenly her grip tightened, which was in vast contrast to the broken weakling of the previous hours. It was hard to explain how I felt at that particular moment as inside I knew I had enjoyed all the pain, lapping up her words like a drug.

I had no doubt that she now looked at me as some sort of Our Saviour-type figure. Whether or not this was slightly self-absorbed on my part, it was definitely disturbing on all sorts of levels. I had started the afternoon embracing a change inside of me, but now the old me was stronger than ever. I could feel all her angst, anger and pain as though it had refuelled all the demons that coursed through my veins. I liked this girl but today had been valuable lesson that I was stronger. As she sat up I could see the show was over, her mask had slipped back into position and now the Nellie of before began to speak.

"Fucking Toby Johnson, I want to kill that piece of shit!"

The mystery of Toby Johnson would have to wait for another day as Nellie wasn't even sure if he was still alive. The half-time break in our weekend for floods of tears and the outpouring of truths had passed almost as quickly as it had arrived. Nellie refused to comment any further on this Toby character, so I didn't push her. I already knew we were looking at our next potential victim and I could already picture his name printed in the newspaper as deceased. All this seemed extremely harsh seeing as this was still a person I knew absolutely nothing about. It was just that I was keen to get back to killing and the look of animosity I saw in Nellie's eyes as she had mentioned his name was enough for me to know this man had done something bad which this time I was sure was personal.

Our emotional detour that weekend had brought us even closer and to me demonstrated the small margin between pleasure and pain. I noticed the difference in the way she fucked after all the cleansing, it was as if the release had made her stronger. An added bonus for me was that for the first time Nellie had succumbed to anal sex which just proved every cloud does has a silver lining. To be honest I didn't feel that much difference in the sharing from my side but I had been empowered by her pain, which curiously left me wanting more.

Of course, I had been pleased that I could now add the role of listener to my skill-set but the way she clawed at my back and bit me during the throes of passion proved she still had a lot of anger to give. I was intrigued to find out what other darkness lay within her and had a feeling that "fucking Toby Johnson" would be the key.

15

An interesting weekend as always had ended way too quickly as the reality of returning to work soon came into focus. There was no doubt that Mondays and I had a particularly difficult history but today I was seeing everything from a slightly brighter perspective. For me the world may have fallen into a deep sleep but today I was feeling wide awake, almost reborn. The weekend's sideshow albeit an out-pouring of darkness and hurt seemed to have affected or maybe even infected me with a wave of positivity. My ringside seat had allowed me a close-up to Nellie at her most vulnerable yet this experience in hindsight had somehow been an uplifting one for me.

Let's face the truth because one thing life can guarantee is that eventually pain will find its way to your door, it's just how you deal with it when it comes a knocking that counts. I had seen Nellie as my equal up until Saturday morning but after a bit of thought I came to the conclusion that her frailties made her weaker, a lesser being. This realization had re-fuelled me with a new feeling of self-belief and confidence. Yes, Nellie may have been the most perfect person I had ever met but I was evolution in the making and now my mojo was back. I was beginning to feel unstoppable.

As I sat myself down for another long day of mind-numbing boredom I noticed my screen saver had been changed. My favourite image of Quentin Tarantino with a gun to his head was gone, having been replaced by a visual abortion of moving words. My first thought was that it had been Nellie but then as I scanned the screen it was quite apparent it wasn't unless she had gone completely mad overnight. In the midst of a ghastly, sky blue, bubble background floated such words as: "Positive", "Productivity", "Focus" and "Team Work". Sitting back in my chair I stare blankly, almost hypnotically as these words continue to randomly bounce side to side, then up and down across my screen. My bewilderment is finally broken by a voice behind me.

"It's William; he has the whole floor set the same."

I span around in my chair to be confronted by a mass of white clothing that was more appropriate for an Ibiza beach party than a City office. It was Annie, the office manager or section head as her position had recently been renamed. Knowing she now had my full attention she continued with what could only be described as mindless workplace small talk.

"I think he's trying to create a form of positive energy within our team. Off the record of course, I feel all these changes are, shall we say, over the top."

I wasn't sure what was more alarming; Annie's choice of an all-white trouser-suit for work or William's efforts at motivation. I didn't have much time to dwell on either as she seemed to be intent on not letting me get a word in.

"I don't see you in the gym so much these days, Mr Shelton which is a shame. That place is so dull and a young fit gentleman like yourself does make those sessions pass so much more, enjoyably, shall we say?"

Well that came out of left field and with a cheeky smile she disappeared back into the office abyss. I had got to know Annie quite well over the past year as she acted as the bridge between us small fry and higher management but I couldn't remember her being so flirtatious. I had to confess, I liked it and started to feel all sorts of urges as I watched her work her way back across the office. The brightness of the fluorescent lights just for a second made part of her white trousers appear almost see-through, I could have sworn she was wearing a black thong, which made me surprisingly hard.

"She likes you, that one."

Nellie's voice seemed almost out of place in my office space but still, it was good to see her so early in the day. I smiled up at her as she leant over the top of my cubicle holding a mug of coffee.

"Good morning sweetheart, all good?"

74

I knew she could sense something as the thoughts of Annie's black thong meant she'd caught me off guard. To be honest I was quite surprised to see her hence my selection of the word "sweetheart." I pushed myself closer to the desk hoping to hide the Annie-fabricated bulge in my trousers as she continued.

"Don't worry, I'm not the jealous type but women just know and that one wants you pretty bad. Hey, I got to get back, let's meet for lunch, say one at the basement bar across the road, unless you have plans with the ultra-vixen of course."

The sarcastic look I gave her was maybe more me covering up my shock at her female intuition than a denial. She obliviously found the whole thing very amusing as she departed giggling to herself once again leaving me to the solitude of my work cubicle and the beauty of that screen saver.

Of course she was right and of course she was jealous as Annie was some woman. The thing that was always going to upset poor Nellie was that Annie was her physical opposite and in my experience women who were what we would describe as flat-chested always had a hang up over their big-breasted sisters. In my opinion Nellie had a kick-ass body, but I knew she had issues about it so an Alpha female like Annie was always going to make her a little insecure and understandably so.

Now the mundane craziness of the end of the financial year had passed the office had returned to its unspectacular normality. This morning like most mornings was dragging with today seemingly even worse than normal. My mind kept wandering back to Annie's athletic body and the outline of her thong that the light had so kindly gifted me. The more I thought about it, even the white trouser suit and short haircut aroused me somewhat. I had never noticed her smell until this morning which was something else and a brand of perfume I just couldn't place. I would have guessed she must have been approaching forty but then they do say to be with an older woman blows your mind.

I knew I could bed her and this morning's little signals had become all the more interesting since Nellie had mentioned them. The forbidden fruit always tastes best but seeing that I was now Nellie's partner it would obviously be morally wrong. But then saying that surely fucking someone when you don't care for that person is more animal instinct. In fact there was a case to be made that it isn't so much cheating but more an advanced type of masturbating. My train of thought was broken by my boss' booming voice as he entered the room.

My brain went instinctively into shutdown the second the first word left his month. He must have yapped on for at least two minutes before leaving to a round of applause. I had found my hatred of these people mellowing over the last month but it was moments like this that put me back to square one. You couldn't really say my boss was a bad man he was just a complete cock.

In fact, William had been looking alright of late as long as you didn't stare at him for too long. It had been rumoured he'd been given a Japanese book on team-building and this, combined with some weight-loss had given him some much needed confidence. Of course now that a samurai sword had gone up in his office we may have only been a small step from doing weird group breathing exercises in the morning, silly cunt.

I sat there looking around wondering what these people would think if they actually had the ability to read my mind. I laughed silently to myself, then settled down for another dose of boredom knowing I was only an hour from my lunch date with Nellie and some much-needed alcoholic relief.

As I walked down the stairs fond memories returned of the night I had met Nellie here the first time. Her copy of the Wasp Factory now sat proudly in my flat and I looked to the table where that night we'd gotten to know each other so well. To both my surprise and disappointment it was empty as she had sat herself at the bar and was currently nursing herself through a pint of Guinness. Taking the stool next to her I sat myself down, yet she didn't acknowledge me or even turn in my direction.

"How's your girlfriend, Annie?"

Fuck, she was jealous, well I guess that was one up for the female sixth sense, still it was best to play denial.

"Really, I didn't think you were the jealous type?"

This time she did turn to face me and I was greeted by a face like thunder, she was angry.

"One thing you need to learn about us women is that we are all fucking jealous, I know you like her, I can just tell and I fucking hate that bitch."

I wasn't completely surprised as I could see it in her eyes this morning. Her stock with me was falling rapidly; first we'd had the emotional breakdown of the weekend and now this. It is amazing how the human mind can be clouded by good sex. Getting closer to me had weakened her yet for me absorbing her problems had made me stronger. It was even possible this whole interchange of emotion was actually now responsible for allowing me to see this for what it really was, wow.

"So you're not going to deny it then?"

The tone of her voice meant this was far from over, but what the fuck was going on? Unless she had suddenly obtained the ability to read minds there was no way she could have suspected anything. What the fuck was wrong with me, suspect anything; I hadn't done anything wrong, well not yet anyhow. Still I didn't want things to end like this especially now we were having anal sex so I needed to tread carefully this was a moment to boost her fragile ego, not destroy it. I reached across to touch her, yet she pushed away my hand, standing and downing the remains of her pint in what has to be said was a very impressive manner before turning away from me again.

"I need to use the toilet."

With that she picked up her bag and was gone. I sat there for a few seconds trying to comprehend the whole situation then caught the bartender's eye and ordered a pint. Come to think of it, this was kind of fun, what if she had actually caught me fucking Annie and imagine if she had caught me fucking Annie up the arse. I laughed out loud causing the couple next to me to look over.

I suddenly started feeling alone again but this time totally in control, this girl was great but like me had some serious issues. The difference was I was drawing strength from mine and strength from hers while she was turning into a car crash. The next five minutes could be very interesting, maybe I would be fucking Annie tonight after all. As I thought about Annie's firm sporty body I slipped off into a sexually charged train of thought.

I suddenly felt a hand on my shoulder that startled me for a split second, even more so as I had been picturing Annie's breasts springing from her bra. Nellie was back and I braced myself for the next barrage of craziness or pearls of madness. This time however she appeared calmer and taking my hand sat herself back down at my side. The tension between us instantly disappeared almost deflating as she gave me one of her amazing smiles she was so capable of. All a bit too bi-polar for my liking but I would give her the chance to speak.

"Hey babe, I'm sorry. I am such a fucking idiot, look, it's not an excuse but I got my period and I'm an emotional train wreck. Fuck, this now and what happened over the weekend you must really think I'm a bit of a basket case."

How could I be mad at her, I couldn't, as all she was being was truthful. Honesty for me was always something I found refreshing and even though her woman's sixth sense had picked up a bit of sexual energy with Annie she hadn't been scared to voice it, that I respected. Her period was an excuse, I knew that, maybe she was just testing me and testing herself at the same time. I knew this girl was special but now I was the one whose voodoo was working and I wasn't ready to cast her aside. I needed her if I was to fulfil my desires for killing and that was easier to do as a team. But first things first, I needed to reassure Nellie everything was great, bringing her back under my spell.

"Look, I haven't fucked her and I have no intention of doing so."

Straight to the point I knew would appease her and it worked almost instantly as she leant forward and gave me a hug followed by a long lingering dirty kiss. She was a basket case but she was my basket case, now however I was sure of one thing: I had no doubt I would fuck Annie. The human idea of monogamy was flawed; we were top of the food chain but maybe the only species to believe in one sexual partner. Nellie may have ended a barren patch but now she was my sex on tap, I had had an awakening, I was the predator, I could see that now, I needed to hunt, to kill, to fuck and now it was time to start living that way.

16

Confrontation was something I rarely had to deal with in my life up to this point and honestly I had found Nellie's behaviour quite unsettling. Our rare lunchtime encounters had always been light hearted yet this had been an intense affair which I had been grateful had ended almost as quickly as it had started. I had breathed a silent sigh of relief when Nellie had excused herself to buy what now appeared were much needed tampons. It was a nice feeling being alone again as once again my world returned to a plane of solitude.

As I sat there nursing my second pint I could feel a calm returning to my world and more importantly a balance to my thought process. The frustrations of her time of the month issues were obvious but the idea of a couple of sex-free days was surprisingly not at the top of my list. The confirmation that her period was not an actual excuse but the truth was a big worry, which now concerned me deeply.

The appeal of being in a relationship suddenly seemed to be wearing thin with me as my more primitive urges grew, rising to the surface almost dying to be satisfied. A bit of guilt tripping could maybe combat mother nature as she played her cruel game but I wasn't sure even a blow job or some anal would be enough to quench my thirst.

It was a strange feeling to be confused but that basically was what I was. Nellie had been great up to the last few days but now lines had been crossed. A part of me knew that she completed me but was that more an insecurity on my part that I had never really fully explored or addressed? It was hard to know.

I tried to clear my head by downing what was left of my pint and ordered another accompanied with a shot of Bourbon. As I felt the whiskey slip down my throat, my mind for some reason slipped back to earlier in the year when a giant Jenga had appeared in the office. Why this came to me at this moment I didn't know. I was happy for the respite but for sure higher management's idea of team bonding needed some work.

It was hard to imagine or wonder what aliens would have made of us humans if this had been their chosen moment and place to make their first contact. I pictured their E.T like faces as they wandered into the office with so much hope then had it crushed within seconds. Let's face it: to be confronted by a bunch of suits complete with crash helmets balancing on a step ladder as they played with wooden blocks wouldn't have been very inspiring.

It was just so wrong and I had no doubt they wouldn't have hesitated to vaporize the lot of them before getting the fuck out of Dodge. As I pondered the affect of an alien vapour gun on the accounts department I caught my reflection staring at me in the back-bar mirror. I was looking gaunt, which was maybe the effect of drinking on an empty stomach and seeing as how I was daydreaming about aliens committing mass murder maybe it was a good time to head back to work.

A sense of alcohol-induced naughtiness came over me en route to the office when I spotted a perfume shop. I was determined to figure out this erotic fragrance Annie was wearing which would no doubt aid in my new-found quest of getting into her knickers. It was quite ironic really that today's drama with Nellie was now acting as a catalyst pushing me to pursue and have some fun with another woman. My mind had been made up and although hurting Nellie could be a side effect of such activities the blame would lay directly at her doorstep.

I can't say I had ever had the pleasure of being in a perfume shop before and was pretty sure this would be a one-off experience. At once I felt out of place, my senses coming under attack from all directions as I was confronted by walls of garish packaging and a ghastly cocktail of different aromas all fighting for my affections. I guess the whole thing was designed to make me consume but all I could think of was a boy at school who had to have his stomach pumped after downing a bottle of Old Spice as a bet.

A tinge of disappointment filled me as I found the

particular brand I had been searching for. It was a rather tacky product in a star-shaped bottle called "Angel". According to the box which of course I had no reason to disbelieve, "Angel" contains a chocolate essence which gives it a unique quality. Well, I guess they had a point but unique quality or not there was no way I would ever pay for such a vile item although the bottle would have made a nice weapon. The shop was busy so I removed the security tag without a problem and slipped the bottle effortlessly into my pocket. It was time to let the games begin.

Returning to work, I had an urge to strike while the iron was hot. Women, like the weather, could be changing constantly and no matter how many compliments about hair, shoes or loss of weight at times they experienced bouts of erratic behaviour. Nellie had already proven this so wonderfully today and that was why I couldn't let this opportunity slip. As I made my way back to my work station I made a deliberate effort to pass her office. The door like always was open and I gave her a smile with enough hint of eye contact for her to think it could be on. Instantly I knew my subtlety hadn't been wasted as although she was talking on the phone the reaction had been to look me up and down with a hint of innuendo. Turning away and playing it cool I now knew it was only going to be a matter of time before she would be mine, it was on.

My mind full of sexual desires, I headed to the coffee room in need of a little caffeine pick- me-up to help me through the afternoon. As I pushed the door open to my surprise I was confronted by Nellie with two of her very blonde female work colleagues, one who instantly spoke up.

"Seems like another good reason to keep our coffee machine broken ladies."

The three of them laughed in a way that only women can, full of filth with a touch of low class. Without skipping a beat they picked up their coffee cups in what seemed perfect synchronicity and headed for the door. Nellie paused as the others disappeared from view and fell out of earshot.

"Hey babe, look, I just feel so shit about today, please don't think of me as a complete cunt."

I couldn't deny her sincerity was genuine but it still didn't change that I was now living with a bipolar freak. I really wanted to give her a hard time but knew this was neither the time nor place to do so and so decided on a more delicate response.

"Don't worry about it, everything is fine and these things happen, look, I will see you at home later, if you want to talk it's never a problem, come here."

She took a quick glance to make sure we were alone then stepped across the room quickly slipping her tongue into my mouth. I still could feel how tense she was as the kiss, although short, was a passionate one with a hint of violence about it. She pulled herself away then came close again, this time to whisper in my ear.

"You're fucking great and I want to be great with you, I think it's time, we should kill again."

A look of naughtiness came over her face then with a wink she was gone heading back towards the office. So she wants to kill again, I have no problem with that, couples should do shit together but our relationship had changed and not for the better. Time would soon tell me which path I needed to take and if that journey would be taken alone then so be it.

I quickly poured out a coffee and returned to my cubicle, hiding the stolen perfume in my bottom draw. How about a threesome with Nell and Annie because that would work. Men always seemed keener on the threesome front than the ladies but this was something that needed serious consideration. I had never done a real threesome except for ones I had paid for so this could be a real opportunity. I don't know why but all of a sudden I had a desire to ram a dildo into Annie's ass. Jesus, where the fuck did that come from? My mind at times even had the ability to surprise me. I laughed out loud which drew a few sarcastic comments from across the room but letting them go I took a sip from my coffee got back to work.

My morning slackness and slightly longer lunch break meant I had a fair bit to catch up on but that was never going to be a problem. I often found myself falling behind but due to the simplicity of this retarded, far below me work it only ever required a simple shift through the gears to catch up. It wasn't long and that was exactly where I found myself, all up to date which would allow me the last hour of the day for more pressing matters. Nellie had already gone home by four thirty so I decided that my little game with Annie needed to start.

She wasn't looking for love, of that I was sure and I anticipated her pussy dampening on the thought that someone had smelt her or knew her scent. The message I needed to send had to be not too weird but enough for her to want to get her vibrator out when she got home tonight. I intended to lay the trap with a note but it was important that the words would have her hoping it was me but still not 100% sure, hence starting our little game.

Not for the first time today my mind started to wander, which it had been doing a lot of lately. I still wasn't sure what was happening to me as I seemed to be transforming on an almost daily basis. My life had always been this roller-coaster of weirdness but these changes were different and I wondered where they might lead to.

I had come a long way since meeting Nellie which was incredible seeing that just over a month ago she hadn't been a part of life and I had been creeping once again towards a full meltdown. Memories it seemed no longer haunted me as they had in the past, it was as if now they only seemed to make me stronger. Other people's actions suddenly didn't make me so angry yet I now felt more capable of acts of violence and punishment than ever before.

I was reaching higher by the second with a fog that may

have clouded my mind for years parting before my eyes, showing me the way ahead. Where was I going? Who was I becoming? Was I the recluse, the killer, the lover or even a God? My devilish mind had me by the balls and my lust for everything life could give me was exciting. If Nellie had been a drug that had awoken me then I had to question what others could do for me. The key was energy and no matter if it was negative or positive I just needed to feed.

"Lee, Lee, Lee! Are you alright?"

I hadn't heard or even seen Annie arrive but suddenly there she was standing right in front of me, white trouser suit and all. I wondered how long she had been standing there; some work was required to make me not look like a complete weirdo and I couldn't let this fish off the hook.

"Sorry boss, I didn't mean to be disrespectful, I guess I'm still a bit jaded from all the long hours last week, I must have just zoned out. Don't worry about me, honestly I'm fine, I'm sure you know how it is; all work and no play."

She had a bemused look on her face to say the least but seemed genuinely concerned for my well-being, which was kind of nice. All that aside my "all work no play" line would get her thinking. I detected a sense of nervousness as she shifted her weight from one foot to the other, then ran her hand through her hair. If I was not mistaken I think she was about to make her move. With a cute little laugh, then cough she cleared her throat.

"Yeah, I think we could all do with a bit of a break after the last couple of weeks. They work you all too hard in my opinion not that the big bosses upstairs care as it's all about bottom lines to them. Hey, I have a crazy idea, how about blowing off some steam later, you fancy grabbing a drink after work? You won't have to call me boss, I promise."

Well, all my plans of games and chases seemed to have suddenly moved forward a few steps. I have to say I found it such a turn-on when a lady asks a man out, fuck all this chivalry shit

85

that's so sexist, we live in the age of equality and it's about time the ladies took the lead. She handed me a card with the name of a bar: "O'Malley's," saying it was nice, quiet and that she would see me there around six. I reckon it was a good forty-minute walk from work, so that told me she didn't want us being disturbed by any fellow work colleagues and that she wanted me all to herself.

17

O'Malley's Bar, what could possible go wrong with a bar that shared its name with one of the most violent songs of all time? I saw its green shamrock shaped neon sign punching the night sky the second I stepped out of the train station. The bright glowing green light seemed to almost take over the street, beckoning for me to follow it as if it was some sort of crass Irish version of the Star of Bethlehem. A sudden tinkle of anticipation ran the length of my body as the bar's entrance finally became visible. I knew my prize was close.

Fate wasn't something I normally subscribed to yet recent history told me that situations with girls in this type of establishment, which was once again a basement bar, tended to end well. Pausing momentarily to gather my thoughts my mind turned to Nellie. It was imperative to be neither careless nor selfish so I needed to send Nellie a message as if I wasn't home early it could lead to some sort of period-induced panic attack or worse. Leaning up against a wall I drew my mobile phone from my bag and began typing:

PLEASE DON'T GET UPTIGHT, BUT I JUST NEED TO HAVE SOME ME TIME FOR A FEW HOURS. IT IS NOTHING TO WORRY ABOUT I PROMISE YOU BUT NOT SURE WHAT TIME I WILL BE HOME, DON'T WAIT UP

This was hardly the perfect crime but I was feeling both impulsive and lustful plus "the painters were in," so what else was a man meant to do? People tend to forget that after all we are only animals at heart and I am doing what animals do best which was to hunt and fuck. Turning my phone off I slipped it back into my bag briefly touching the stolen bottle of Angel. The perfume was a sweetener if things started to go south but I was in a confident mood that it would be surplus to requirements this evening. In fact, it would be safe to say the only perfume I would be coming in contact with tonight was that which I got to lick off Annie's body.

As the large door shut behind me my first impression was

that the bar appeared to be a nice place but obviously Irish and disappointingly not a Nick-Cave-themed establishment. I took a moment to scan the busy room then headed down the last few steps towards the bar to join the jovial crowd. Annie was nowhere to be seen but then a sudden squeezing of my buttocks told me she had arrived.

"Nice buns, you really do work out."

Turning around I was taken aback as what I found before me was a much different looking creature than my white-trouser-suited boss from the office. Ironic really that I thought I was the one transforming, but wow, leather trousers, biker boots but an unfortunate Bon Jovi T-shirt. Still first impressions were important so best to gloss over that particular musical transgression.

"Goodbye office manager, hello rock chick, all I can say is I'm impressed. Wow, you look great and Bon Jovi, nice."

This was obviously the reaction she'd been looking for and fair play to her she got it. I would have to say this was a very different start to the evening than the one I had expected but I knew what she was doing. You see, by catching me off guard she was taking control, the combination of the bum squeeze and now the surprising choice of clothing meant she had now taken centre ring, which was a very interesting turn of events. Just the gleeful look on her face at my mentioning of her T-shirt told me I'd started well, confirmed by her positive tone as she continued to speak.

"Yeah! I love Bon Jovi, I must have seen them like twenty times, they are just soooooooooo fucking amazing live, guess you must be a fan?"

Of course, I didn't like Bon Jovi and that combined with the drawn-out use of the word "so" already had me thinking about heading for the exit. Saying that her tits did look fantastic in that T-shirt pushing out Jon Bon Jovi's face and making him almost look retarded, which I guess kind of balanced things out somewhat.

I didn't need to say a thing as just a polite nodding of the head combined with a smooth smile was sufficient to please her. It was important to keep this ship on course as being tactful was never my strongest suit especially where music was concerned. I bit down on my tongue and clicked my mind into the charm setting.

"Yeah, they're great and I just love that T-shirt, in fact I must say you look amazing."

I hated myself and imagined my records at home shaking their heads in despair; still best not to slaughter her favourite band if I was to have any chance this evening of seeing what lay under Jon Bon Jovi's head.

It shouldn't have been the greatest surprise that she'd changed out of her trouser suit. Yet I almost felt a sense of disappointment as it had played a large part in how I perceived our forthcoming sexual encounter was going to play out. I guess she must have detected something as she suddenly went on the defensive.

"Don't look so surprised, we're not at work now, look, between the two of us I fucking hate those trouser suits, so come on, let me get some drinks in."

Once again, she was playing the dominant role, this time taking me by the hand and leading the two of us into the main bar area. The large hordes of people didn't seem to bother her as she whistled catching the eye of the bartender, who instantly blew her a kiss, what the fuck was going on?

Now in my experience a bartender never likes to be whistled at yet there she was doing exactly that and not only did he smile but blew her a kiss for her troubles. All this seemed pretty normal behaviour as no one batted an eyelid. Her voice continued to compete against the strains of Thin Lizzy's "Whisky in a jar" that vibrated from the speakers as she shouted across the bar.

"Two pints of the black stuff and couple of large Bushmills please Jim."

She turned to me as if she had forgotten something.

"That's alright with you, yeah?"

Of course it was, as any sort of alcohol would improve my chances of getting laid. I nodded, touching her on the arm not only as further acknowledgement of a yes but also first contact as I started to plan my strategy.

The night was already taking a very different turn to how I had imagined and now I found myself once again being led by the hand but this time towards the back of the establishment. Making a beeline towards an empty booth we soon found ourselves sitting across from each other in a dark corner when suddenly it hit me, she smelled different. What the fuck happened to the "Angel?" I needed an inroad and this was it as just noticing she smelled differently would please her and bring her under my spell, women loved that kind of shit.

"If I'm not mistaken aren't you wearing a different perfume? I could have sworn you wore Angel, it smells nice but I prefer your work smell."

Boom, right back at you sweetheart, enough with all this jabbing business, I was taking control and landing the first meaningful punch meant centre ring was mine. As I waited for her response it suddenly dawned on me that maybe I had underestimated my prey as the expression on her face changed to one of an almost sarcastic contempt. Looking straight at me she gave out a cheeky laugh before firing back.

"Just because you recognised the perfume I wear doesn't mean I am going to fuck you darling. I am two very different

90

people at work and at play. Just remember I am older and wiser than you and don't forget, you know what they say about older women?"

She thinks I will be intimidated by this but I won't bite. I like all this playing hard to get especially with this edge of flirtation, now we can start the real games, time to set the tone.

"What do they say about older women, what, that they are older? Anyway, who said I wanted to fuck you, maybe you're too old for me, darling."

I read the situation right as she isn't offended in fact she smiles then does her little lip pout thing that is just so sexy. Jesus, she has great lips which would look even better clamped around my cock. She is enjoying this little game just as much as me, which means all is on track.

Our sparring is momentarily halted as a cute waitress appears at the foot of the table with our drinks. I sit there in polite silence as the two of them make conversation about some guy called Roland who appears to have been very sick. Fuck Roland, I want to play, not to sit and listen to this meaningless bollocks. Thankfully the waitress gets the hint that she is a third wheel and disappears leaving the two of us once again facing each other. Annie reaches for the Bushmills first, raising her glass.

"To older women, who know how to fuck and have great tits."

There wasn't much to say to that so I raise my glass in agreement and we both down our whiskeys in one. The moment after a shot is always pleasant as the alcohol trickles down the throat giving the body a little jolt. We briefly sit there in silence just looking at each other like poker players. I was having fun, it wasn't an uncomfortable silence by any means, in fact it was sexy as hell. After maybe ten seconds of arousing eye contact she leans forward resting her elbows on the table and breaks the silence.

"You are different to the others, I can see that. There is

91

something very playful or evil in those brooding eyes of yours, I just haven't worked out which yet. You know most men I meet at work are scared of me but you don't show any sign of fear or intimidation, I like that. It's almost as if you are this cold silent killer hidden in that office day in day out hoping nobody will notice you, tell me I'm wrong."

I felt quite one-dimensional all of a sudden and although I knew she was joking, her "silent killer" comment hit hard. I needed to steer this boat back onto my chosen path as I didn't like to be analysed, ha ha, how ironic, Annie-lysed. Time to step it up with a bit of humour.

"Don't good people pay for this kind of shit? I didn't realise I was here to be analysed or in this case.......Annie-lysed."

I couldn't just leave comedy gold like that in my head, it was just too good, however my timing is off. Yes the desired effect had been achieved but maybe would have been better delivered in-between her intakes of Guinness. Poor Annie is now sat in front of me covered in beer; it's amazing really, the power comedy has as I think that her Guinness may have actually come out of her nose. We both continue laughing at the mayhem my one-liner has caused as I hand her a packet of tissues I luckily have in my pocket, still best to apologise.

"I'm so sorry, I didn't mean to be quite so funny, you OK?"

She was fine but the same couldn't be said for her Bon Jovi T-shirt, which may never be the same again. One thing for sure the power had now swung back in my direction as I had caught her with a punch she never saw coming. It's always nice to know people find you funny and normally from my experience it helps when laying traps for the opposite sex. Annie wiped her face clean glaring down at her Guinness stained T-shirt; it could have been so much worse if she hadn't been wearing a Wonder-bra which had shaped her huge breasts into a flood-like barrier.

At least she'd seen the funny side of things as this could

quite easily have been end of proceedings for a more fragile individual. Annie was made of sterner stuff and was actually seeing the funny side of it all.

"Well look at you Mr Shelton with the witty mind, very fast and very funny. Of course, your humorous turn now means we may need a trip upstairs to change my T-shirt."

I like the "we" bit of that statement but what the fuck, upstairs? We were in a basement, don't tell me we would be fucking in her car, unless...

"What, you mean you live upstairs? Aren't you a bit old to be living above a pub?"

For some reason she seemed to find this hilarious. It was if I was suddenly God's gift to comedy but on a more positive note if she was laughing I guess she liked me. Still, I had to admit I was a bit taken aback that a woman of this obvious quality lived here. I had pictured us going back to her luxury flat in some tree-lined street no doubt overlooking a canal.

"Yeah, I live here, what, you want the gory details?"

There was no sign of shame but more defiance in her voice but if her idea of gory was woman in her late thirties living in a pub then maybe I would save my murder story for another day. Still I wanted to know more.

"Gory details? Wow, sounds kind of intriguing, I don't mind a bit of blood, so do tell."

The word blood made me think of Nellie's period and then for some reason Joe of the 12-inch cock lying there twitching on the floor. If Annie had secrets I wanted to know them, I was curious. I went to further my investigation but stopped short of speaking as she stood up.

"OK maybe, but give me a second, don't worry, I will be back."

I wasn't going to argue so I sat back and watched as she quickly slipped amongst the customers in the main bar area then disappeared from view. She really had the most amazing arse, one just made for the tight leather trousers that she was using so obviously to show it off to the maximum. Thoughts of her rear-end suddenly faded as once again my mind flashed back to the night I had killed so violently.

I remembered the ease the broken bottle had ripped into his neck and how his body had just so pathetically crumbled to the floor. That was the night that my great potential had awoken. I had felt so powerful as he had lain there dying before me, he was scum and that part of him had found me, it was as if I was its new host. It had been a similar feeling when Nellie was telling me her darkest secrets, it seemed the more she hurt the stronger I had felt. This was the key, I was onto something I was sure of it.

"Daydreaming again there junior, penny for your thoughts."

I sat back and smiled as she placed an almost completely full bottle of Bushmills onto the table before once again sitting herself down in front of me.

"I was actually thinking about how great you looked in those leather trousers, you have an incredible body."

Nothing subtle about that but then I would have quite happily bent her over the table and fucked her, right here, right now. Women always loved a compliment especially one about their body. I had always been a play-it-nice sort of guy but sometimes you've just got to be more direct. I didn't want her little trip to the bar to give her the chance of changing the subject matter. I wanted to hear her pain and see her suffer in front of me then drink it all up; time to start digging.

"Anyway, as much as I would love to discuss what lies under your clothes and believe me I do, you promised gory details, so come on, spit them out."

With a polite smile she poured out two shots pushing one over to me without a word then raised her glass once again in a silent toast before knocking it back. I followed suit then as she poured a refill.

"They are hardly gory to be honest, it's not like I killed anyone although I maybe should have. Hey, I don't know why I'm telling you this, it wasn't really in my plans for tonight."

Her tone had completely changed, the confidence she had so forthrightly displayed before draining from her by the second. She paused, this time looking down at the table before downing the whisky. I was eager to hear her misery but then at same time I wanted to fuck her and if she kept drinking at this rate that wasn't likely to happen. The time was right to play a friend and lighten the mood; I reached over taking her hand in mine.

"Annie, look, we all have secrets and problems, I guarantee you that if everyone in this bar was to lay down their troubles on this table here in front of us we would soon pick up our own."

What a load of crap, I wanted to hear her problems, her dirty secrets and the darker the better. I knew they were my fuel and I wanted to be stronger, I would have her body later but now I needed her pain. My words seemed to have an instant effect as she continued to hold my hand then started to stroke it gently. Amazingly it was Nellie who had shown me this little trick and now it would almost certainly result in me bedding another woman. Annie was now on the verge of opening up and I gave her my full attention as she continued.

"You're sweet, I never knew you were like this, Lee, your parents must be so proud."

Fuck off, my parents, fucking hell don't make me laugh, where are your analytic skills now sweetheart? You really think you can read me, please you wish, here you go darling some reality for you to chew on let's see how your issues match up to mine.

"My parents are dead, my dad of a heart attack, no doubt caused by his hedonistic lifestyle and my mum killed herself shortly after in the bath courtesy of a razor blade."

Talk about a mood killer but hey, if you live by the sword you die by the sword. A look of horror filled her face as her hands instinctively covered her open mouth, I guess I had shocked her somewhat. Sitting still I decided to milk the moment, peering down at the table as if I was suffering. The ball was back in her court and once again she reached across the table for my hand.

"You poor soul, I am just so sorry, that must have been awful, terrible, I don't really know what to say?"

I wanted her to pity me, however now it was crucial to rebuild her self-confidence which was disappearing quicker than the whiskey. She was already my prey caught in my web and now I would change the mood again before sucking her dry which in turn would lead to a more physical outpouring of emotions.

All it took was a stroke of the hand and a calming smile, then she was back. The next hour flowed almost as well as the whiskey as I basically charmed her knickers off. She did start to open up a bit telling me her tale of a failed marriage as if it was part of a stand-up routine and in these fucked-up times probably could have been.

Even though I now had my own partner I still didn't fully understand the human need to couple up. In her case it had obviously been a rash decision to marry as she had found her husband in bed with another man not once but twice.

The pub was her father's and she had returned there only recently after the break-up. "Three generations of O'Malley's," she had said as she led me through a fire door then up some metal stairs and into a fenced-off alley that ran along the side of the building. The highly stacked cases of bottles and empty barrels not for the first time that evening reminded me of the life I had previously taken.

We reached a door, then as she looked for her key I took my chance grabbing her from behind and forcing her against its frame while kissing the back of her neck. I knew through her moans she could feel my erect penis fighting to get to her and the more my body ground against hers the louder they grew. Finally she could take no more, spinning round grabbing my cock through the fabric and at last our mouths came together as our passion spilled over into pure lust and desire. She smelt so good, pure sex. Joe's dead body filled my head again as my tongue worked my way up her neck, was I meant to kill this woman? I pushed her away and stepped back which startled her.

"Someone is a bad boy that likes it rough I think."

Maybe it was a good thing that she didn't know exactly just how rough I was thinking. I couldn't be sure how much self-control I had left, fuck, what was wrong with me? I knew I was very drunk yet still I reached for the bottle of Bushmills in her hand and took a huge swig. This just wasn't who I was, this woman was one of life's victims and wouldn't be one of mine. I needed a physical release and needed it quickly.

"Get that fucking door open and you'll see how bad I really am."

She stepped forward standing right in front of me unzipping my flies then slipped her hand inside my trousers to grab my erect penis not once breaking eye contact. Once again I brought the bottle of whiskey up to my lips and took another long drink. I lowered the bottle, giving out a little joyous breath that brought a smile to her face as she pushed herself against me first grabbing my hair pulling my neck down to her mouth. Slowly she ran her tongue up the side of my face until she reached my ear then stopped before biting it softly and quietly started to whisper while continuing to fondle my manhood.

"You know the real reason I wear a trouser suit to work is, when I used to wear skirts I would get so fucking bored that I used to end up fingering myself behind my desk. I haven't been with a man in a while, so promise to fuck me good and fuck me hard, I want it to hurt."

97

18.

One of the recurring problems that constantly seemed to rear its ugly head in my life was my inability to know when to stop. It was just a trait or flaw in character I guess as I tended to be extreme in a lot of both my normal and more destructive activities. Tonight it had once again been the turn of alcohol with the whole Annie adventure ending in a blur as I awoke on a park bench. It must have been close to midnight when I stepped off the bus to make the short walk home still very much under the influence of a hard night of drinking.

I stopped to regroup a bit sitting myself on the wall across the road from where Nellie had murdered poor Stinky Pete. His departure from this world hadn't gone unnoticed as now several bunches of flowers lay at the top of the alley where he'd met his demise. I was still feeling a bit overwhelmed by the events of the evening as from what I could remember I had been truly tamed. I don't think I had ever been fucked like that, every thrust of Annie's body felt as if she'd been ridding herself of all this rage and hatred she had built up inside of her for years. As I stood up I took a deep breath and I wondered if Nellie would still be up when I arrived home. To be honest I hoped not as I was still quite drunk and didn't fancy facing any more emotional turmoil today.

Pushing the key into the front door I open it as quietly as I can then step into to the dimly lit front room. The silence is punctuated by the sound of my record player making a strange clicking noise giving the room an awkward type of feel. I imagine Nellie must have been waiting for me as she is now asleep on the sofa snoring peacefully. Walking across the room to the turntable I carefully lift the needle off the still spinning record which places the room into silence that is instantly broken by the sound of Nellie's voice.

"You're home late and Jesus, you stink of booze."

I didn't detect any anger in her voice and reached down to kiss her then sat myself down on the coach beside her, lifting her feet to rest them on my lap. Of course I stank of booze, after all I had consumed way over a bottle of fine Irish whisky and was still far from sober. I started to massage her feet as she lay there motionless, giving the impression that she was not happy; maybe time to smooth things over.

"Yeah sorry, one thing led to another but hey it's good to be home, how you doing?"

My words were clumsy and slurred but the foot massage was definitely winning her over as she rested her head back onto the pillow, shutting her eyes. I knew I wasn't getting away with it that easily and sure enough with her eyes remaining firmly shut she began to speak.

"Look, I am not your fucking owner so you don't technically answer to me, I get that. However, what I do ask for is some fucking respect, so when you get home at way after midnight not just stinking of booze but FUCKING PERFUME!! What the fuck am I meant to think?"

The whole rant had been delivered calmly until the heavy emphasis on the words "FUCKING" and "PERFUME." It seemed I was well and truly in the doghouse but all was not lost. Pushing her feet to one side I stood up and headed back across the darkened room. Turning on the light didn't exactly improve the situation.

"Fuck, Lee, turn the fucking light off will you!"

I don't do as she commands, instead I go for my work bag, which doesn't go down well as she sits up with a face of pure anger and starts to shout.

"FUCKING TURN IT OFF!"

This time her blood is boiling as she throws her body back down into the sofa with a scream placing a pillow over her face to shade it from the light. Quickly I retrieve my bag then hit the light switch again, plunging the room back into near darkness.

"Sorry about that Nell, it's just I got something for you."

I am still a little drunker than I had realised and as I go to sit back down on the sofa I almost fall to the floor. Somehow I just manage to perch on its edge and turn to face Nellie, who responds by throwing the pillow straight at me, hitting me square in the face before launching into another tirade.

"What the fuck has got into you? You're acting like a complete fucking nutcase."

I ignore her, then resting my work bag on my knees take a deep breath to try and compose myself. In all my life, I have only ever had amazing sex with two women, one is asleep above her father's pub and the other is no more than a metre from me, imagine that threesome, wow. Nellie sits up again.

"Really, what the fuck is wrong with you? If you got nothing to say then just fuck off because you are really starting to piss me off!"

Adjusting my position on the sofa I raise my hand in a calming manner, which doesn't seem to relieve the tension but at least gets her lying down again. She does deserve an explanation and now it seems our relationship will turn a new corner as I lie through my teeth.

"Please I beg you to hear me out, I've had such a fucking awful day. I know you're feeling shit and a bit vulnerable so all I can do is apologise for my actions. I don't really know why but I just felt I needed to be alone for a bit today and just get drunk. That was some nasty shit you laid on me over the weekend and then with the craziness at lunchtime it was all too much. It's hard to explain but I guess it was like I had the weight of the world on my shoulders."

I pause with the hope of inflicting some guilt, lowering my

head for extra effect then waiting for her. I knew she would've been suffering all night thinking she had scared me off and that was exactly what I was trying to tap into. Slowly she sits up pulling herself close before running her hand over my back in an affectionate manner. Her whole demeanour has now been turned on its head and she starts to speak, this time in a guilt-ridden tone.

"Look, it's me who should be saying sorry, not you; I really need to man up. Things haven't just been great with you, they've been fucking great and I am so lucky to have found you. All night I've been lying here thinking I had fucked everything up and all because I laid all that emotional baggage on you, which wasn't fair. I always get a bit crazy when I'm about to get my period and worse when I'm on it but that shouldn't be an excuse, you don't deserve that."

Managing to dig myself out of this very deep hole would normally be impressive but in my current state was more of a miracle. All I needed now was some icing on this cake as I didn't want to lose her and in future would need to be more careful. She was far from stupid, in fact she was good for me and I was sure we had some sort of destiny together which I couldn't afford to lose.

Still there was hole in my story I still needed to address to complete my comeback. I reached into my bag and handed her the box of Angel I had stolen with a rather different objective in mind. She seems lost for words and even surprised I have brought her a gift, now for that icing.

"I knew you were hurting, Nell, and wanted to get you something. I had originally planned to head into town and buy you a record, something soulful to give you a lift, maybe some Marvin Gaye, Wilson Pickett, a bit of Stevie. Well, as I said before one thing led to another and before I knew it I was pretty drunk. Anyways, as I walked towards the train station I somehow found myself in that perfume shop close to work, hence how I smell. Being wasted isn't an excuse but drunken guys do silly things and when I saw something called Angel I instantly thought of you. Of course now I have sobered up somewhat I feel a bit of dick but hey, that's your lot."

She threw her arms around me giving me a huge hug and I felt no guilt, she wasn't a pawn in my game, she was my Queen. I looked forward to more encounters with Annie and many others but they would be distractions whereas Nellie was now a part of me.

As she opened the box a large smile fell across her face, actually making me feel good. Holding the bottle up, she gave it a little squirt releasing the chocolate essence into the air instantly making me think of Annie and giving me an erection. Looking at the garishly shaped bottle she shook her head in almost disbelief at what was happening.

"You're one crazy motherfucker and you know what? It is tacky as hell but actually, it smells surprisingly nice, thank you."

I wasn't crazy; I was in control and had her wrapped around my little finger. The train was back upon the track and Nellie pulled me close kissing me softly. She ran her hand down my body to find my erection then unbuckled my belt, I guess she still liked me.

"I hope you don't mind fucking a girl when she is on, because I am horny as hell?"

I had no problem with such things as it was normally the lady who objected, us men were just not fussy. I did however have one request and a sexual bucket list item I felt was close to being struck off.

"It's not a problem with me babe, but with one condition: You let me remove your tampon with my teeth."

She didn't need to answer as she pushed herself back into the sofa pulling up her t-shirt to reveal a huge pair of underwear which caught me by surprise, compelling her to make an excuse.

"Sorry about the Bridget Jones knickers, but mother nature made that call, not me."

I sank down to my knees in front of her and as she opened her legs slipped off her knickers in quick fashion then dived in for the kill.

19

My early start was greeted by a killer hangover which was brutally reminding why I didn't normally mix my drinks with Guinness. To add insult to the way I was feeling my daily routine had been broken as the little coffee shop next to the station was closed. According to the sign in the window they were shut due to a family bereavement, I only hoped it was the old man as he was a miserable fucker. I settled for a Red Bull from the newspaper kiosk knocking it back in one before heading to the platform.

As it was every day at this ungodly hour the place was packed with the same faces, in the same clothes and carrying the same cases. I was no different of course so who was I to judge but after my complete misreading of Annie I wondered what secret lives these people were hiding behind their work camouflage.

The train seemed more packed than usual today, which was probably more to do with a hangover-induced bad mood than actual reality. As the doors closed for the first time I could already feel the alcohol sweats soaking into the back of my shirt under my jacket. Then there she was again, I say again but as I had only seen her maybe a couple of times in my whole life that seemed more than a slight exaggeration.

I wouldn't say that she was unattractive but it was her mind that interested me as she was always reading cool books. People didn't read books any more as they had fucking Kindles, tablets or other shit on their phones to amuse them but she was like me still going old skool. I had noticed her the first time during the summer with a copy of "Girlfriend in a coma" by Douglas Coupland, then once again about a month ago reading one of my personal favourites, "American Psycho". She must have been going through some sort of Easton Ellis phase as today she was reading "Less than zero". The Red Bull was working its magic giving me a much-needed caffeine boost and suddenly I felt compelled to converse with this interesting young lady.

"Hey, Less than zero, cool book."

My yelling across the crammed carriage instantly drew about 30 dirty looks. I knew she'd heard me as it would have been impossible not to yet she dared not look up, maybe hoping I would go away. I was going nowhere and now with the predictable reaction of all these average Joes felt an urge to address the whole carriage.

"Come on people, what the fuck is wrong with us? Why does no one ever talk on the train? Every fucking day the same fucking silence."

"Fuck you, weirdo!"

The voice rings out from the back somewhere winning a few cheap laughs, but I refuse to be disheartened and once again address my fellow passengers.

"I will take that as a sign of life, first contact even. Thank you for your contribution, sir, wherever you are, but come on, no more fucking bad language, please."

This throwaway line doesn't exactly get them rolling in the aisles but does at least get a half decent reception. I would say that now 70% of the carriage was looking my direction, most I imagine thinking "Who dare break the taboo of talking on public transport." My momentum is broken for a second as the train stops at a station and the robotic voice of the tannoy system takes centre stage. Like every day I watch as the doors open then close yet nobody gets on or off.

"Is it just me or does anyone wonder why every fucking day we stop at this station? Does anyone actually live here? Think about it, as this station is robbing me, in fact robbing us all of at least 2 minutes extra in bed every day."

I must be winning them over as this time my rant receives a good slice of healthy laughter and even a few cheers. Through the crowd I can still see the "Less than Zero" girl seemingly pinned to her seat, obviously hoping I had forgotten about her, which of course I haven't, and again I go to address her directly.

"Young lady, please, Less than Zero, I know you can hear me."

This time she does look up with an embarrassed look on her face giving me a kind of half wave and a shy smile. The whole moment is played out as if we are on stage in maybe the world's smallest theatre as the morning crowd watch waiting to see what happens next, better not disappoint them.

"Hey, don't be shy, I just want to say I love that fucking book. Easton Ellis must be nailed-on my favourite writer, he is just so original, so enjoy that ride but never watch the movie."

She gives me a polite nod before looking back down at her book again, obviously praying inside this whole saga is over. I take stock but notice people still staring in my direction so for the last time I address my new-found audience.

"Now that's all I got to say people, I am all done so as you were, back to the silence."

I gain a strange sort of round of applause before the carriage slips back to normality once again descending into silence. I watch her through the crowd but she doesn't raise her eyes from the book, which is understandable due to its content but still a little disappointing.

My urge to kill it seemed had been turned into the urge to fuck as I started to picture her naked in an assortment of different positions. One stop from my own she gets up to leave so I decide to follow, I felt at least I owed her an apology but really, I just wanted to fuck her.

She hadn't seen me get off the train and I soon caught up to her on the platform before she had a chance to exit. I reached forward lightly touching her on the shoulder, which causes her to stop in her tracks. As she turns around her face fills with horror, I need to say something quick or this could get messy.

"Hey, I just wanted to say sorry, I didn't mean to embarrass you back there. I remembered you from a few months back when you were reading "American Psycho" so when I saw you today reading "Less than Zero" I just had to say something."

I give her my best puppy dog eyes and innocent smile routine which she just doesn't seem to be buying. Now it was my turn to suffer it seemed as she just stood there staring at me just long enough to make me feel uncomfortable. The silence was suddenly broken as she started to laugh then as I went to speak she beat me to it.

"What the fuck! Are you some sort of stalker, and besides that what kind of weirdo talks on the train, don't you know the unwritten rule?"

She was already starting to play games; it seemed all was not lost after all.

"Sorry again, but I just hate that rule and by the way this weirdo is called Lee."

She gave me a lovely smile which was a good sign also meaning it was maybe on.

"Well Lee, I'm Lisa and I am also late for work, you got a pen?"

I reach into my jacket pocket handing over my pen. Without taking her eyes off mine she grabs my arm, pushing up my sleeve then steadying herself writes out her name and number on my lower arm before placing the pen back into the palm of my hand.

"Well Lee, I guess you know how to read, so call me some time, you never know it could be fun, you're kind of different, I like that. Anyway, until the next time as I really must run, but please, no more shouting on the train."

After a couple of seconds of lingering sexual tension she gave me one final smile then turned to walk away. I watched her as she headed down the platform but after maybe no more than 15 steps she turned back to face me again and started to shout.

"And you're right, "Less than Zero" is a fucking awful movie, needs a remake."

I start to laugh but when I look back in her direction she is gone, lost instantly in the rush hour crowd. I wasn't sure if I would call her or not as she seemed too nice to fuck up. Besides that I already had my brainy pussy in Nellie so apart from another body to explore she gave me nothing. Of course, there was always the chance she had some darkness she needed to share which I would happily help her with.

What could have been an awkward morning at work turned into an anti-climax as Annie was a no show. I guess I was kind of disappointed in a way as I had been looking forward to seeing how she dealt with the dreaded day after. I couldn't remember how our night ended as I was quite out of it by the end but was certain we hadn't said goodbye. There lingered an element of the unknown or "what would happen next?" I wondered if she remembered telling me how she liked to finger herself behind her desk and I laughed to myself as I turned on my computer.

The morning dragged as always at its normal snail´s pace and I counted the seconds until freedom. I briefly caught a glimpse of Nellie leaving for lunch with a few work colleagues but given the unfortunate business of yesterday´s rendezvous I decided not to follow suit choosing to eat in at the staff canteen for a change. I knew that last night had been wrong but it was something different to the guilt I was feeling. I sat alone and played with the processed cheese sandwich in front of me pausing for thought. With Lisa I was at it again, why this need for human contact suddenly? I had never needed it for years and now it seemed to have gotten hold of me like some sort of drug.

I started to panic about Annie and how she might take my

rejection. Could I even resist was another question that only time could answer, what a mess. If Nellie found out it would surely break her but the sex had been so wild and carefree whereas with Nellie it almost seemed too much. Of course fucking her was great but my sex on tap was turning into an intense experience the slower and more intimate it got. I had liked the way Annie had begged me to hurt her, she liked it rough and wanted me to pull her hair, bite her and drive into her as deep as I could. Just hearing her howl with a mix of pleasure and pain was ecstasy in itself.

I wasn't sure what the fuck was wrong with me or where my self-control had gone. As I sat there suddenly the whole fucking of Annie just felt so wrong to me. I knew I had been going through changes and I was pretty sure this transformation was making me stronger but at what cost? I was the kind of person who needed routine to keep me sane and had found exactly that with Nellie who it seemed had stabilized me. This was against the grain for me but had felt so right up until that bloody Saturday night that's when something had changed inside of me.

Could it be the evil this man Joe had possessed had absorbed itself into me? Maybe yes, but if that was the case it was making me stronger if not more erratic. I had been going soft, letting my self-discipline slip; I needed to get back in control. Nellie was the best thing that had ever happened to me yet it seemed since we had become closer I was hell-bent on destroying us. This would have to change now if I was to evolve. I looked down at my arm, rolling up my sleeve where Lisa had written her number then spitting into my hand wiped it clean. Tonight I would build bridges with Nellie then we would move forward together. I had a calling, we had a calling and now it was time.

20

His body had gone limp with the minimal of struggles as you would have expected from a man of his advanced years. Now he just hung there ever so slightly swinging from side to side as we stared up at a lifeless body. Nellie had fallen silent, almost tongue-tied in what seemed to be a moment of reflection, however there was a coldness in her eyes which told me differently, I needed to break the tension.

"Well, I guess that's the end of Toby "fucking" Johnson."

I reached out to touch her but she angrily pulled away raising her hand, pointing it directly at the swinging corpse.

"Fuck that piece of shit, we should have tortured him and made him suffer, this was the easy way out."

She was right of course but we had no choice but to be careful as if you tended to go around murdering with spite, malice and with a bit of torture thrown in you tended to get caught. We had got lucky before so if this was to turn into an ongoing project we needed to act in a more professional manner. For Nellie this had been all too personal, which I guess was understandable under the circumstances but still unacceptable. For me it was simpler as we had achieved what we had intended to do, which was kill Toby Johnson. There had been no argument that he had deserved to die and now he was dead so our work here was done.

"Come on Nell, let's go, he's starting to stink."

I guess it was true what they said about hanging someone after all and that people actually did shit themselves. Judging by the smell coming from Toby that certainly seemed to be the case anyhow but it had been a long day and we needed to go home.

Our weekend project had started on the Friday night a good 48 hours earlier when I arrived home from work early to be greeted with a "I've found him, that motherfucker is still alive!" Of course she was referring to the now deceased Toby Johnson. It seemed Mr Johnson had been a truly nasty piece of work and Nellie's desire for redemption was justified in my eyes. The story was an all too familiar one these days of someone in a position of power abusing it to take advantage of their perverse desires. The news was full of them at the moment as everyone from celebrities and clergyman to teachers and politicians were being put in the dock on what seemed an almost daily occurrence. I guess the easiest route would have been a public exposé, but that was too simple, plus it was so much more fun being judge, jury and executioner.

To say the early part of Nellie's life had been a turbulent one was definitely an understatement. The bleak early years as a toddler spent with her mother had been bad enough but largely forgotten over time. However, the soul-destroying experiences she'd had in various state-run children's homes still lived very much within her.

It seemed all these places were pretty grim but nothing had scarred her more than the months she'd spent at Saint Luke's Home for Children. I remember sitting there that night in shock as she told me of the horrors of this place. Of course you hear and read about these kinds of things in the news but to hear such first-hand details from someone you actually knew was nothing short of horrifying.

Although my own desires had questionable values in this modern society I felt they were explainable whereas what could drive a fellow human being to abuse a child wasn't. The lowest form of child molester had to be the ones whose job it was to look after children and then worse than that got paid to look after troubled ones. Nellie had been in the troubled camp but at least got through her ordeal without being sexually abused which I guess in hindsight seemed a good result.

To her credit she had struck out at the system, fighting back, but had ended up being beaten black and blue for her troubles. The instigator of this had been one Toby Johnson and for years she had dreamed of paying him back with interest. Her desire for revenge wasn't so much for her beatings but for her friend Tammie. This poor girl was one of life's true victims and suffered over a year of sexual abuse at his hands as a minor. Stuff like this doesn't go away and years later she had taken her own life.

"I was a tough little bitch at that age so when he tried it on I was more than ready. I wasn't weak like some of the others, like Tammie, as my childhood had already been tough. General bad behaviour was the excuse he gave to summon me to his office that night, big mistake. I can still see him now undoing his dressing gown to reveal his small pathetic penis then hear him asking me if I wanted to play a little game. He never saw it coming as I rammed the shard of glass as hard as I could into his leg with all my strength. His screams were beautiful but my victory was short-lived as I may have won the battle but I didn't win the war, that blow was for all the girls and boys he abused but now I want more."

She may have been a heroine to the other girls but her fame had come at a price as the next morning she found herself locked up in the cellar. Every night for four nights he visited her to inflict his revenge, beating her with his leather belt. She knew he had enjoyed these violent moments as said he had always left drooling and aroused. This all came to a halt on the fifth morning when she had been shipped out to a young offender's prison.

"Believe it or not the prison was better than the children's homes because at least you knew where you stood. The guards were just cold with us but in reality, it was just like school except you didn't go home at the end of the day. In fact, thanks to that place I got an education but then that came at a cost. Tammie and I had been thick as thieves but without me she had no shoulder to cry on as I was not only her friend but also some sort of mental crutch. I remember we would write to each other and the despair of those letters will live with me forever. Her abuses at his hands never stopped and if anything, they actually got worse; she just wasn't strong enough to fight back, easy pickings."

112

It was a sad story but now Nellie was determined to finish it by writing her own ending. With the help of the internet she had managed to track down Mr Johnson to a country house in the middle of nowhere where he now lived alone surrounded by just solitude and trees.

"I want to go to this man's house and kill him, Lee, no more, no less."

I knew instantly I would have no problem killing this man as these kinds of people didn't deserve to live. I guess our weekend plans were set and a sense of excitement spread through my body. I lay in bed that Friday night trying to picture what this man might actually look like, first alive and then dead. Nellie was angry and wanted vengeance but we still needed to play it cool.

It was close to dusk when he finally appeared in what had been almost four very frustrating hours sat hidden in the woods that lay directly behind his house. Mr Johnson was a frail man who must have been easily in his eighties and for what I could see struggled to walk without the aid of a stick. There was no doubt that either Nellie or I could have killed this man with our bare hands but unfortunately that was not what we had in mind. The plan was simple; we were going to make it look like suicide but just needed to be sure he was alone, which now after our scouting mission appeared to be the case.

The night would run smoothly, of that I was sure, and as we approached the house we held hands. I rang the bell twice then a few seconds later a light came on and we could hear someone making their way to the door. He didn't open it but we could now see his small crooked crow-like silhouette through the coloured smoked glass that separated us.

"Who is it?"

His voice was rough and cruel-sounding but with a hint of caution. Nellie spoke up and for some reason put on an American accent.

113

"Good evening sir, I was hoping you might be able to help us, you see our car has broken down up on the top road and they're say it will be at least an hour wait for the tow truck. I am 8 months pregnant sir and would really appreciate if I could use your bathroom if it's no bother."

As improvisations went it was poor and I was pretty sure he wouldn't buy such a crock of shit. But then by some miracle and after a short pause the key turned in the lock opening the door. Mr Toby Johnson was now in front of us looking directly at Nellie seemingly confused.

"An America eh, I have a great affinity with, oh, I thought you said you were pregnant young lady?"

Nellie smiled then kicked away his walking stick, which instantly sent the old man off balance and onto the floor. I knew she had wanted to punch him but we had a plan and needed to stick to it. To be honest even a gust of wind would have been sufficient as up close he looked even frailer than he had first appeared. Nellie took a step inside and stood over him as he cowered on the floor.

"I fucking lied."

Following her in I closed the door behind us before we dragged him into the living room sitting him up in what we thought was his chair. He sat there trembling, with his eyes closed and hands in front of his face, almost anticipating he was about to be hit. Nellie was not happy.

"Open your fucking eyes, you piece of shit."

She gave him a hard slap and then as he sat back up emptied the contents of a glass she'd found on the table next to him into his face, which sprang him back into life.

The next hour was pure theatre as Nellie broke him. I knew how much she had wanted to physically harm him but in many ways what she did was worse as she raped him mentally. His tears were for no-one and I guessed he knew he was going to die the moment he found out who she was. She made him stand to drop his trousers so she could see the scar her shard of glass had left all those years ago.

It was there too but as he stood with his trousers around his ankles he got an erection that if I hadn't held Nellie back would have cost him his life there and then. I managed to calm her down but after that he was really scared and must have used the word sorry a hundred times. She just kept going, letting him have it with both barrels.

"Say her fucking name!"

"Tammie Peters, I'm sorry."

"Fuck you, now say it again."

"Tammie Peters."

His crying now seemed genuine, which made me wonder if it was actual regret he was feeling. It was funny how people always have remorse or look to God for forgiveness when they're staring death in the face. I never believed in God but if I was to die and then come across him or her in the afterlife I would quite happily apologise and admit I was wrong. The "Death to Toby Johnson Show" was now coming to its climax as Nellie had him standing on a stool with a noose made of his own bed sheets around his neck.

"Not that you deserve it but any last words?"

This was probably the first sentence she had used in an hour without the words, fuck, cunt or shit in it. However, in a show of misguided hope Toby was clinging on for his life.

"Please, I don't want to die like this; I have money, I can give it to you, please."

115

Now that was a mistake as the offer of money didn't go down well with Nellie.

"You fucking think you can bribe me, fuck you Toby; I don't want your fucking money. This is mercy motherfucker as if I had my way we would have tortured and then crucified you."

He knew it was the end at that point and just bowed his head in surrender. She had made him write a confession of his wrong-doings in the style of a suicide note, which was now tucked into his trouser pocket. Nellie looked him up and down one last time then stepped up close.

"Fucking look at me old man!"

He raised his head in an almost defiant way looking her straight in the eye, she paused for a second not breaking eye contact.

"Fuck you Toby Johnson this is for Tammie."

One kick and it was over, I was pretty sure life would never be the same again after that night. His death had been cause for reflection and as I drove the rental car back to the city we sat in silence for long parts of the journey. Our body count was now three and the question now was how far would we go? Nellie had fallen asleep and looked so peaceful in the moonlight but there was nothing peaceful about the two of us as we were killers. It was as if I had found a new drug and now I understood how Nellie had felt left out after the first kill. To take someone's life from them was real power and a power that now both of us were gifted with. I felt good, I wanted more, besides now it was my turn.

21

This Monday morning like most Monday mornings work seemed insignificant for me but now for very different reasons. Today I stood higher on the mountain as I had been elevated to a greater plain feeling more alive than ever before, almost reborn.

Despite all this new-found belief I had still shown up to work, maybe out of habit more than anything else. As I looked around the office I felt myself elevated above these people who surrounded me day in and day out, I was capable of more than they would ever achieve or even dreamed of achieving. I had woken up a much different person than the one the day before, my transformation was going through stages but whereas previously I had questioned it today I embraced it. I could feel an excitement building inside of me as I pondered just how far I would go and what I was to become.

My work station was a self-contained pod amongst a hive of similar non-descriptive man-made capsules. The height of the sides meant when sat it was impossible to converse face to face with fellow workers, which in itself was a bonus. However, now as I sat there alone my personal space was under attack as one of the many tie-wearing clones was trying to communicate over my left-hand wall.

"Earth to Lee, Earth to Lee, hello, anyone home?"

I could hear him but chose not to answer taking a silent pleasure in feeling his frustration at being ignored.

"You're such a fucking weirdo Lee and I know you can hear me. Anyway, Annie wants to see you in her office, so message delivered, do what you fucking wish, I'm out of here."

Annie was back; the information momentarily confused me as she had been away ever since our night together and with so much happening since I had almost forgot she existed. Getting to my feet I paused for a second, peering across the large office where everyone seemed so lost in their work lives, either locked to a computer screen or telephone. Slowly I weave my way through this vile cocoon of stale activity making my way to Annie's office door, which surprisingly I find shut. This is a bit unusual for her but still best to play it formal, so I give it a polite knock.

"Come in and shut the door behind you please."

Her tone was puzzling and it almost felt like I was about to lose my job. I stepped through the door closing it behind me as instructed, then stopped in the middle of the room. Anna was sat at her desk with her back to the door yet even as I entered she didn't turn to face me or say a word. What the fuck was going on? Someone had to break the tension and I guess that someone was me.

"Hey Annie, I had a great time the other night, is everything OK? You've been away for almost a whole week."

It was suddenly apparent even with her back to me that she was very tense; you could see it in her shoulders.

"Go fuck yourself, Lee."

She span around in her large leather office chair and looked awful, her face was a mixture of heavy make-up and what appeared to be bruising.

"Jesus, what happened to you?"

My concerns for her well-being didn't seem to improve matters as she sat there momentarily opened-mouthed, then shook her head in what appeared to be disgust.

"Really! Are you seriously going to ask me that question? I should get the fucking police in here right now. Men like you should be locked up, you're one sick fucking puppy you fucking son of a bitch."

I wasn't going to take this, I could feel my whole body growing tense as my legs started to shake and my breathing shorten, who the fuck did she think she was?

"Fuck you Annie, it takes two people to fuck and if I remember correctly you were gagging for it. So don't go throwing your guilt trip back in my face and don't even think of mentioning rape, that was consensual sex and you fucking know it."

Maybe fighting fire with fire hadn't been the best move but fuck her, this was some Fatal Attraction bunny-boiler-type shit. I wasn't going to stand for this, she was nobody compared to me and I was in control. I could feel my eyes narrowing and my teeth started to grind against each other as she once again started to speak.

"You really are a piece of shit. Yes, it was consensual sex, but the beating you gave me afterwards wasn't, because of you I haven't left my fucking home for a week. Men who beat on women are cowards, fucking cowards!!"

A fucking coward? I could feel the blood boiling in my veins and had an urge to hit her. What was wrong with me? Had I hit her before? I remembered a few dark thoughts that night but I hadn't acted on them, not that I knew of anyhow. I tried to think back but was confused; I knew I'd had a few blanks from that evening as that tended to happen when I drank heavily but could she be right? However, I had no time to answer such questions as she launched into another rant.

"What, nothing to say, you coward! My brothers will find you and fuck you right up. We are Irish and us Irish never forget."

I wasn't lost for words any more but was however fighting a seemingly losing battle to control my inner animal. Noticing a letter opener on the desk I reach forward picking it up, then point it straight at her. Remaining seated she laughs with a kind of contempt but quickly her face turns to pure anger.

"What, you going to do finish the job here and now? What, your fists not good enough so now you want to cut me? You sick fuck."

Every one of her poisonous words hurts me yet I refuse to be imitated and take another step closer to the desk. This is now a battle of wills and as I approach she stands, leaning forward on her desk with her hands outstretched in front of her, looking straight at me. For a moment I am distracted as the angle she has chosen to lean at allows me to steal a good look at those great breasts of hers. Of course they no longer interest me but that doesn't change the fact they are amazing. This time she really is mad.

"What the fuck is wrong with you, are you looking at my tits? How fucking dare you, now get the fuck out of my office!"

As quick as a flash I raised the letter opener bringing it down on one of her outstretched hands that was supporting her weight on the desk between us. The scream was blood curdling as you would expect from someone who has just had their hand pinned to a desk by a letter opener. The silly cunt didn't have much to say now did she? Now it was my turn to speak.

"Not much to say now bitch, I look forward to meeting your Mick brothers. Maybe I will fuck them in the arse like I did you, keep it in the family yeah. Nah, fuck that, I'll get them down on their knees taking turns to suck my dick before I fucking kill them and by the way, I fucking hate Bon Jovi, they are the definition of shit."

The office door slams open and Annie's secretary Kim rushes into the room. She doesn't even have time to say anything before she starts to scream at the sight of Annie's now red right hand pinned to the desk in a pool of its own blood. A few seconds later she is followed in by the big-nosed guy from marketing whose name I can never remember, a look of shock fills his face as he looks at Annie then Kim before turning his attention to me.

"You fucking psycho!"

He came at me in what he would now surely always remember from this day onwards as his "regrettable hero moment". I couldn't miss his nose and with a quick side step connected with a short right hook making sure I followed through with my elbow for good measure. The double impact of both elbow and fist combined with his incoming force leaves him in a heap on the floor as Kim lets out another scream. Who the fuck did these people think they were? They were nothing but insects to me. I step over big nose spitting on him for good measure, then blowing Kim a kiss make my exit. I guess this was going to be my last day working here.

I hadn't even stopped to clear out my desk, just grabbed my jacket and bag en route as I headed straight out the door and into the outside world. My first moments of freedom were greeted by the rain, the cold drops hitting my face revitalizing me as I peered up at the clouds that now opened almost symbolically above me.

The many people that passed me meant nothing as their faces faded into the colours of the tall buildings now surrounding me coated with a fresh skin of rain. There was nothing like a good downpour to clear the air, it was like watching the world consume a fresh glass of water that hydrated it almost instantly breathing new life into its dying body.

It took a couple of minutes of walking before what actually had happened finally started to sink in. It had truly been a spectacular morning but still I wasn't completely sure what had come over me or had even possessed me. After all the self-control I had displayed with so much discipline over the weekend I felt disappointed with myself. This time for sure there would be consequences as my actions had been way too public, which I had no doubt would now lead to some sort of police intervention.

I must have been walking in no particular direction for at least an hour if not more. I decided to stop when I came across a nondescript pub on a quiet side street. The pub was like the land that time forgot decorated with printed plates, velvet style seating and old photos of the area. The best course of action after the events of the morning was to keep a low profile, so taking my freshly poured pint I sat myself at a quiet table in the corner underneath a picture of Winston Churchill.

My entrance hadn't really attracted much attention as the pub was dead as you would expect for that time of day. I presumed the elderly lady behind the bar who had served me to be the landlady. Her face was coated with a thick layer of foundation as she fought a losing battle against the ageing process. She hadn't struck me as a conversationalist so I had chosen not to engage in small talk, hence now finding myself sat alone away from the bar.

The only source of entertainment apart from the bland music seeping from an old jukebox in the corner was a table of old gentleman playing dominoes. I watched them from a distance, sat there in their Sunday best, sipping at their pints. A few wore medals so I guessed due to their age most they had to be war veterans living out their final years. It struck me how they sat there with so much calm and peace poise slowly drinking their pints. No doubt they would understand me as taking lives had been their business back in the war.

My mind slipped away from the old men's domino game and back to earlier in the day. The way Annie's hand had been pinned to her desk had been quite mind-blowing, stunning even. The beauty of the moment reminded me very much of one of my favourite movies "From Dusk Till Dawn". Selma Hayek's brilliantly named character "Santanico Pandemonium" changes the whole direction of the film when she reacts to something very similar as it happens to Richard Gecko played by Quentin Tarantino. Like in the movie, the blood this morning had been such a crisp red, almost magically as it had shone so majestically against the bland colour of her desk. I guess it would have made the fight a bit more even if big nose like many in the movie had turned into a vampire. Poor bastard, at least he had a go.

I knew in my heart that Annie hadn't lied so hitting her was an unforgivable act and even though I couldn't remember doing so something inside me told me I was guilty. I deserved to be punished as one of my moral codes had been broken by attacking an innocent woman not once but now twice. Annie had been right to call me a coward and although that maybe wasn't the right choice of words any man who hits a woman is in the wrong.

I thought back to a piece I had read recently about "Opus Dei". Those celibate religious freaks loved a bit of self-punishment and maybe that was the route I should take. Fucking madness, looking to religious folk for guidance or punishment but there was definitely something in that wire chain thing they wore around their thighs. Come to think of it self-harming was no doubt something I would enjoy, maybe I should just chop off one of my fingers or toes instead, self-mutilation seemed about right.

22

The old men started to drift away as lunchtime turned into afternoon and the darkness began to creep in through the windows. You could see in the way they parted company that a certain sadness filled each of their eyes not knowing if this was to be their last game before the Grim Reaper came a-knocking. As they took their leave it wasn't long until just one solitary member of this band of brothers was left sitting at the table all alone staring into the emptiness. A quick nod to the bar and soon the landlady was at his table with a fresh pint in her hand.

"I'd like to buy that one for this gentleman, please."
My shouts from across the room startled the two of them and now they both turned to look at me in a suspicious manner. I continued, this time more on the back foot.

"Sorry, I didn't mean to offend, I just saw the medals and felt the urge to do something, I have had a funny old day so just thought it would be a nice thing to do."

The old man smiled, he had a warm face and as he turned in my direction I could now see he had three medals pinned to his suit jacket.

"Well young man, in all my years, of which there have been many, I have never been known to turn down the offer of a free a drink, so good health to you sir."

He raised his glass slightly off the table, nodding his head in my direction and I followed suit.

"May I join you?"

The landlady gave me a dirty look as soon as the words had left my mouth pointing a finger in my direction but before she even had a chance to speak the old man raised his voice.

"Now now Peggy, this gentleman is only showing respect, so come on, don't be so judgemental and let's embrace the kindness of strangers."

She still seemed suspicious of my motives, her eyes trained on me like a hawk trying to work me out. I spoke up to calm her.

"Peace and love sister, I have no beef with anyone, well, not here at least. Look, I'm not trying to buy some company so if this gentleman wishes wants to be left alone, I will respect his wishes and remain in this corner whilst continuing to purchase and consume more of your fine ale."

George was his name, a war veteran from the Second World War and at ninety-two he felt his best days may still be ahead of him. I instantly liked him as he had a certain wit and a very dry sense of humour which are fine but rare qualities to find in anyone these days or even yesteryear as he pointed out. Even the landlady dropped her guard after a while, loosening up enough to buy the two of us a couple of whiskey chasers, which was nice.

People often underestimate the old, casting them to one side, secretly hoping they would just hurry up and die to relieve themselves of their burden. When an old person makes a mistake people are far too quick to blame old age; yet if someone half their age does the same it is instantly written off as one of those things, that's just not fair.

Slowly as the drinks started to flow I began little by little to drip the war into our conversation. I don't know why but I was quite taken by his medals and wondered what tales of glory lay behind them. Finally in a rare pause in our conversation I plucked up the courage to bring up the subject.

"Do you mind if I ask you about your medals?"

Without even answering he looked down at his chest, cradling them in his hand and making me instantly regret asking him about them. I needn't have worried as he started to smile

125

almost as if it was directly at the medals themselves and then in a soft voice began to speak.

"What, these old pieces of tin? Worthless trinkets, I honestly don't even know why I still wear them."

His humility was quite humbling, even refreshing, especially when compared to the self-important modern times today's world seemed to run on. However, I couldn't let him off that easily now the subject had been breached.

"Come on, you can't put yourself down like that, if it hadn't been for your generation we would all be speaking German, right?"

He smiled at that as if he had heard it a thousand times before, which he probably had seeing it was the cliché thing to say when mentioning the war. Slowly he started to unpin his medals one at a time, laying the first two on the table in front of us. However, when it came to the third of his collection he held it tightly in his hand as if it was some sort of priceless jewel, then once again went to speak.

"Those two on the table were a token gesture from His Majesty that all surviving military personnel received after the war. Even old Jonesy who just fleeced the lot of us at dominoes has a pair of them and he never once looked the enemy in the eye, in fact the old boy never even left this country. So to say they are worthless is a bit strong but they are lesser medals nonetheless. However this one."

He paused as if just the thought of it hit a nerve, then opening his hand slightly took a moment to just look at it.

It wasn't hard to gauge that this particular medal was special and I felt a rush of guilt as if I had awoken a memory that should have been left firmly in the past. Maybe it was time to change the subject, but now I was really curious.

"I am guessing that one in your hand is very different? If I am not mistaken out of all your little group you were the only one who wore a medal with a purple ribbon. There is something special about it, I can tell just by the way you cradle it in your hand like it's some precious jewel."

This seemed to amuse him somewhat but at the same time also sadden him ever so slightly. He took a moment to gather his thoughts then licking his lips took a sip from his pint before continuing the conversation.

"Very observant of you, but a precious jewel, I don't think so, all this is in my hand is a memory and one I will never forget. It's not that I can't, but more, I refuse as I know the story behind this one like I know the back of my own hand. People of your generation think that war is romantic in some way and maybe that's Hollywood's fault, but I am telling you this, there is no romance in war."

Maybe for the first time he had agitated me and I felt to respond in like.

"Don't go painting the whole of this generation with the same brush, some us are different, we aren't all sheep. I for one see glory in the victory but there is no glory in war."

He paused again seemingly wanting to reflect on my response, then taking another sip of his pint turned and looked straight at me, now we were starting to get somewhere.

"With all respect son there is no glory in victory once you've seen the things I have. Victory brings only one thing, relief and that is a relief in knowing that at that moment you are safe again. You may have seen a thousand war movies but with the odd exception nothing was like being in the reality. I have seen men reduced to the size of an apple by flame throwers, had my face covered by the blood of my friends and nothing prepares you for the sound of a body being crushed under a tank. Death and killing were everywhere so that in the end you become numb, blocking them out. Well I say that but those images never leave you, they are tattooed to your soul, forever."

Just by the look in his eyes I could see quite clearly there were still horrors living within him. I wanted to hug him, telling him it was alright, but knew it would have been inappropriate. George had been the only one of his fellow domino players who had seen any real action during the war and was truly haunted by the experience. I too now had killed but the experience could never haunt me; it just empowered me to a higher plain. This man had regret which made him weak, he hadn't been ready to take lives, he'd just had no choice. Time to see what this old man really thought.

"So, you say you are haunted by these memories, which I understand but seeing these things must have at least made you stronger? I don't know if you ever took a life but if you did the feeling of pure revenge must have been overwhelming. The power to bring down vengeance on another human being is a gift not a burden."

I don't think he was fully ready for my rant and by the look on his face seemed somewhat shocked as he tried to digest my words. He looked away, then back again, but this time with a hint of anger. I had got my rise.

"People who talk power, glory and vengeance know nothing. I was a shoemaker when I was drafted, I didn't want to kill and didn't even know if I could but I had no choice. Yes I survived but I'm not a proud man, I am a tortured one."

People paid good money for therapy sessions like this, he was offloading his hurt and I was drinking it up. I wanted to know what happened and knew he would tell me, he was ready to unburden himself; he just needed another little push.

"OK, you say you were one of four survivors from a two-hundred-man troop, all seems a bit Hollywood to me, is that really true or has the war story taken on a life of its own over the years?"

This time I had him, and whatever nerve I'd hit was now drawing the really George out. His whole demeanour seemed to be changing in front of me as his eyes narrowed, but if anything he seemed calmer than before, almost focused. Without doubt I had offended him, it was just a question of how much.

"You're a strange one, we came across lads like you in the war. You like to pretend you are all brave, trying to get an upper hand with some backhanded compliment but you're lucky today is today son, and not sixty years ago, believe me. And yes, some war stories do take on a life of their own but not mine."

This was the real George in front of me now a much more centred individual now oozing a sort of confidence. Still I felt a little hurt by his previous comments and needed to readdress the balance.

"You know what, if you don't want to tell me your story, then don't. We've both been sitting here now for a couple of hours and I am a little oiled to tell you the truth. Maybe my tone has offended you and for that I'm sorry but I've nothing against you old man, in fact I actually think you're fucking great. But just don't go round judging every book by its cover because that's a mistake. Maybe I didn't fight in the war but that doesn't mean I haven't suffered, but for my victories they don't give medals. Go ahead, tell me your story but don't hold back on my account."

He was taken aback by my forwardness, but now I could see he was enjoying our banter. Taking another sip from his pint he placed the glass back on the table, I gestured with an open hand that was all his then with a chuckle under his breath he began.

"It was shortly after the Normandy landings our troop arrived in France and were sent straight out to patrol some farmland about fifty miles inland. Pockets of Germans still remained hiding in the area and we had been given the job of finding them, then flushing them out. For a couple of days we came across no-one apart from thankful locals, so our mood was good knowing the war was almost over, but we were wrong. It all happened so quickly as we came down the side of this grassy hill and next thing we knew we were being fired on by a German foxhole that had somehow escaped the air raids. These foxholes were often only manned by two or three men but nearly always had an MG34 gun. Now this is no ordinary gun it's more a killing machine, a weapon that could fire off close to a thousand rounds a minute from distance. We were no more than sitting ducks out there on that hillside and it mowed through us in seconds. I don't know how many men it felled but it was pure chaos, I got lucky and hit the deck but all I could see around me were the dead bodies of my comrades who had been savagely ripped apart by the bullets. As I lay there I knew I wasn't alone as I could hear voices which gave me hope that a few like me were still alive. I would say that burst of shooting took out maybe one hundred and fifty men in less than a minute. Some who'd survived the initial slaughter were foolish enough to try to escape but even before lifting themselves off the ground they were gunned down, which told the few of us left we were trapped. I remember hearing both crying and praying as we just lay there motionless too scared to even scratch our noses, that is a strange feeling. I guess the only positive thing about the attack was it had happened late in the day and night soon fell. The foxhole was close as I could hear the German voices and even smell the smoke from their cigarettes. I reckon there must have been half a dozen men still alive so the only hope of saving them and myself was to get to that foxhole. It was a moonless night and I started to drag myself through the bodies in the direction of the voices. Every move I made I knew could be my last but I just refused to give up. Slowly I managed to move away from the fallen, getting to the shelter of some bushes. I could now see how close the foxhole was, even picking out the glow from the ends of their smokes, hatred filled me at that moment and I just knew I would kill them all. From the cover of the bushes and then some trees I now made quicker progress, so soon ended up only a few feet from my destiny. I counted three voices so I was outnumbered, but just the sound of their laughter gave me the fuel I needed. I waited trying to decide the best course of action, laying there for what must have been a good couple of hours and then an opportunity presented itself as one of the Germans left the foxhole to take a piss. He didn't even hear me coming and I slit his throat as he stood there with his penis in his hand, covering his mouth to ensure he didn't alert his comrades. It was now or never, so I turned towards the foxhole and charged, diving in feet first. My entrance had caught them by surprise with my boots catching one of them square in the face. There was no room to move and I remember one of them going for his Luger, but I was quicker planting my knife into the centre of his chest. The other jumped me from behind and as he held me I could feel him fumbling for his gun. We both fell backwards in the struggle, yet in the fall I somehow managed to break free but my knife was gone. What we had was a kill-or-be-killed situation leaving me no choice but to go at him with my bare hands. I was like a rabid animal punching and pummelling his face until finally he went limp. I remember getting up, then looking down at him, all that was left was a bloody mess where once had been a face. That's why I have this medal."

He took a deep breath and looked away, picking up his pint and downing its contents before signalling the bar for another. It was an amazing story and this man was a true hero. I sat in awe as he now placed the remaining medal on the table next to the others, then turned his head and looked at me with a kind blank expression; I felt inspired.

"Wow, that is some tale, you should be proud of what you did. Everyone has the beast inside yet it's only a chosen few who ever see it surface. In many ways those chosen few are evolution, remember it's nature's way to kill and we humans have gone soft, we have become domesticated."

He seemed slightly horrified by my statement and my rant, turning his attention fully back in my direction.

"That is not a tale, story or part of a movie, that was reality. As I said before, I am not a proud man, I just did what I did to survive and as for domesticated?"

He didn't understand me and of course he wouldn't as he was blinded by these events of the past. He had allowed them to consume him when he should have learnt from them and grown stronger. I needed to explain.

"Of course domesticated, as it's nature's way to cull but we breed more than we kill which creates generations of useless beasts, sad domesticated creatures that serve no purpose. Life needs cleaners and if there are no wars to do the cleaning then what?"

I was done here, George may have seen death and his hands had blood on them but he just didn't see the bigger picture. The kind of mission I was on I guess was very different to anything he had encountered in the past. Whereas I had found clarity in killing, he had been emotionally scarred by it. To separate right and wrong gave me my edge, leading me to a yet undetermined destiny, fuck I was drunk.

23

I left George to his thoughts and after what had been an interesting afternoon decided to walk home in the rain rather than take the train. There was no doubt in my mind that his generation contained a far more evolved type of human than the flawed model we saw today. War had been savage at times but throughout history had always acted as a way to control population and cleanse the weak. Our animal instinct was to survive yet we cradled the weak rather than erasing their stain from this world without actually seeing this was making ourselves weaker. Creatures we looked down upon as inferior were now more evolved, could such a vast range of species be wrong? Spiders, bears, sharks and cuddly little hamsters all ate their young if they didn't make the grade. I'm not saying we should eat our babies but if we are to grow as a species we need to act before it's too late.

The rain had almost washed away my drunkenness by the time I approached the front door so I was feeling more sober than drunk for the first time in a couple of hours. It was close to nine and Nellie was up waiting for me, jumping to her feet and running across the room to hug me as I entered the flat. It was good to feel her touch and now I kind of regretted not taking the train to get home earlier.

"Jesus, you are soaked to the skin; let me get you a towel."

Her caring instinct instantly filled me with a kind of happiness which surprised me as my emotions towards her had flat-lined a bit over the last few weeks. I was a colder person inside, more calculated but obviously still capable of random acts which now in hindsight appeared to be spikes of emotion. Taking the towel I wipe the cold rain from my face and arms before drying my hair roughly with the towel. Nellie sits there silently looking at me then reaches to the table and holds up a business card and starts to speak.

"The police have been around looking for you, a Sergeant Richard Wright, actually he wants me to call him on your arrival, someone has had quite the day it seems."

I sit down on the sofa next to her as she passes me the card, reading it before throwing it on the table in front of us.

"Richard Wright, wasn't he a member of Pink Floyd? I guess times are hard."

The mood in the room isn't tense but there is a definite undercurrent of uncertainty coming from Nellie. I need to address the obvious elephant in the room before she does.

"You heard what happened at the office then?"

This has to be one of the silliest questions ever asked and I burst out laughing as soon as the words leave my mouth. Of course she would have heard, how could she not have, drama like that just doesn't happen every day.

"I guess you're referring to the coffee machine breaking down again or was it something else? Oh, that's right, didn't you pin a woman's hand to her desk with a letter opener and then break someone's nose?"

The sarcasm was justified and the conversation that followed could have led to more questions than answers, but Nellie was cool. To her it was all about the future, even saying she just didn't care if Annie and I had any sort of sexual history. Saying that I was quite sure her reaction would have been slightly different if she knew exactly how recent that sexual history was but decided not to elaborate. I made a promise to myself that when the time was right I would come clean, but today wasn't to be that day.

It seemed if anything that my reputation in the office was a lot more high profile than I ever realised. It was funny to think that after all this time I had never noticed that my stock had been raised somewhat after rumours of my sexual prowess had done the rounds. The events of the day had actually turned me into some sort of true office bad-ass. I wasn't sure if the women would be queuing at my door but at least now I was infamous albeit in a despicable way. Nellie had found it amusing that the man she had chosen to share her bed and life with was now the talk of the town.

"I can't believe you slept with that Aussie tramp on reception, how many notches did the office actually provide your bedpost?"

It appeared there was nothing like a bit of in-house violence to get the office talking. To be fair, there had been a six-month period of mindless fornication with some taking advantage of various temps, but in reality, most of my conquests were not in house but caught in a wider web. As for notches, it all depended on how many different bedposts we were counting as normally I preferred to dine out, with Nellie surprisingly being my first meal prepared at home.

I wasn't sure what I was going to do about the police, so decided to sleep on it, which was maybe not the worst idea. Nellie had the opinion that I wouldn't be going down as it was my first offence but I didn't share her confidence. Ending up in prison was something I hadn't even considered up to this point, but in hindsight this was a serious offence, so in the eyes of the law I could be in trouble. Just the thought of doing prison time for such a trivial thing disgusted me, seeing I was yet to reach my potential. Acts I was yet to commit would surely command more gravitas and to be the thought of being derailed by a letter opener was almost incomprehensible.

It must have been close to 5am when Nellie found me curled around the toilet on the bathroom floor. It had started with the shits followed by a violent batch of puking, meaning I had remained clinging to my porcelain friend until she'd discovered me. Things were better now but I still felt a bit rough and thought back to the hot-dog I had bought off a street vendor on my walk home. Slowly I sat myself up on the sofa glancing over at the clock, wow, it was coming up to eleven which explained why the house was so peaceful. I was one of those lucky people who never got ill but after years of avoiding all sorts of sicknesses they seemed to have finally cornered me last night all in one hit. Maybe it had been unfair to blame the hot-dog vendor but something had really fucked me up. No point dwelling on such things but still I felt grateful it had passed and started to think forward to the day ahead.

I knew I needed to address the police issue sooner rather than later as it wasn't going away on its own, so I made the call. Dealing with the police was something I had limited experience with and so I wasn't really sure what to expect. I remembered as a young boy my father saying on more than one occasion that all the stupid people he had grown up with were now either plumbers or policemen. Sergeant Wright seemed OK on the telephone and we arranged that I would meet him down the station at three. I guess after all these years I would soon be putting my father's theory to the test.

It was a weird feeling being off on a weekday and seeing as I had a few hours to kill I headed out for a late breakfast. There was no shortage of places open, yet even with all the choices I ended up buying myself a very unimaginative bacon baguette and a strong coffee. Yesterday´s rain had now passed being replaced by blue and sunny skies so I decided to make my way to the park to enjoy my breakfast al fresco for a change.

What I hoped would be a bit of peace couldn't be further from the truth as the daytime park seems to consist entirely of old people or mothers with prams. I thought again of George picturing him as a young man ramming his knife into the chest of the German soldier. I wish I had been born in his generation as being given a reason to kill would be better than looking for one. I wanted to kill again but now chances were I would be banged up, maybe not for long but still behind bars. I laughed as I remembered how last night Nellie had tried to lighten the mood by offering to buy a strap-on dildo to prepare me for life inside, funny girl.

Like yesterday's rain the sun felt good albeit for less

sobering reasons. It was a good reason to take a walk. The area around the park was new to me and I headed down a small path that led surprisingly to a canal. The man-made river flowed slowly past me as I sat for a while watching the dark water moving gracefully in the sunlight. A few joggers and cyclists passed me but disappointingly not one boat. I noticed a couple of drunks huddled under the bridge, which reminded me of Stinky Pete, making me feel sad for some reason. Death and killing had scarred poor George yet it seemed this pain or remorse didn't exist for me or maybe just refused to surface yet.

Heading back up onto the high road I left the canal and its drunks behind me emerging in front of a large church that for some reason caught my eye. I wandered into the graveyard which surrounded this vast building and started to read various gravestones that littered the area. The church was old with many of the stones unreadable mainly due to decay with the oldest I found being from 1879: an Eliza Day, who had, it seemed, been taken too early at twenty-three. I peered up at the church, its spiral pushing up towards the clouds and noted how the stained-glass windows looked so incredible, especially when caught by the sun. Meandering my way around to the front to my surprise I found its large doors wide open and for some reason wandered in.

It was hard not to be instantly taken back by the beauty of the inside, the stained-glass windows that had already impressed me so much from outside casting beautiful colours across the floor. Several candles were burning, which gave the whole place a wonderful smell, drawing me towards the back of the building and the altar. The whole set-up was quite overwhelming and as I stood in front of the large statue of Mary cradling the baby Jesus that towered over me I felt a kind of peace.

You could see how the masses fell for the charms of religion as the church and its idols gave off a very powerful image. The gold candlesticks were a perfect example of this sitting on the altar giving off an impression of success rather than greed. Yes, the church was a con-job in my mind but you couldn't argue it was a very impressive one.

The whole church experience was having a strange calming effect on me, which I knew was wrong. I hated the whole idea of organised religion but couldn't deny the peace I felt here. My whole thought process was making me feel a touch confused to say the least, so I decided to take a seat on one of the many empty pews.

I scanned the room for flaws yet was left gasping at the imposing sight of the organ with its beautiful long pipes reaching up to touch the sculptured roof. For a second I lost myself, maybe even dropping off momentarily but was brought back to the real world by the opening and closing of a door. Swinging around I saw a man of the cloth making his way up the aisle in my direction his gown following as he walked. As soon as I had clocked him I knew he was going to attempt conversation, making me wonder where murdering a man of the cloth in the house of God would sit in the grand rankings of sins.

"Good afternoon and please forgive me my child if I have disturbed your prayers."

He was far younger than I had expected a man of the cloth to be, with his eyes giving off an impression of pure tranquillity and calmness. I had no desire to engage in petty small talk so took his eagerness to start a conversation as my cue to leave.

"Don't worry Father, I was just leaving, trust me, a place of God is no place for a man like me."

I went to stand but hesitated as a sad glaze fell came over his face. I guess the Church membership numbers were dwindling somewhat and I was being perceived as a potential member. Still there was no real reason for him to look so sad as surely in this day and age with the church's tarnished image he must have been used to rejection. Saying that I was a gate-crasher in his house so he deserved an explanation.

"Look Father, I was never here to sign up so nothing lost and nothing gained."

He acknowledged my words with a kind of acceptance and a half smile; who could have thought that my good deed of the day would have involved a holy man, go figure. Despite this it was time to go so I stood, drawing him to respond.

"My child, what makes you think you are not welcome here? I believe there is a place at the table for all souls."

There just seemed something instantly and innately wrong with a priest or whatever he was referring to me as a child. Didn't he read the fucking news?

"I know you fuckers like them young, but a little tip for you mate, don't go referring to people as your children. All it does is conjure up images of....you know what I'm talking about."

It was a silly reply really, my aggression no doubt hangover-related but still I had no desire to hear about God and all that bollocks. You would have thought just my use of the f-word would have been enough to scare him off, yet he appeared unflustered once again addressing me in a calm and controlled manner.

"Sir, I assure you I mean no harm, the church is a place for all faiths, a gathering point for the local community and a place to feel at ease. If you wish to share your thoughts or troubles I will be here to listen, if you wish for advice I will guide you the best I can but please there is no need for hostilities. I detect much anger in you young man but you must not feel threatened by me."

Really, fucking threatened by him, what a fucking joke that was. I turned to face him square on then taking a breath looked him up and down debating my next move. You had to give the man credit where credit was due he truly was unflappable and in a funny kind of way I found his voice almost relaxing.

Laughing to himself he took a seat at the end of the pew and gestured for me to join him. I have to confess I was starting to like this guy but still had no desire to discuss my life with him especially my more recent activities. Maybe it was a touch of guilt that was the deciding factor in persuading me to sit down again as I had been quite unnecessarily rude; there was no doubt I owed this man an apology.

"Look, I'm sorry I didn't mean any harm with my words and I apologise for my cursing. I have a rotten hangover and I'm kind of going through a strange sort of passage in my life at the moment, a kind of resurrection for want of a better word."

I instantly regretted using the word resurrection as unless he was a Stone Roses fan he would interpret that in only one way. He didn't disappoint.

"You must remember that the Gospels teach us many things, take Luke 24 for example."

I sank my head into my hands exhaling loudly which was enough to stop him mid-sentence. As he paused yet again a feeling of guilt gripped me. What the fuck was wrong with me? I was being rude, this was a good man and despite his misguided beliefs was not an evil one. Not only was bad language out of order, I also had to remember I was sitting in his house showing him disrespect, which in any culture was inexcusable. I lifted my head from my hands giving him a smile to try to put him at ease.

"Hey Father, forgive me for my lack of courtesy, my bad, it's just I'm a non-believer so your Bible references are lost on me. Look, don't get me wrong as there are plenty of good messages in that leather-bound book of yours but I'm not here to buy so, just don't talk to me about Jesus, miracles or commandments and we will get on fine. Come on, let's change the subject, how about telling me about this place. I mean with all the crazy people in this world, how can you leave the door open, don't the candlesticks ever get stolen?"

Six times in the last three months was the answer proving two things: people ain't no good and junkies are desperate.

"We may be religious but we are not stupid, those

candlesticks are plastic with the real ones locked away for show time."

I liked the way he spoke as there was a touch of rock'n'roll to it. No surprise really that junkies and your average thieves were stupid, but saying that they were impressive fakes, still I couldn't resist picking holes in his answer.

"Of course, some would say you are stupid for being religious in the first place, you seem like a smart man, so why throw your life away on something that is nothing more than an urban myth?"

He took a moment to think before lifting his feet up on the pew beside him placing his hands behind his head, which would have made for a great photo. I had taken for granted his acceptance of my rather flimsy apology but had a feeling things were about to get a lot more interesting as he started to speak.

"OK, what other stereotypes can we bring up? Of course it's par for the course we're all child molesters but then you got the dinosaur evolution argument, good people getting cancer, why pray if he never answers and a new one I heard last week, Jonah!!"

It was hard to believe that someone had actually used a nature-based TV channel to dismiss the Bible as fake but that's exactly what had happened.

"You see, in his own words he said, "the Bible was a load of bollocks," based on the fact that it was actually impossible for a whale to swallow Jonah as its throat was just physically too small, apparently he'd seen it on Animal Planet."

A good sense of humour is a redeeming feature for me in anyone, so Father Conway, as he had introduced himself, was certainly winning me over. I had prejudged this man with my stereotypes but allowing myself to converse with him had just proved to me how wrong I had been. I could never have imagined myself sitting in a church for a couple of hours with a man of the cloth but that's exactly what I had done. We had discussed everything from great Westerns to albums by the Cure and I had enjoyed his company immensely. I am not actually sure what he may have made of me but from my standpoint those couple of hours were the closest I had come to making a new friend, maybe ever. As I stepped out into the open air again I made a mental note not to judge every book by its cover.

24

It's funny the way life steers us upon all sorts of different courses almost testing our fragile make-up with its random events and encounters. I had been riding its wave for a while now from finding myself on the ledge of a building debating my own demise to having conversations with war veterans and now holy men. Fate is normally associated with love but it is far more complex than that.

Most would say falling into the arms of a beautiful woman had its plus points but I was now starting to feel the non-sexual random encounter with a stranger gave me more. I always knew I had this ability to read people mainly by their eyes but that was now proving not to be as revealing as I had first thought. We as humans have developed this defence mechanism to hide our true selves which I too was guilty of. I was now considering the possibility that I had been wrong all along and the whole idea of the actual existence of interesting people started to excite me.

My recent experiences were nagging at me making me re-evaluate the whole concept or prospect of new friends. Of course, when I say a new friend I'm talking of people I wasn't intending to fuck, just learn from. Although with the church's bad rep that may have been on the table, not that I had picked up on that vibe. I had always made my way through life without the need for friends but in hindsight that was maybe a mistake. Often I'd found myself nodding in agreement as people talked with pride, boasting they could count their true friends on one hand, in my case that never was going to be a problem. I didn't want to jump the gun and go from loner to social butterfly overnight but the events of the last few days were certainly giving me food for thought.

The loneliness of a boarding school upbringing combined with a rather strange home life meant I learned to enjoy my own company at a very early age. Many a good book at school kept me company while from a distance I watched others fall into tribal-like groups. For me I just always preferred to be on the outside looking in rather than trapped amongst the herd, it just felt more comfortable.

You could never say I was unpopular, only I never chose to be close to anyone as I never felt the need to. As my life had moved on through the years it had always been the same both at university and then work.

More recently as I had unfortunately become part of the office furniture the concept of the work friend had raised its ugly head. The problem with this type of situation is that they are always more work colleague than friend meaning any out-of-work conversing always led back to work. For this reason I always avoided any work-type-related-drinks gatherings with the only exception being made for the ladies whose out of work detours tended to lead to, shall we say, happier endings.

The strange thing about this self-imposed exile from friendship was that I was actually quite good company. When thrown into a social situation I always managed to hold my own and come across as what I considered well. Recent examples of this of course had been both Father Conway and George, who I believe had enjoyed my company. Saying that I was a slightly different proposition to your normal average Joe fuckwit so it was quite understandable really.

Maybe the peace I had found with Nellie or with the taking of lives had mellowed me. I knew I didn't fit into modern society or how this modern world dictated we should live but still maybe it was possible I had been missing something. The conversation was an art form but my problem had always been that I tended to analyse everything and everyone. What this would lead to was a likelihood of me being pushed over the edge at some point, which these days seemed quite dangerous. It was possible I was being a bit harsh on myself but kind of knew I was not completely in control yet and maybe until that stabilized it was best to stick with just Nellie. Still, although I had probably burnt my bridges with George I was convinced I would come back to visit Father Conway again one day. Yes, Nellie was great but he gave me a different outlook on things which I had actually enjoyed.

As life tended to do the remainder of the afternoon had

taken a downward spiral after I had been charged with "Actual Bodily Harm." As this was my first offence they had released me after a couple of hours to reappear in court three weeks from tomorrow. Sergeant Wright not surprisingly turned out to be a complete cunt seeming taking great pleasure in informing me that I was guaranteed jail time for my little stunt. It was maybe a touch harsh to refer to such a glorious work exit as "my little stunt" but now I was starting to feel a bit worried at the prospect of actually doing time.

As self-pity tried to overwhelm me I debated what to do with the rest of my afternoon; Nellie wouldn't be home until well after six so I still had a few hours to kill. The little voice inside my head was telling me to get high or drunk but although that was tempting I voted against it, albeit by a split decision. Besides, I still had to carry out some form of self-punishment for my cowardly act of hitting a woman, so destroying myself with drink and drugs was just inappropriate when that needed to be addressed.

I continued to just walk in the vague direction of home but stopped as I caught my reflection in the window of a shoe shop. The man I was looking at could still get away with being called young, but even if I appeared to be in good shape something didn't feel right as I looked too normal. For all these years I had just wanted to blend into the crowd and be unnoticed but that wasn't my agenda any more, I knew I was different and this transformation or metamorphosis I was going through needed to express itself.

When I finally reached home the weight of the potential trouble with the Police still lay weighed heavily inside me refusing to stop asking me questions. There was no way I was scared but I did feel a little bit helpless not knowing what path my rash actions had set me upon. Three weeks was still a while away though so I decided to calm myself by taking a long shower.

The water felt good as it ran down my face and I shaved like I always did under its flow. As the blade cut smoothly through my stubble I moved downwards removing all my chest hair followed by, with a little help from scissors, its pubic brothers. As I turned the water off I peered down at my penis admiring how much bigger it looked without its shelter or scenery. The hair removal wasn't to stop there and after drying myself down I set to work on my head.

The electric clippers cut through my hair until I was left with a military style flat top but I wasn't finished there. Retrieving my razor from the shower I started to shave the sides, then the back of my head leaving just bare, fresh and shiny skin. The effect of the razor felt kind of weird at first but then gradually so right that it was almost liberating. My reflection was that of a different man now and impulsively once again I grabbed the cutters turning my new flat top into a Taxi-Driver-style Mohawk. The mirror didn't as now what faced me was a true bad motherfucker, I couldn't resist.

"You talking to me?"

As I sat myself down on the sofa I began to realise the parallels between the movie Taxi Driver and how my life was going. Was my new haircut a sign of how my brain was now wired? Travis Bickle was a loser but was I really so different? I had loved that movie so much when discovering it as young boy that I had even stolen the copy from the local video store. It now felt as if the movie had tattooed itself to my subconscious and all these years later those memories were resurfacing to guide me in some way.

I reached across to the table picking up Nellie's laptop and started to Google Taxi Driver quotes. Straight off the bat I was hit with the image of the famous haircut that I too had given myself this very day. But it wasn't until I started reading down the page that the connection truly sunk in, it was as if I was reading my own mind, quote after quote:

"Loneliness has followed me my whole life, everywhere."

"All my life needed was a sense of direction."

146

"Listen, you fuckers, you screw-heads. Here is a man who would not take it anymore. A man who stood up against the scum, the cunts, the dogs, the filth, the shit. Here is a man who stood up."

"Someday a real rain will come and wash all this scum off the streets."

I knew it that very moment; it just felt as if the penny had finally dropped. It wasn't just Taxi Driver but also American Psycho and the Wasp Factory, the list just went on. I was blessed that these wonderful works of greatness had been delivered to me, but I just hadn't seen it. These were more than mere works of fiction or art they were tools or guides, maybe I was to be the third instalment to complete my own saga of hope. I had found my answers and now I needed to carry them through with actions to complete my purpose on this planet. I was a chosen one, a gifted one and those who refused to fall at my feet would be punished, I would be redemption.

It was important in this moment of clarity not to get carried away as first things first I needed to pay for my crimes. The last thing I wanted was to be tainted by shame; self-punishment would cleanse me and prepare me for my battles ahead. Moving into the bedroom I pulled out a small chest from under the bed then returned to the living room table. This chest had been with me since childhood, its contents a collection of various items both old and new I always knew would come in handy one day.

Lifting the lid off I started to search through its contents, the channel knife was there as was my childhood magnifying glass which had brought me so much pleasure as a kid. Then I found it, a beautiful stainless-steel cigar cutter, a gift for my father that his death had cruelly robbed me the chance of ever giving to him. I paused as I held it in my hand remembering the ghastly smell his cigars had given off. A part of me still missed him but that part of me was now dying as every day I grew stronger. Taking it from the wrapping it was hard not to admire what a beautiful piece of kit it was. The stainless-steel surface was so shiny it was almost mirror-like, but more importantly it was still as sharp as the day it had been purchased.

147

The next 30 minutes of my life demonstrated how serious I was about redemption and punishment. I had to live by a code if I wanted to succeed and that code had been broken. I believed retaliation was fine under provocation but an unprovoked attack was just wrong unless deserved. With this rule in mind I could maybe justify the letter opener but not the beating I had inflicted on Annie the week earlier.

I should have waited for Nellie but that would have led to more questions and I didn't want her talking me out of this, it just needed to be done. As I slammed my foot down on the cigar cutter I was surprised at first at how easily it went through my little toe and then secondly at how little it hurt.

I sat there watching the blood seep into the towel placed under my left foot, almost breaking into laughter. To see my severed toe just lying there against the blue of the material was a bizarre sight to say the least. Reaching down I took the end of the string noose I'd previously wrapped around the base of the toe and pulled it tight. Ironically this actually seemed to hurt more than the actual removal itself, forcing me to give out a small cry of pain. Finally placing my makeshift ice-pack that was really a bag of frozen peas on top of my foot I sat back and took stock. The cold created a strange throbbing and I could feel my heart quicken as the blood raced through my body to come to the aid of the wound. I wasn't finished yet but the sealing process could wait as my mind turned to the more pressing business of trying to work out where I could buy a gun.

25

I awoke on the sofa realising I must have passed out, then a sudden bolt of pain rose from my foot to remind me what I had done. The whole toe-removal process had ended up being surprisingly easy, proving anything is possible with a bit of mind over matter. However, when it had come to the sealing of the wound, things, although straightforward, had taken a twist. First, I'd heated a stainless-steel knife on the hob and then returning to sofa had pressed the hot blade to the wound. It's safe to say I'd never experienced pain like that before and the smell of the burning flesh still lingered in the air.

Sitting myself up I winced as my foot hit the ground sending another wave of pain through my body. I guess I'd been lucky as I'd had the sense to return to the sofa before applying knife to skin or may have found myself in a slightly worse state on the kitchen floor. Leaning forward I peered down at the ugly stub that had once been my little toe, then threw a towel over it.

As I sat back on the sofa I heard the sound of the front door meaning Nellie was home.

"What the fuck have you done?"

She stood in front of me in a state of surprise, which was understandable under the circumstances. I couldn't help but smile really as even the coolest of customers would have been alarmed to come home to find a Mohawk boyfriend and pools of blood.

"OK Robert De Niro, I am going to the kitchen to get myself a glass of wine, but when I get back you can tell me what the fuck has been going on."

I couldn't be sure if she had noticed my foot of yet but it would only be a matter of time and I wasn't completely sure how to explain it. On the whole it had been a weird 48 hours, that was for sure, but I still had a very good feeling about everything. I heard the fridge door close and in a flash she was back glass in hand, sitting herself down at my side.

"Busy day it seems; how did things go with the Police?"

The whole Police thing had slipped my mind and just the thought of it filled with the same dreadful feeling as earlier. Of course I had expected to be in trouble as it was basically assault with a deadly weapon. However the prospect of actual jail time hadn't really become a reality until Sgt Wright had so happily teased me with it earlier.

As I went through the events of the day she must have detected a sadness in my voice as she came over and gave me a huge hug. Maybe I needed it more than I realised as my eyes started to well up and then the floodgates opened.

"Come on, let it all out babe, it's good to cry."

She was right as it did feel good but it also made me weak and pathetic. I remembered my reaction after seeing Nellie crying and now imagined her judging me the same way. I didn't understand where the tears were coming from as I just wasn't this kind of person. In fact, I couldn't remember the last time I cried at all, oh fuck, that's right, the day I almost jumped off that building.

"Hey, I'm sorry Nell, I don't know what has gotten into me, the funny thing is I don't even feel sad or like crying, they just appeared as actually I feel great."

It was true, I felt good almost reborn despite the unfortunate police business casting its shadow over me. The toe cutting had been liberating and now that burden was lifted I wanted to move forward. My life now had purpose and direction, meaning I could feel the drive inside wanting to be fuelled. However, whatever had cause my slight breakdown needed addressing as my position at the top of this particular food chain was in jeopardy and more importantly I couldn't let Nellie think I was weak. I pushed myself free of her and running my hand across my face in a crude attempt to dry my eyes began my recovery.

"Fuck my tears and fuck sorrow, fuck my new look, fuck pity, fuck work, fuck shame, fuck regret in fact fuck this whole fucking damn world! There is a storm coming Nell and I need you to believe in and more so trust in me, we are the future!"

My "there is a storm coming" line had been stolen from somewhere so may not have been the most original but it was still dramatic. Nellie looked a bit taken aback by my mood swing which I guess was understandable as I was being a touch Jekyll and Hyde. I smiled trying to comfort her but she looked away, but then almost instantly looked back with a look of pure joy on her face.

"I believe in you Lee and have done since the very first day we met. You are my destiny, of that I have no doubt and without you I feel so weak, incomplete even, wherever you go I will follow. I know you won't want to hear this but
.... I love you."

My sudden recognition that I had stolen my previous line from a Batman movie was replaced with a feeling of pure horror. As she rolled herself onto me we started making out but I was now distracted by her inexplicable use of the L-word. Why are we humans so flawed to believe in such shit? With Nellie it had all started out so well, so rock'n'roll even, but now this? She obviously detected something pulling herself away from me.

"What is it?"

She may now have been playing the innocent child but she knew precisely what. It had been her poor decision making that led unwisely to open that door, uttering that shameful word now meaning playtime was about to come to a very abrupt end.

"Love! What part of this world you have lived in has shown you that? It is pain that makes us feel alive and this love you speak of is nothing more than a self-fabricated dream. I thought you were better than that, a connection sweetheart, that is what we have as we share pain and hurt, that is what makes us stronger, this is what forms our bond as nature intended, I would

151

kill for you Nellie, so fuck love!"

She reached over touching me softly on the arm, then once again pulled herself close. My rant hadn't rattled her cage as I had intended and now she placed both her hands on my face looking deep into my eyes.

"You have to believe sometimes Lee, this world can't just be pain, hurt and misery; there has to be space for good as well as evil. I'm not some stupid schoolgirl so I know what I feel, you may wish to hide from it, labelling it as a connection or a bond but it's more than that. I eat, sleep, and breathe you every day; not a waking second passes without me not wanting to be with you. When you are in me I feel complete as if we were meant to be joined, love is not the enemy, it is just something that happens. I never asked for this but I found it and I'm so glad I did and hope it never dies."

She hugged me so tightly I could feel her heart beating as our bodies came together but chose to think rather than speak again. I wasn't sure how much of what I was thinking or feeling I could tell her as the whole game had now changed. I didn't like unpredictability but now in my eyes Nellie bringing love into the equation meant just that.

The way my mind was focusing and developing still felt relatively new to me but was a thing of beauty in which I had found clarity. This talk of love just proved to me that her thoughts of the future and destiny were very different to mine. Losing her at this point was not an option as we had set off on this journey together but now it was essential she would never be allowed to take the wheel.

I was suddenly brought back to the here and now as by complete accident Nellie kicked my foot. Not for the first time today a shock of pain raced through my body as I gave out a loud scream causing her to recoil away from me. Almost instantly she pulled herself back close again glancing down.

"Trust me I want to know what the fuck happened to your foot, but first you're going to fuck me. "

Her chameleon-like ways were so apparent at this moment as the difficult "love" conversation was quickly cast to one side. She knew exactly what she was doing with her weapon of choice being sex so cunningly used as a distraction tactic. Of course it worked as my hand was now halfway up the back of her top undoing her bra as I kissed her neck.

She obviously knew that something wasn't right with my foot but it actually appeared that she hadn't spotted the missing toe. There was no point in killing the mood with that bombshell but tomorrow I would get that gun and the real games would begin.

26.

Any plans I'd harboured of purchasing firearms were suddenly put on hold as the reality of my wound kicked in. Although the level of pain had dropped, my movement was now restricted confining me to the four rooms of my flat and two days of sitting at home doing nothing. Of course my self-inflicted exile from the outside world should have given me time to think but in fact did just the opposite. In the past these welcome invitations of spare time had always ended in a drunken haze or worse but on this occasion I decided to remain sober and drug free, instead choosing to lose myself completely in my record collection.

The release that music gave me had always been amazing but it seemed I had forgotten exactly how great it actually could be. My collection of records was now vast and for me a good way to reconnect with its contents was spending hours reorganising it. First like always I went with the standard A to Z, then into genres and decades before finally going back to A to Z. The whole procedure was like a game; throwing out problems like not knowing what to do with solo projects by members of bands. This in turn led to rediscovering forgotten gems, LPs like the magic of George Harrison's "All Things Must Pass," and the glory of Iggy Pop's first few solo efforts. I had removed every record from its sleeve, cleaning them almost robotically before carefully returning them to their section. Just experiencing the smell of the vinyl and sleeves themselves made the process worthwhile to me, there was something almost romantic about the whole thing.

The escapism of these days in truth had done me a world of good allowing me to recharge my batteries with some decent food, sleep and of course the music. I reckoned in forty-eight hours I'd played no more than twenty percent of my records so the possibility of a few more days in that groove was becoming rather appealing. In all honesty, I could've stayed like that forever as the appeal of not working was a great one especially when trapped in my personal vinyl wonderland.

Although this was indeed a fine plan I was in fact stalling

and needed to get back to reality. Walking now was more discomfort than pain but in this short period of time my foot had healed remarkably well. However, as I sat there pondering my next move it ever so slightly started to throb, as if trying to tell me something.

Glancing up at the clock I yawned as it was already well past three, which meant Nellie would be home in a few hours. These daytimes alone had flown past but now my decision was made, tomorrow I would return to the outside world. The next phase of this journey awaited me and I would hunt down the tools needed to help me complete it.

It was funny how life was more stable being both sober and work-free, allowing me to once again enjoy my own company. The situation with Nellie had also improved as we seemed to reconnect, casting her use of the L-word into the past as a distant memory. Last night just proved we were on the same page again as after dressing and cleaning my wound she had come up with a quite brilliant idea. Placing her recently purchased black nail polish on the table she insisted we would now paint one toe for every kill. I liked this, plus the polish looked good even though my number of kills would now be restricted to nine.

Friday morning was completely uninspiring with the dark clouds and rain outside telling me to take another day off. As tempting as it was to dig out my Blues records and use the weather as the perfect excuse I had to refuse. There was no more time to waste so dressing accordingly I headed out of the stale air and into the wide world again wondering what today might throw in my direction. Sex had been a great painkiller as had the music, but now away from the comfort zone of inside my movement would be truly tested.

It maybe took all of five minutes before the remains of my toe started throbbing under its bandage almost as if it knew its holiday was over. I say bandage, which it now was but originally I had crudely wrapped what was left of my little toe with electrical tape. Since the discovery of my handy work to her credit Nellie had done a good job. She seemed quite at home playing the nurse which had led to some erotic role-play but more importantly had treated the wound.

Her initial reaction to my missing toe was one of amazement that I hadn't ended up in hospital, or even worse, dead. I had expected her to question my sanity but once I had explained my reasons for the self-mutilation as the letter opener she'd understood. Of course, she was also right as a man should never use violence against a woman but rather than being scared that I had committed such an appalling act she had applauded my ability to self-punish.

The ever-changing weather wasn't disappointing and after a mid-morning of sunshine the sky returned to a familiar grey with a steady flow of rain. As I started to walk I had found a rhythm and stride that worked although, hopefully temporarily, I was now blessed with a limp. I hadn't planned to go far and hoped my main man still lived at the same address as before or it would be back to the drawing board.

Finally I was on the train, grateful for the respite as now my foot had really started to ache. Taking off my old beaten-up New York Yankees baseball cap I ran my fingers over my scalp. The skin now felt so rough as hair started to return to what before had been such a smooth surface. I was happy with my new look but for the purpose of today needed to be low-profile so replaced the cap back over my rather distinctive haircut.

Where I was heading was perceived to be a bad part of town but an area I already knew well having lived there for my first six months in the big city. In many ways I actually preferred the high levels of immigration and old tower blocks to where I lived now, which was just so middle-of-the-road stale. As in most areas like this in big cities drugs and violence were everywhere, meaning I dangerously adapted to life on the wrong side of the tracks.

My penance for drugs meant the area fast began a utopia

for me with crack cocaine being the drug of choice. Through my short life there weren't many substances I hadn't tried but crack was by far the most addictive and dirtiest of the lot. As soon as I left the station I caught my first whiff of its presence, telling me things hadn't changed that much although the graffiti had definitely improved. The good thing was that I was entering a no-go area for the police, not that they would ever admit that, but it wasn't them I was worried about. Pulling my cap down to shadow my eyes I lifted my hood to cover my head then started to make my way across the park through the rain.

The area was quiet with the combination of the rain and grey clouds making things seem bleaker than I remembered. I laughed to myself as I thought of Taxi Driver and another one of Travis' gems:

"Thank God for the rain to wash the trash off the sidewalk."

It was an interesting quote really as society had forced these types of people to adapt if they wanted to survive. Although prejudged you had to ask yourself: in reality were they really any worse than today's politicians or bankers? Cutting through the kids' playground that was no more than a set of frames where the swings had once hung I headed through a space in the railings, turning towards the large tower blocks that loomed in front of me.

There were six blocks in total and I had lived in block three, which had been inexplicably named after Nelson Mandela for some obscene reason. The only people visible were drunks or junkies sheltering from the pending storm as the rain now started coming down in an alarmingly violent manner.

My timing was good as a large clap of thunder disappeared behind me as I pushed open the front doors of the building that had once been my home. It was good to get out of the rain but there was something all to uncomfortably familiar as the smell of crack and piss hit me reminding me of my past. The lift, like it had been years before was out of order so I headed up the stairs towards the third floor where I hoped my dealer from my time here still lived.

I now realised how much I hated this place as several bad memories seemed to swamp me as I climbed those stairs once again. It had been a turbulent time in my life but just seeing how dirty and grim everything was made me want to vomit. Finally I reached the third floor and was greeted by a large black gentleman smoking a joint who stepped across my path.

"And where you think you going Mr. New York Yankees?"

His fake Jamaican accent did nothing for stereotypes but I remembered him from when I lived here. People referred to him as Horse which I'm guessing was more to do with his manhood than his equestrian skills. Obviously I had somehow amused him as he was now bent over laughing and slapping his leg in what was quite frankly an over-the-top moment of joy. At last he straightens himself up and with a chuckle he points at me.

"I know you, white boy; you're that banker who used to live up on the fifth."

It was always nice to be remembered but I hated being referred to as a banker almost as much as "white boy." Jesus, what the fuck is wrong with people?

"Please don't call me a fucking banker, trust me, if I was a banker I would have killed myself by now in the hope of starting some sort of chain reaction to save the world."

I don't know why I even said that or where it had come from but it sets him off again. I guess he liked my dark material, but I wasn't here to entertain as a one white man stand-up show and needed to get moving.

"OK Horse, timeout buddy, it's been great to catch up and all but I'm looking for Juice, does he still live here?"

Just the fact I have remembered his name seems to go down well as he stops laughing and his face fills with a look of pride.

158

"Yeah baby, number thirty-two like the legend himself, you know the way. He'll be happy to see you, bro, as you were a good customer and not the kind a brother wants to lose."

A quick fist bump and I was back on my way heading down the open hallway, pausing for a second to take in the view across the city. From this elevated position I had a good view of not only this rundown neighborhood but also in the distance the buildings of the financial district and my previous employment. I didn't miss work as I had needed to move on and turning a corner I blanked out any thoughts of it as I arrived at my destination. The door of flat thirty-two was a place I had found myself on many occasions in the past. I hesitated briefly recalling what a piece of shit Juice was. I mean anyone who named himself after OJ Simpson was a bit unstable but then to move into flat thirty-two because it had been OJ's number was downright strange. I rang the bell and waited.

I don't know why it was taking so long but the wait was making me anxious. At last the door swung open and there he was, the famous Juice in front of me in all his glory. In what could only be described as a very uncomfortable moment he embraced me with the kind of hug you give an elderly relative, then gestured me inside.

"My man from the city has returned back to my flock, motherfucker, it has been a while, where you been at, I have missed you bro, come on, come inside, mi casa es tu casa."

Juice hadn't changed, still sporting the cornrow hairstyle which I'd always hated and the over-sized clothing which made him look just so stupid. The flat's interior just stank of low class trash with money, complete with its huge flat screen TV, tacky white leather sofas and lava lamps. We weren't alone as a dower-looking big dude was playing some sort of war game on the TV while smoking a huge joint. I couldn't see his face but his failure at not acknowledging my arrival was just rude. To his credit Juice sensed my annoyance at the snub.

"Don't worry about Lance bro, that motherfucker is a zombie when he be playing that video game shit. I like my sports games but with this motherfucker it's all about the killing."

As if on cue and rather ironically a zombie walked on to the screen that Lance instantly blew away with an annoying shout of "boom motherfucker!" Juice found this all too funny, obviously picking up on the irony of the situation and his previous statement.

"Fucking zombies being killed by a fucking zombie, how fucked up is that shit?"

I took an instant disliking to Lance; he was almost a perfect example of all that was wrong with today's youth. Manners were a simple concept and not a difficult one to grasp so his lack of them made me angry.

"I fucking hate video games, shouldn't young people be out fucking or playing sports, not trapped in front of a fucking screen all day?"

Surprisingly Lance now appeared to be aware of my existence and looked around for a split second to see who was talking then spoke while continuing to play his silly game.

"Who the fuck is this motherfucker Juice, and who the fuck hates video games? Hey white boy, they have fucking Olympics and world championships for gamers, this is some serious shit and I be training bitch!"

Really, he was trying to justify the whole video game shit like that, how pathetic. I had no time for such a waste of life and wanted to get back to what I came for then be gone. Turning to Juice to speak I stopped as he to seemed a little taken aback with my attitude.

"Hey bro you need to take a chill pill, Lance is one bad motherfucker and a domesticated cat like you going to get hurt if you keep letting that mouth of yours go."

He walked across the room and gave Lance a fist bump which went into some sort of fucked-up handshake routine. These creatures actually thought they were top of the food chain but in reality, they were no more than the dog shit you find on the bottom of your boot. I was beginning to lose my patience.

"OK, when you faggots finally finish shaking hands can we get down to some business? I'm not here in a social capacity so let's cut the crap so I can get the fuck out of here and you can get back to sucking each other´s cocks."

Both men looked at me as if they wanted to kill me where I stood but that would soon change. Reaching into my pocket I pulled out a large stack of notes dropping it on the table in front of them. Both men relaxed instantly as their breed tended to do when confronted by such a materialistic vision. Juice was first to speak up.

"Smart ass motherfuckers like you don't forget and yous a knows where to come a calling, because Juicy baby he got it all. Now it looks like Mr. City Boy been doing alright for himself, that's a lot of coin bro, so what's your poison motherfucker, you want to pop, snort, smoke or spike?"

Motherfucker was hands down my favorite swear word if not my favorite word in the whole English language but these clowns were just cheapening its beauty. I didn't want his drugs, I wanted something else and it was time to test the waters.

"I want something to shoot and I don't mean heroin."

Both men started to laugh like I had said the funniest thing ever, Lance even stopped his video game, which was a miracle in itself. However the laughter stops suddenly as they pause as if it was part of some routine, Lance stands and then points his finger at me.

"You got some stones motherfucker coming in here and asking to buy a gun. What is today, black stereotype day?"

I really was in the presence of dumbness, to think that these two blinged-up black drug dealers were complaining about stereotyping was maybe the most idiotic thing I had ever heard. Saying that the situation was maybe spinning a little out of control and I could do with bringing it down a notch.

"OK guys let's chill. Lance, I have known Juice for a long time in one of my many previous incarnations, so no need to get angry. As for guns, I know he has them, as when I used to get high here back in the day he would always be showing them motherfuckers off. Now sit back down big man as I mean you no offense and if I have offended you, I am truly sorry. Now I have a big pile of money and it's looking for a new home, so it's simple. Do you motherfuckers have a gun I can buy or not?"

My words must have worked as Juice gives Lance a nod and he disappears into the bedroom. As he lights himself a joint he sits himself down at the table. The money has done the trick and Lance reappears with an old sports bag, which he passes to Juice before turning his attention to me once again.

"Well today's your lucky day mofo, take a seat and let's talk some coin."

27

Juice's still but crumpled body was now lying at my feet
while Lance looked almost peaceful slumped backwards in a large
sofa chair that his huge body almost swallowed. It would have
been easy to mistake them both as asleep if it hadn't been for the
blood; Juice's, which ran down his face from where had once been
an eye, and Lance's, which now seeped from his chest giving his
Nike T-shirt an all new designer look. I hadn't wanted to kill them
but they'd left me no choice and to be honest scum like this would
only be missed by other scum, so no big deal.

Maybe 90 seconds had passed since I had gunned them
down and I sat facing the door awaiting the arrival of Horse. He
must have heard the gun shots even over the sound of the storm so
his inevitable arrival was imminent. Right on cue I heard the key
in the door and instinctively raised the gun, but in truth had no
desire to add another body to my kill list today so shouted out:

"Horse, I know that's you, look, I mean you no harm; I
give you my fucking word."

The door opened slightly and although Horse remained
out of sight I could see his large shadow dancing in the hall behind
him. There had been two shots and now only one voice so I
imagined he'd done the math; the allegiance to his now deceased
boss was about to be tested.

"What you done white boy? I heard shooting."

Horse may have been a big powerful man but I could hear
the fear in his voice as he cowered safely behind the front door. All
sorts of things must have been flying through his head and there
was no doubt he was on edge making him dangerous. I needed to
calm this whole situation as there was a capacity for it to spin way
out of control.

"Take a breath Horse; I have no grudge with you. What
lies on the other side of this door is one thing, a fucking large

business opportunity, all you got to do is think, anyways how can we celebrate your promotion with you behind that fucking door, come on big man, Lance and Juice are dead."

I could now hear him talking to himself, obviously in a combination of trying to comprehend what had happened and mustering up the courage to come inside. Finally he pushed the door open leaving us face to face. I kind of felt sorry for him as he stood there with his hands aloft trying to appear as non-aggressive as he possibly could. My eyes shot to a knife in his hand which he quickly proceeded to shut by pushing the blade against the side of the door with his other arm held aloft.

"Don't go shooting me now bro."

I paused like always to give these kind of moments the theatre they deserved and then laid the gun down on the table to my side. He seemed relieved as I took my hand off the weapon and rested it under my chin.

"Don't you watch the movies Horse? Never bring a knife to a gun fight."

Just the use of the word fight seemed to strike fear into him again but I crushed the tension with a smile before continuing, pointing to the weapon on the table.

"That is one quality gun, .38 Smith and Wesson, yes sir, that is some kind of old-school cowboy shit right there."

Horse had now noticed the two bodies in the room but wasn't taking his eyes off me. You could see by his body language he was thinking vengeance but was also weighing up the situation that lay before him. I let him think, and then after ten seconds he spoke assuredly.

"So what now, boss man? I know where he keeps his stash."

164

It was more a "kept" than a "keeps" but I let the grammatical error go as I had no axe to grind with this man. Not much had changed for poor Horse as even when I'd lived here Juice had him outside on look-out in all types of weather both day and night; this was all about to change.

"You fill your boots big man, I've got what I came for so the rest is yours as far as I'm concerned. Just remember, when the police come a calling it was a nasty drugs beef, not some white boy banker, Okay?"

He nodded, then with a more relaxed look spoke up:

"It was only a matter of time bro, these were bad men and bad men make bad enemies."

It appeared Horse was already at peace with the not so sad passing of his now previous employers. His better world would start here allowing him to turn this whole affair into the business opportunity which he was due. I watched as he stripped the sofas pulling out large bags of drugs and cash bringing a look of satisfaction to his face. We had an understanding and I knew we wouldn't have a problem, it was just how business got done sometimes. Picking up the backpack of guns I stood looking over to Horse who was in the process of loading the Xbox into his bag.

"We cool?"

He briefly stopped what he was doing to nod then frantically headed towards the bedroom and out of view. I took this as my cue heading out the door and down the stairs then back into the outside rain. As I walked across the park the storm was now raging with the ground around me flooding, giving the impression I was walking on water and maybe I was. Once again the shallowness of people had disappointed me forcing my hand and leading to me once again having to strike out. The evidence of how the universe worked was apparent for all to see as two people were now worse off while two more had gained; the yin and the yang.

As I trudged through the puddles making my escape I thought back to my victims. Greed was without doubt one of the uglier of human qualities but in this case, it had been a fatal one. Really what was wrong with people? Why on earth hadn't they just completed our business transaction? There was legitimately no-one else they could blame apart from themselves as they alone had acted as the catalyst to their own demise. The whole thing was almost comical, my mind took me back to the moment Juice had shown me how to use the gun, basically all this idiot had done was load the bullets that would ironically kill him. His arrogance and need to show off were sad traits but also nothing less than you would expect from his kind and neither man would be missed by this world.

The risk of being caught on camera in this city was high as big brother always seemed to be watching, and although the area I was now leaving behind me was never going to be an issue as destroying CCTV cameras was a local hobby, the same couldn't be said for the train station. Maybe paranoia was already kicking in but still why gamble? If everything went pear-shaped the station´s cameras could be my undoing, so I stayed on foot. Heading off roughly in the direction I needed to go the sky continued to be lit by flashes of lightning and filled with claps of thunder seemingly guiding me. Even though the area was empty I stuck mainly to the back streets, which if it hadn't been for the weather may have been a far more dangerous prospect than being caught on any station camera. It wasn't long before my toe started to play up, aching once again which made it uncomfortable to walk. I needed to stop so I headed down a street of boarded-up-buildings, taking shelter in one of the many abandoned shopfronts.

The relief was almost overwhelming as I came crashing down to the floor, my foot not surprisingly tensing up sending a now familiar spike of pain up my leg. Stretching out I ungracefully slumped myself up against a boarded-up door of a deserted building.

Stopping to get my breath back had been a good idea especially now as the rain if anything appeared to be getting harder. I watched as the drains started to overflow forcing the water to look for alternative escape routes as another clap of thunder sounded above my head echoing in the narrow street. I was wet through and resting the bag at my side I slipped off my cap banging it against the wall frustratingly sending a spray of water back into my face.

Surveying my surroundings I started to gather my thoughts closing my eyes for a moment to enjoy the sound of the rain falling and the water flowing down the gutter. I couldn't have been any more than a ten-minute walk from the financial district where only a week ago I had so painfully plied my trade. It was amazing really as these could have been different worlds with the contrast of my present rundown surroundings to that polished turd of a hellhole. The rich-poor divide was huge in this city but strangely and tellingly they were only separated by the smallest distances.

Of course this area would have its day as the roots and branches of this corporate world looked to find the next cool neighbourhood. I could see it now, a hipster coffee shop with those bearded fucks smiling at the customers ordering their special brand of coffee. Almost certainly there would have to be some sort of deli-style restaurant and a cocktail bar which no doubt would be some old converted pub selling overpriced drinks including a selection of cool beers that no one had ever heard of. I loved the idea of things being different but it all lacked an edge as the corporate world sadly evolved camouflaging itself under some so-called hip banner.

I was suddenly struck with a feeling of self-doubt which momentarily disorientated me, maybe it was the discomfort coming from my toe but I knew really it was something different. What was I doing? I was no God and who was I to judge who should live or die? My growth as a person was spinning out of control and I now could feel it festering inside of me. It all now just seemed a long way from scratching cars and playing gym bingo, this was serious and no longer a game.

I wasn't quite sure how I had got to this point in such a relatively short time; Yes Juice and Lance had been scum but did they really deserve to die? I was struggling to find answers to my questions, which was an altogether new experience for me. I had convinced myself that today's killings were justified because they had planned to rob me but something didn't fit. My mind paused for a second as once again it was drawn to the water flowing away down the gutter crashing into the drain. I was feeling nauseous and turning to one side was sick.

The rain was still not showing any sign of easing up and now quickly washed away my vomit as I looked on. Suddenly another clap of thunder boomed out sending me momentarily into a panic and frantically looking around as a feeling of being watched gripped me. Fuck, paranoia had well and truly kicked in as I now realized these latest killings had affected me, leaving me on edge. Of course there was no one here and taking a deep breath I wiped my mouth clean as I tried to calm myself. Shutting my eyes for a second my mind slipped back to my previous train of thought as flashes of Joe, Toby, Lance, Juice and then Annie's bloody hand filled my head. What was going on with me? Fuck! Who am I? Fuck another question, I want fucking answers what was it with me and all these fucking questions? Fuck another question.

I needed to relax and just remember I was still here even though I wasn't sure I morally deserved to be. My body count was rising yet I couldn't say when or where or even how it would stop. A part of me always hoped that my killings were to be restricted to those who deserved it but now I wasn't so sure. My changes were now leading me, meaning I had become judge, jury and executioner but maybe more worrying was that I was enjoying the act of killing and was craving more.

The power of taking someone or something's life was a great one and I thought back to the insects I'd so happily tortured or killed as a youth. At the time the whole experience had given me immense pleasure albeit a rather watered down version to that of now but still joyous nonetheless. I believed that everyone contained the ability to take a life and countless wars had proven just this. We were animals after all and this is how they acted although maybe in a more primitive form. They were right actually making me consider there was something to gain from me eating my victims.

The rain was falling at a more frantic pace and again the sky was alive, this time with a more rapid-fire combo of thunder and lightning. The storm was here, but then it always had been, it was just now it was learning to surface and express itself with the difference being these were no longer insects. I don't know why but my mind suddenly locked on to a memory that had been long forgotten, forcing itself into my consciousness as clear as day.

While at school my mother had befriended a single father of a boy no more than a few years older than myself. I was still very young at the time but now in hindsight I realise they'd been fucking. For the few months this affair lasted we would drive out to this old farm in the middle of nowhere where they lived. I couldn't remember the boy's name but did remember his long blond hair, blue eyes and the fact he never said more than ten words to me. Apart from our strange friendship it was a small boy´s dream exploring that farm with all its different barns and machinery but there was something about this kid, like me he was different.

One time we sat on the roof of one of the many barns while I watched him shoot pigeons with his BB gun. He was good too, killing three in a row until he wounded one, leaving it struggling on the floor of the yard below us. We both just sat there watching this bird dying until suddenly he calmly jumped down then stamped on the poor creature's head. I was no stranger to killing animals at this point of my life but the coldness he showed to finish the pigeon off had not only been impressive but clinical.

A few weeks after the day of the pigeons we returned for what would be our last visit as the affair must have come to an abrupt end. On arrival I was told my so-called friend could be found at the back of the house in the orchard so headed in that direction. As I made my way through the many beautiful trees and fallen fruit I soon came across him chasing butterflies with a large net. As usual he didn't say a word so I just sat there on the ground watching him dancing through the trees in the pursuit of his prey. It was fascinating watching as every butterfly he trapped would be stored alive so carefully in a plastic box. After about twenty minutes he just suddenly stopped, dropping the net at his side before picking up the plastic box and gesturing for me to follow him.

We headed towards a garden shed situated at the back of the orchard then slipping a key from his pocket he opened the door leading the two of us inside. As I stepped through the door it was like entering a magic kingdom as all over the walls must have been hundreds of dead butterflies all pinned symmetrically to large polystyrene sheets. It was an impressive sight with an array of sizes, colours and even an eerie looking caterpillar section. I now watched as the young boy placed his box of fluttering butterflies on the work bench before opening its lid allowing them to fly free.

They immediately headed towards the window but any sudden bid for freedom was short lived as they found their exit cruelly blocked by the pane of glass. My host found this all so amusing watching them flutter until one came to rest on the glass then quick as a flash and rather expertly he caught it by its wings. He held the creature up to the light looking it over in great detail before reaching into a draw and pulling out a pair of pincers which in turn he used to crush its little body.

Whereas with the pigeons there had been no emotion here we had the complete opposite as he became aroused. I have never found another man attractive but just the sight of his erection pushing against the fabric of his tight football shorts gave me the same effect. He noticed then smiling removed his penis taking it aggressively in his hand and starting to masturbate in front of me; for some reason, I followed suit.

There was nothing sexual between the two of us and we

both came, as boys of that age do in extremely quick fashion, me first then him a few seconds later. The moment was over before it had even begun and quite calmly he returned his penis to his shorts then went back to his butterflies catching another by its wings. I never saw him again after that day but left confused by the connection we had established. You had to wonder where he would be today and on what path his life had taken him. All these years later I now understood our connection; we both had a bond and that bond was killing.

I don't know why that memory had been suppressing itself inside of me until now or why it would have chosen such a time to reappear. Maybe my mind was trying to tell me something and connect the events of today with that particular moment from my past. I couldn't see it apart from the recurring theme of today being yet another strange day in my life. My journey had begun and now a wide road lay in front of me but how would it play out before fate finally conspired against me and it was my turn? One thing was for sure, fate was a curious reality to live within as today had proved by turning the courses of three men's lives on their heads and by presenting an opportunity to mine.

I reached down to the bag between my feet and placed it on my lap. All this talk of fate made me think it needed testing and I wanted to see what it had in store for me, let it judge me for my actions. Looking left then right to make sure I was still alone I opened the bag and reached inside. It seemed fate was all too keen to show its face as my hoard was far more fruitful than I had originally thought. Whether that would be a good thing or not only time would tell as alongside the two handguns I was already aware of I found a rather crude looking sawn-off shotgun. There would be time for that later but if there actually was to be a later would be another matter altogether.

The pistol was a six shooter, which meant the odds were against me but still good at six to one. This was the gun that had already taken two lives today but the question now was would it be taking a third? Soon it would have its answer and I would also know what card the hand of fate was destined to deal me. I pause before once again looking up then down the street but there was nothing but rain and the ever-increasing puddles. Peering down I manage to load the gun with a single bullet without removing it from the bag. It feels cold as I turn the cylinder with my hand watching it spin while it makes that lovely clicking noise. I freeze for a split second as if I know this is to be my final moment then in one swift movement I pull the gun free, pushing the barrel into my mouth. It's time to see if this game has run its course as now fate will decide my path. I close my eyes and squeeze the trigger.

28

"These are just so fucking mental!"

I had laid all the guns out on the living room table and to say the least Nellie was more than impressed. Two handguns with almost a full box of bullets and a sawn-off shotgun with nine shells was quite the haul and yeah that was fucking mental. I needed to broach the subject of today's killing sooner rather than later but couldn't be totally sure how Nellie would react. Without having to state the obvious I'm sure she'd already put two and two together as you don't just go out and buy these sorts of weapons over the counter. She would have already been stewing inside and seeing how eager I was to break out the nail polish it seemed best to break the ice.

"I guess you're kind of wondering where all these guns appeared from?"

It wasn't exactly subtle and in all honesty a bit of a leading question but I needed to address the matter before she had the chance to. Rolling her eyes she gave out a little laugh before shaking her head then started to speak in a sarcastic tone.

"Really? Trust me, I want to hear everything but first things first, I really need to change the dressing on that toe of yours."

As she disappeared into the bathroom to retrieve her first aid kit I swung myself round on the sofa to take a more comfortable position. I had to say I was feeling a lot happier about life especially after the test of fate and of course at what had been a rather productive day. Leaning back I shut my eyes imagining how Horse must have been getting on tonight free from the shackles of Juice for the first time. Apart from my own personal gains I felt good that the events of the afternoon had also led to helping out a fellow human being.

"Well someone is certainly very pleased with themselves, aren't they?"

As Nellie sat herself down I opened my eyes giving her a smile which not for the first time was greeted by a very sarcastic roll of the eyes. Lifting my foot up onto her lap she started to cut away my dirty and wet bandages.

"I will never know what on earth possessed you to go for a walk in the middle of that storm in your condition. Well I say that but judging by what's in front of us that statement does now seem rather redundant and quite self-explanatory."

Of course she was right: I had been an idiot to go out with my toe in such a state and especially in those conditions. Yet I had acted on impulse which had now born fruit so in the end it had proved to be the right decision. My new collection of guns seemed to be smiling at me as they lay there and it was a good feeling to now have this power so readily available. My toe hadn't bothered me that much during the day but now with the imminent application of that brown alcohol shit I hated so much it had started to ache as if it knew something was up. As Nellie returned to the bathroom to retrieve the vile liquid I sat myself up hearing a crash as something hit the floor.

"I just hope for your sake that is not the nail polish? Because I will be needing that."

Maybe there were better ways to break the news of a double homicide to your partner but that was just the way it chose to surface. A silence fell over the bathroom as she stopped what she was doing then as I looked across the room her head appeared around the side of the door with a curious look etched across her face.

The good thing about Nellie apart from her being great in bed was that she wasn't stupid. To be fair a big pile of guns and nail polish was never going to be the most difficult of connections to make but still she remained remarkably unflustered. I guess in many ways this was testament to how far we'd come and maybe how comfortable the whole taking of lives was becoming. She continued to clean up my toe as I told her the tale of my afternoon adventure with her heart seemingly not skipping a beat.

"Well if you're going to play with matches it's only a matter of time before you get burnt."

Once again she was right and her wise words were maybe something that we ourselves would be sensible to take on board. Having the guns was a real game changer which meant we were suited and booted but could also lead to a lot more complications. There had been no real doubt that in all the cases of Joe, Stinky Pete and Toby Johnson we had got away with murder. Even with today's victims the police would have little to no interest as chasing down the killer of two local drug dealers was never going to be marked as a priority. However saying this, the bullets I had so clinically used would now be traceable so the next time I killed with that particular gun there would be a chance of a match and then maybe a paper trail. I had to confess that using the broken bottle had been satisfying but the power of a gun was a different world almost completely intoxicating. Still we needed to take heed and be more careful from here on in with that statement maybe directed more at me rather than Nellie.

"Which one did you use to kill them?"

She'd now finished dressing my toe and once again was sat peering at the guns. It was strange really that she had no desire to handle my new toys just looking at them as if she was studying some sort of work of art. I pointed to the .38 recalling how it had tasted earlier when its barrel had been so ominously placed inside my mouth. Luck was just something I'd never subscribed to, so the fact I was still here after my little game of Russian roulette meant fate was well and truly on my side. It was time to grab the moment by the balls.

"There is no stopping us now Nellie as these bad boys change the game, I hope you're ready to raise some real mayhem, who's next?"

She paused before replying not taking her eyes off the

guns then raised her head and looked straight at me.

"Raising mayhem seems a great idea and I'm seriously up for this ride but maybe for now, with the police sniffing round you like they are, the best course of action would be to hide these 'bad boys'."

I detected more than a hint of sarcasm as she'd repeated my cheesy selection of Hollywood words but couldn't dispute the fact that she was right. I had the perfect place as in the kitchen just above the fridge there was a loose ceiling panel where I used to store my drugs in my more paranoid moments. Not only was it perfect but also discreet and slightly out the way with still enough roof space to fit both the bag and guns. Placing the bag on the table I took every gun in my hand one by one examining them individually before returning them to the bag. We sat in silence for a moment then as Nellie stood I passed her the bag and she spoke up in a very gentle tone.

"You know this is all going to end really badly don't you babe?"
I was a little lost for words but she did have a point. Although for me it wasn't so much about things ending badly but how far we were willing to go before they actually did. I kind of gave her a half smile then replied in what I hoped was a reassuring tone.

"Okay, point taken, hide the guns and let them rest, but tomorrow is another day and we need to keep moving forward."

Maybe not the best effort at reassuring someone but we had come too far now for cheap words. I always said what was on my mind so she needed to choose either to follow or leave and that would be her decision. Picking up the bag she avoided eye contact completely, which told me she was confused.

"Look, let me get rid of these guns and then I'll knock up some food, it will give me a chance to think; later we can talk about all this and maybe even form some sort of plan?"

I couldn't really blame her for feeling overwhelmed as I had put her through the wringer this week. The whole Annie thing was bad enough but then the toe removal combined with today's guns and murders was all a lot to take in. I tried to catch her eye as she made her way towards the kitchen but she didn't look back closing the door behind her. She needed time to think so I would give her some space. I reached for the remote for the music system and hit the play button.

Suddenly the room was filled with the beautiful sounds of PJ Harvey and Nick Cave's wonderful duet "Henry Lee" bringing me a warm feeling of joy. Before the music had a chance to consume me completely the moment was lost as there was a knock on the front door. Nellie wouldn't have heard it through the music plus needed her space so standing up I hobbled my way down the hallway. I opened the door but before I had a chance to see who it was I was struck in the face with an almighty blow which knocked me clean off my feet. I could taste the blood in my mouth and tried to sit up only for a foot to pin me to the floor.

"And where the fuck you think you're going you fucking cunt."

His accent was thick Irish and from the floor I could make out he was large man sporting one of those annoying hipster type beards. From my limited position, I was pretty sure he was alone but given the pure size of this big bastard there might as well have been two of him. Pushing myself up onto my elbows I go to speak but receive a kick in the face for my troubles. Then before I even have time to contemplate the pain he takes hold of one of my feet and drags me towards the living room. The friction of the carpet burns my back but then suddenly I find myself being lifted and flung through the air.

I land right in the middle of the coffee table, which smashes under my weight, leaving me in a pile of broken wood. Quickly I take my chance reaching out to try and grab one of the short-broken table legs but once again he pins me down as his large boot finds my arm. At last I start to catch my breath amongst what remains of the table as my tormentor takes a knee down at my side.

"You been a bad boy Lee, my sister sends her regards."

From his low position he punches me in the side just under my rib cage, which instantly has me struggling for air once again.

Fuck, this has to be Annie's brother. That fucking bitch must have got my address off human resources, fucking Data Protection Act my ass. As I roll onto my side I need to speak but am struggling for air. But then behind him I see the kitchen door is now slightly open then briefly catch sight of Nellie through the gap before she disappears out of sight.

"You see this, Sonny?"

As I rolled onto my back I looked up to see him now brandishing a large knife and looking very pleased with himself. His moment of smugness at least allows me to get a word in.

"It's ok Paddy, we got no potatoes that need peeling today but thanks nonetheless."

My comment was met not unsurprisingly with another blow to my side but this time delivered with a kick.

"I don't find little pricks like you very funny; I think will be having ourselves some fun and games tonight."

He pointed down at me as he spoke but out of the corner of my eye I caught Nellie coming out of the kitchen with the sawn-off in her hands.

"But not half as much fun as we're going to be having with you big boy."

Her words stop him in his tracks and I smile up at him

through my teeth as the realization that we aren't alone hits him. More by instinct than anything else he turns on the spot coming face to face with Nellie who taking a quick step forward smashes him square in the face with the stock of her gun. The blow seems to stun him sending him to one knee but he's still not completely out and raises one of his hands in a show of defiance. It's all too late as a trickle of blood starts running from his nose and Nellie waits a second before delivering the second blow which this time sends him down collapsing on top of my legs.

As I manage to pull myself free she holds out her hand helping me to my feet before calmly walking to the front door and shutting it. I sit myself down on the sofa as Nellie returns to the room giving our new friend on the floor a kick in his side which neither moves nor wakes him.

"Fuck me! I don't know about you Lee but Jesus Christ I hate a fucking Irish accent."

You had to feel sorry for this man really as he had come to restore some family honour and now found himself tied up with electrical cable on the floor and gagged with a dirty kitchen cloth. He was a big cunt so we had acted fast as we knew he wouldn't be out for long and we had been right as he came to after only a few minutes.

As he opened his eyes he stared up at us sitting on the sofa, he had been felled and was now our prisoner. Nellie raised the gun from her lap and pointed it at his balls instantly causing his eyes to open wide as he tried to speak in a mad panic through his gag. She then stood kicking him hard in the stomach then waiting for him to make eye contact before again repeating the action. Hovering above him this time she raised her finger to her lips, he got the message and remained silent.

29

"You all done Baz?"

As I pressed the phone to my ear Annie's voice had sounded so full of hope. It was as if I could feel her excitement racing down the line as she waited for her brother to pass on all the gory details. Of course, now there was one small problem as this may have been her brother's phone but I was most certainly not her brother.

"Hello Annie, how the devil are you?"

My words were greeted by a wall of silence as reality dawned on her as she realised who was on the other end of the line. It was tempting to give out one of those evil callous movie-style laughs but I refrained deciding to continue with a more direct approach.

"I think you and I need to have a little chat sweetheart and judging by the state of Baz, it was Baz wasn't it? I would advise you to do exactly what I say."

"What the fuck have you done with my brother?"

You couldn't blame her for such an aggressive response as the call she had been expecting had now taken a rather unexpected twist. Her brother was fine as I had no desire to start killing random Irishmen in my flat, even those who'd been sent to harm me. Yes, maybe his pride had taken a hit and certainly he'd a few more bruises than yesterday but at least he would live to fight another day. What was most important now regarding this current situation was that a window of opportunity had presented itself and I wasn't intending to let it slip through my fingers.

"Judging by the shit music in the background I'm guessing you're at O'Malley's, no?"

The ball was now in my court and all I needed to do was

finish the job with no extra drama. As I spoke I looked across to Nellie who was a picture of calm sitting on the sofa not once taking her eyes or the gun off poor Barry. Almost comically Nick Cave's Murder Ballads had not stopped playing through the whole ordeal giving the mood a sinister feel but also making the case for choosing CDs over vinyl.

"I asked you a fucking question, what the fuck have you done with my brother?"

Annie's tone now was more desperate than angry but I still needed to stamp my authority on this situation giving her no option but to comply.

"Look, you need to fucking listen or the gun that is now pointing directly at Barry's head will do what it was built to fucking do, you fucking understand?"

Just the word gun got her full attention and I was pretty sure she was now crying but clearing her throat she composed herself to answer

"Yes, I understand, please don't hurt him."

"OK, I will see you within the hour and I expect to find you alone in that shitty little flat of yours. No tricks or this evening will not have a happy ending, oh and one more thing, bring me a bottle of Bushmills up from the bar."

She she had no choice but to agree and I had no doubt at that moment she would have been in a complete state of panic. Not only would she be reliving our more violent moments together but also now hoping her brother wouldn't fall to the same fate. I had once again turned her world completely on its head being the catalyst to all sorts of terrible thoughts and scenarios now running through her head; funny how things work out really and all this because of a little bit of lust.

As the taxi dropped me across the road from O'Malley's I

pulled my phone from my pocket just to check in with events at home before proceeding. Apart from Barry pissing himself everything appeared to be fine and under control, well almost. Nellie wasn't happy, complaining that "Unknown Pleasures" kept jumping halfway through "Dead Souls" and was somehow blaming me for the condition of my records. I wasn't sure how much of a music fan poor Barry was but felt pretty certain that the musical combo of Joy Division and the previous "Murder Ballads" weren't exactly relaxing him. I hung up the phone laughing then headed across the road towards the bar and my pending reunion with Annie.

I only knew the one way to her flat so pulling my cap down to hide my eyes walked straight through the front door into the bar area. Luckily for me the place was busy and I quickly blended into the crowd retracing the path that Annie had led me on the night we had fucked. Pushing my way through the fire door I headed up the metal steps and then into the alley that led to her door. It was open and I found her sat on the step waiting for me to arrive with an obviously premeditated greeting.

"If you have done anything to my brother I will fucking kill you, you understand that?"

The Irish were such stupid fucks, brave yes but always so fucking stupid. Had she not heard anything I had said to her? I turned to walk away, which instantly changed her tone.

"No, no, stop, I'm sorry."

I don't know why but a sudden feeling that I could fuck her came over me which was of course just ridiculous. Saying that some women do have a history of staying with violent partners so maybe it wasn't completely out of the question. Plus, I couldn't help but wonder what lengths she may have been willing to go to for the sake of her brother.

A punch of reality hit as I caught a glimpse of her bandaged hand, which instantly reminded me that I needed to start playing nice. Despite her being a wild fuck and a tingle of lust that was now grabbing my body it was properly best not to rock the boat by making a pass at her. If any sort of sexual reprise was going to happen I would allow her to make the first move as I needed to get on with the matter at hand.

"Hey Annie, there's no need to apologise this has all just got way out of hand and the blame lies completely with me. Look, I am sober and come in peace so I just truly want to say sorry for everything. Now come on, let's go inside and have a drink, please let me explain."

She looked me up and down the same way she had the night we had slept together, which I guess was a good start. However, this time the vibe was very different as it wasn't lust led anymore with her now struggling with deciding if she wanted to trust me or not. Taking a deep breath she stood, then with a nod turned walking through the front door and into her flat. All was going to plan so I followed and then went to close the door behind me.

"No! The door stays fucking open!"

Understandable really seeing our recent history so first raising my hands in an attempt at a peaceful gesture I pushed the door back open. As I made my way into her makeshift living room my mind was flooded with fond memories from my previous visit. Annie however seemed not to be on the same page and was completely on edge sitting herself down on the arm of the chair closest to the door. The Bushmills was on the table so I sat and started to pour myself a glass

"It's just one phone call and your brother is free, in fact just two phone calls."

I couldn't deny that she looked good and I could feel myself getting hard. It was just a simple combination of seeing her again, the flat and those great memories. I remembered how I had bent her over the arm of the chair where she was now sat when we had first drunkenly fallen through the door. Then how she had screamed so joyously as I penetrated her ass for the first time, I smiled and look up to find Annie wasn't enjoying the moment quite as much.

"Ok, you got your fucking whisky and I let you in, now can I have my fucking brother back?"

We had fucked a lot in this room and it had been great, had she forgotten everything?

"We had some great sex that night and don't tell me you're not thinking about it now. You know you are maybe the best lay I have ever had, well 100% top 3. It is so unappreciated a woman who knows the true benefits of anal sex and because of that you are special; no, you are better than that, you are exceptional."

She doesn't say a word, just sits there looking at me with a look of complete amazement and contempt then takes a long breath exhaling before passing comment.

"You are one fucked-up motherfucker. You sit there after beating me, sticking a letter opener through my hand and now kidnapping my brother yet you want to reminisce over our one-night stand, you're fucking crazy."

I could tell she was turned on, she wanted me and I knew it, I would play her little role-play game.

"You know I am hard now, just the sight of you and the memories of this room are making me horny, come on, you must feel the energy?"

She starts to laugh, then putting her head in her hands starts to shake it while giving out a cry of frustration before looking back up again.

"Seriously, you need fucking help."

It was a fair enough assessment to be honest as maybe I had got carried away in the moment, slightly misreading the vibe. I reached into my pocket pulling out Sergeant Richard Wright's business card, throwing it on the table in front of her.

"Make the call and drop the charges then I will call home; do this and Barry comes home breathing, then we can all go back to living happily ever after."

What choice did she have? None was the answer to that question. I knew I had her over a barrel and even though I would have preferred to have her over the arm of the chair it would have to suffice. It was all over so quickly really and to honest I did feel sorry for her as I had treated her particularly badly. There was no point explaining my guilt as that was my personal business and I had already paid for my crimes with my toe. Anyways she wasn't capable of understanding my own form of penance as she just wasn't on my level and never would be.

It was good to end this rather eventful day on a happy note with a different type of closure. It was all about the Yin and Yang and just finding the balance had made me feel good. As I walked through the front door with the Bushmills in hand Nellie's smile filled me with warmth. There she was sat on the sofa still cradling the sawn-off on her lap like a new born child but Barry was gone, meaning our home was once again ours.

30.

It had always been a bit strange to me that I could never remember my dreams but in many ways I guess it was a blessing. I couldn't even start to imagine the turmoil or damage that an uncontrollable video loop of images could have on a person. I mean, it wasn't like you had any sort of quality control or censorship or even a remote control to turn it off. My case was different as my mind was never a lazy one, which meant when I went to bed it simply just shut down going into a kind of standby mode. I often found that when I awoke I was as bright as a button as my brain just seemed to spring back into life, primed for action. Some days I arose so fresh that I would often roll straight out of bed into sets of exercises before even addressing Mother Nature's call or contemplating the day ahead.

This morning, however, was proving very different as I found myself almost pinned to the empty bed with last night's sleep driven show-reel rerunning itself inside my head. It's often said that us humans only use ten percent of our brains so maybe I'd always had the ability to dream just had never accessed it, until now of course. It was almost like a part of my brain had suddenly been brought back online, which was obviously due to my ongoing transformation and evolution. I had become a more complete model and although this new-found ability to dream was puzzling it needed to be embraced.

I continued to lay there pushing my brain to now focus in on my dream. I needed to understand it and work out its meaning so closing my eyes I started to remember.

It was odd really as there I had been looking up at what appeared to be hooded figures who were holding me down nailing my hands to what appeared to be wood. I remembered a kind of joy I had felt as I recalled the music that was building with every blow; fuck, that's right, it had been Pink Floyd's "Great gig in the Sky". I could hear it now and see exactly what was happening as I was being crucified with both my hands and feet now nailed to a cross as I was hoisted up. The music suddenly climaxed as the

186

vocal kicked in and now a sea of these hooded figures surrounded me all kneeling with their arms outstretched as if I was being worshipped. Suddenly I could see my face in pure ecstasy, lit up as the sun rose in front of me, I was their saviour.

Pushing myself off the bed I fell naked to the floor rolling myself over onto my front then went into a mad set of press-ups. I must have done fifty in less than a minute with the pain from my toe pushing me on as the agony acted as a kind of motivator. I finally succumbed, my heart pumping as I lay there allowing my mind to drift back to the dream, what the fuck did it all mean?

Eventually I got myself together then after a cold shower decided to head out for some fresh air. A walk was surely a good call allowing me time to clear my head as I continued to ponder the meaning of my sleep-driven entertainment. It truly was an inspiring morning with the fresh frost slowly being melted away by the bright sun that looked so magnificent against the blue of the sky. I just loved days like this where the sun would warm your face yet you could still see your cold breath. As I wandered aimlessly allowing the pure beauty of the morning to consume me I soon found myself like a few days earlier down by the canal.

There is something calming about water and even the dirty brown flow of the canal put a smile on my face. I sat myself down at the water's edge on an old iron bench watching some polystyrene flow past me, turning in the current. These distractions were short-lived as my mind once again slipped back to the dream. What did it mean, could I possibly be the saviour, the chosen one? Just the thought of me even thinking this made me laugh out loud. Jesus, I knew I was special but was neither mad nor vain enough to believe that I could possibly be some sort of God.

Recently it had dawned on me that I had some sort of calling in this world but I still wasn't sure of what exactly that was to be. The dream had confused me somewhat both in its content and the fact it was maybe the first time I had actually recalled one. Once again I stared into the flow of the water and for some reason

187

thought of Father Joe; fuck, could he have the answers? I was no more than ten minutes from the church but more worryingly this thought process was maybe testament to how desperate I actually was.

After a brisk walk the large wooden doors loomed in front of me but I stopped short from entering as I considered my options. My state of mind was fragile this morning and I could feel my optimism battling with my logic. I had always known that I was highly intelligent but the events of the last few weeks had me thinking of what price I had paid for that gift. Sane people just didn't chop off their toe or commit murder but then who was the rule maker or the judge to decide what was right or wrong. I certainly believed in bettering ourselves as a breed of animal yet this modern world now contained a weak, softer type of person. I couldn't quite put my finger on what exactly it was that I really hoped to change or achieve as I truly hated almost everything.

What the human race had become was alien to me; it was as if we were chalk and cheese. Every day I wandered through its streets and despised what I saw. This constant style over substance and self-obsession people had with their own lives, it was driving me mad. It was as if we had entered into a period of history where the people had everything at their fingertips but were scared to embrace that power. Maybe it was just they didn't have the self-confidence or certainty only feeling secure hidden behind this social media camouflage they painted their lives with.

I hated it all: status updates, selfies, selfie sticks, tweets, Facebook, Instagrammers, blogs, podcasts, hashtags etc etc etc. Where would these people be without a "like" button? And where the fuck was the option to "don't like" or "hate?" I could never understand what someone had to gain by watching the world through other people's photos, video clips or status updates. I don't fucking care about your fucking lives and no I don't have fucking Facebook, Twitter or Instagram, live in the moment you fucking zombie cunts.

Nothing can really prepare you for reality in this sin-filled despicable world we live in, a clergyman's nightmare but now a place that was destined to be my battlefield. Nobody knew I was different but they soon would because I have wandered, I have turned, I have lost, I have won, I have delivered, I have hated, healed, killed, snorted, cum, fucked, stolen, drunk, repented but now I will destroy.

Life isn't meant to be sweet, it is flawed and those within are merely pawns playing some fucked-up game of chess. I never asked to be the King, Jesus I didn't even ask to be the rook or the bishop this world just chose me. My dorsal fin was raised, there would be an apocalypse and I would rain down some serious hurt on this sick world. I could feel the blood and energy racing through me as the anger increased inside of me and started spinning out of control.

"Good morning Lee, what a beautiful morning?"

31

As Father Conway poured me a cup of tea I had to confess I never thought in a million years that my first experience of going backstage would have been at a church. To be honest I felt grateful that he had found me when he did with our morning encounter resulting in me bursting into tears before giving him a long hug. We were now sat in what would be best described as a half office, half living room set up that worked although probably shouldn't have. Religious artefacts were very much omnipresent as you would expect in a church just not in an IKEA-superstore type of style. As I sat on the large garish red sofa I was feeling a little lost and a touch embarrassed by my previous turn outside. I had issues, that was for sure and if I was to understand these demons that lay deep inside me they needed to be confronted head on. Bearing that in mind I guess and like it or not, I now found myself maybe in the right place to do just that.

Father Conway smiled as he handed me a cup then sat himself down on the sofa directly opposite me. I couldn't help but like this man and even if I didn't subscribe to his club a good man was still a good man. He didn't speak straight away allowing a deliberate silence to fall between us which was more comforting than awkward. Leaning forward he returned his tea cup to the table removing the spoon then tapped it on the side of the cup in an almost call-for-arms type manner. Looking up he stared straight at me, once again with a smile across his face, then cleared his throat.

"I know after our last encounter that you are a non-believer, I can assure you it was something that you made quite clear."

He paused, which was so perfectly timed it would have made even the best stand-up comic proud. I wasn't stupid and knew this pause like before was quite deliberate; he was trying to set boundaries and also wanted my full attention which he now had. He was giving me what could only be described as a "I remember, so don't go off on one," kind of look which I acknowledged with a wry smile and a nod before he continued.

"I know you see the Church as an evil place Lee but something has drawn you back here today. OK I am pretty sure you're not here looking for God but today even more so than before you do seem so deeply troubled, so restless, even lost. I can't guarantee the answers but just maybe I can help you so please feel free to open up."

Of course, I was looking for answers as my mind needed to be understood but at this moment in time it seemed I was the person least qualified to do just that. There was little doubt that I was one fucked-up cookie but all the recent violence, death and now dreams were leaving me even more confused. I wanted answers but didn't know the questions; my emotions were an out-of-control rollercoaster which showed no signs of slowing down and if anything was picking up speed. As I looked upon Father Conway I was suddenly filled with a desire to kill and knew I was capable of doing it but why was that even entering my train of thought?

"You Okay Lee? A penny for your thoughts, young man?"

Really!! I wasn't sure he was ready for that as a confession of wanting to murder him would probably be somewhat of a mood killer.

"I think it's best for all concerned if I keep that last thought well inside my head."

He found my reply instantly amusing which gave me a horrible feeling that he was being smug; fuck him, as if he was the holder of all the fucking answers. How could this man even think he could compete with me intellectually? Yes, he appeared smart but you had to question anyone who devoted their life to an organisation like the Catholic Church. Where were all the answers to your prayers motherfucker? Nowhere, that's where they are, because nobody is fucking listening. If you want to be a good man then just fucking be a good man why all these fairy tales and worship, it was just such a load of bollocks.

"I detect a lot of anger in you....."

I started to laugh which stopped him mid flow; obviously I was angry how couldn't I be as living in this pathetic vile world in which we found ourselves was hardly awe-inspiring it was comical. I needed to express myself out loud.

"Well if you're going to choose to live in the shadows hiding yourself away in an ivory tower everything must appear fucking great. The world is flawed my friend, so how can I not feel anger? We as humans need to fight our desire to be comfortable in these fucking false lives of lies and deceit. We are all looking for the fucking answers but it's the questions that need re-evaluating. Your little hypocritical leather-bound book would condemn me as sinner for my so-called crimes, as would society, but who makes these rules? We are animals that have been sedated, domesticated and have been tricked to allow a chosen few to rule over us. Fear has bullied the innocent into believing such shit removing the once proud animal instinct from each of us. I am talking evolution, about putting it back on track, as I no longer will be controlled, I refuse to flee or be bullied, the world needs to change and I am starting the fight back."

To say Father Conway looked uncomfortable would be an understatement as he was nothing short of terrified which made me feel good, even powerful or Godlike.

"Please, calm yourself, you have no fight with me. I am here to help, let's take a deep breath..."

Suddenly his mouth was moving yet I no longer heard his voice as if I'd somehow hit the mute button. Why the fuck was I here talking to this moron hiding behind his so-called good book and to think I actually thought he could help me. Let's face facts: the bible is full of evil, some real dark shit, yet these puppets conveniently manage to skip over the parts about slavery, abuse of women's rights and homosexuality to find a good message, fucking hypocrites, fuck them all. I want to talk evolution, dinosaurs, same-sex marriage, abortion, contraception, murdering in the name of God, paedophile priests and more. I looked up at him still yapping on and started imagining his face covered in blood. My mind suddenly felt enlightened by the whole moment as I found myself flying through the air knocking both Father Conway and the sofa he sat on backwards.

We both fell hard onto the cold marble floor with me the quicker to react getting to my feet and grabbing a nearby statue of Jesus. The father was still struggling down on all fours and once again I went at him this time pinning him to the floor before starting to beat him with the statue.

Suddenly it felt cold in my hand as I peered down at what was now a caved-in bloody face before me. Father Conway still lay trapped under me but now his lifeless body told me one thing: that he was well and truly dead. What the fuck had I done? Frantically standing up I looked around but knew no-one was there; he had deserved to die as he had obviously provoked me and I was not a man to be provoked. Who would actually give a shit as the world wouldn't miss a man of the cloth, in fact I should be applauded for reducing their number by one.

"FUCK, FUCK, FUCK!!!"

What was I thinking? This just wasn't right or meant to be then dropping to my knees I lowered my head onto Father Conway's chest and began to cry. I knew these were hollow tears but I so wanted to undo this but it was already too late. I don't know why but I looked up to the ceiling as if I was looking for a God for answers and started to shout.

"FUCK YOU, FUCK YOU, AND FUCK YOU!"

The shouting cleared my head almost instantly as I started to realise the magnitude of the situation that lay before me. I couldn't afford to lose control, I needed to remain calm and think quickly. Placing the statue carefully on the floor beside me I lifted myself off Father Conway's body then without pause I made my way out towards the main church. Peering through the curtains I saw that luckily the church was empty so taking my chance ran to the main doors and bolted them shut.

It was at least an hour later that I found myself sat on the same iron bench as earlier once again watching the canal roll past. I still wasn't sure how I felt as my mind was a mess which currently seemed to be nothing new. The church hadn't been as big a problem to sort as I'd originally thought and in the end I had done a good job of covering my tracks.

I had debated about cutting the body up but had seen to many CSI episodes to know that never ended well. It was simple really as I robbed the place making the murder scene appear like a robbery gone wrong. At the back of the room I had broken into a locked cupboard discovering some more valuable church items than those displayed out front. These were now the source of infighting as they found themselves in the hands of the junkies under the canal bridge.

They couldn't have been more than fifty metres from where I now sat and I pictured their faces as they must have thought Christmas had come early when they stumbled upon the haul. Of course all they were doing was framing themselves for murder or at worst sending the police on a wild goose chase.

It was amazing to think how the human mind reacted to certain situations. I knew I was far from normal but still I applauded myself at the way I had quickly come up with a plan to cover my tracks under such adversity. If truth was to be told, I had freaked out, but then suddenly my brain had gone through the gears realigning my thought process allowing me to focus.

It had been simple in the end, I had taken everything I could, loading the items into what must have been Father Joe's laundry bag before leaving through a rear exit. Finding the back door behind a huge curtain had been a huge stroke of luck. However, seeing how that led to the old graveyard which in turn backed onto the canal could only be classified as God given luck. I laughed to myself at the thought that maybe even God himself had aided in my escape. Imagine the scandal if the world suddenly found out he too had a certain distaste for the church and organized religion.

The sight of what remained of Father Conway's head suddenly gate-crashed my mind. This time, however it was a wave of calm that embraced me as I knew at that moment I had once again gotten away with murder. There would be no need for self-punishment or to pay penance this time as I already classified this as the past. As much as I liked Father Conway his violent demise didn't make feel as bad as what happened to Annie, who ironically still lived and breathed. Curious as that was and although undeserved sitting there I felt no remorse for taking his life. Suddenly I could hear the junkies' arguments turning violent as they fought over their newly acquired treasure, which meant there was only one thing left to do.

Finding a public phone in this day and age was a more difficult task than it had been a few years previous. The old standby of the train station never fails and picking up the receiver I started to dial the Police. It rang maybe twice before a woman answered and although I didn't have much to say it was important to bring closure to today's events.

"Yes hello, I was just walking my dog down by the canal and there seems to be some very strange behaviour coming from under the bridge behind the church........."

32

By the time Nellie got home from work both the local and national news were covering the "brutal murder" of Father Conway. It was a kind of weird watching a news story I was such a part of being covered on the TV especially with all the speculation surrounding it, as they labelled it "such a ghastly event." Watching the whole media circus unfold kind of saddened me as it had done with the previous killings as my moment of glory was lost through my absence. Of course this wasn't a bad thing but it did niggle at me as any message I hoped to achieve was being lost, today's tomfoolery apart. Nevertheless, it would be wise to keep this murder to myself as not only had it been a rash mistake but also another painted nail would lead to more jealousy from Nellie.

Since we had begun my killing spree not much had reached the public domain apart from the so called "suicide" of Toby Johnson. That particular death had been warranted, so to say it hadn't been in vain was maybe the wrong sentiment. Child abuse stories had been a favourite of the press for a while and now St Luke's was currently going through the wringer. I personally gained a certain feeling of pleasure knowing some good had come from Toby's not so self-inflicted passing. However, what was surprising was how Nellie had shown very little interest in following the fallout from the story but then I guess the whole murder thing must have given her some sort of closure.

As we sat down together that night it almost felt that middle age had kicked in as she sat watching TV while I listened to music through my headphones. The honeymoon period of our relationship was over, that was for sure and even though the sex was still intense it was somewhat less frequent. Something was wrong with Nellie and I couldn't quite put my finger on it but then again it was probably me as it had been an emotionally charged kind of day.

I reckon it must have been at least four months now since we had first met and then three since our first kill. Initially Nellie had shown a real desire to strike out at society with talk of shitlists, anger and revenge yet these dreams seemed to have been watered down somewhat since the killing of Toby Johnson. I on the other hand felt ready to strike out at any time with the guns filling my mind with all sorts of possibilities as I raced forward committed to fulfilling my potential and quenching my desires.

As I looked over to Nellie she indicated she wanted me to remove my headphones, which I did.

"It was you, wasn't it?"

I hadn't noticed her pause the TV and the question took me by surprise leaving me sitting there a little confused.

"Admit it, I know it was you, I could just tell something happened today the second I walked in. It's the look in your eyes, it just gives you away and today it's the same as that night I came home to find you with all the guns."

Even though I was pretty sure it was the church killing she was referring to I wasn't 100% certain. The best thing to do was to play dumb just in case it was something else that I had missed.

"I am not sure what you mean babe?"

This was maybe a mistake or bad judgement on my part as a denial would surely create a crack in our relationship. Honesty had been one of our rudimental rules but then so had the L word and she'd already broken that one. I hadn't started moving the goal posts, she had and it was her who would have to take responsibility. Eventually this thing we had would end but she would be made to remember it was her, not me who initiated the original change of direction.

"You know exactly what I mean because the murder in the church today was you, of that I have no doubt as I see it. Every time you have killed you've seemed different, don't get me wrong, not in a bad way It's just I detect a kind of calm in you, it's almost like you're less intense."

I knew what she was talking about as every kill had left me with a feeling of self-confidence. I guess what she was now detecting or reading was my inner calm, which meant she was right. My life had been a strange course of events that had shaped me as a person, however nothing like the feeling I got from killing had ever come close to calming me.

For as long as I can remember I'd always had the beast inside of me but now knew that was the thing that completed me. It was as if my mind had been in the dark and somehow this animal had found the light switch. I looked up and could see Nellie talking but couldn't hear what she was saying; it was happening again, the same as in the church before when I killed Father Conway, Fuck!! I need to tune back in.

".....and that is how I feel. You just can't go off a one-man crusade, it's like you're cheating on me with all your death and murders, we are meant to be a team and I want to fucking kill too!"

She reaches beneath the cushion on the sofa beside her and pulls out the same gun that only a few days earlier I had used oh so brutally and efficiently.

"Is this the gun you used to kill those drug dealers?"

She was not happy and had the dark tone in her voice that at times I found such a turn-on. The vibe here was very different, something was going to happen and I nodded to confirm it was that very weapon. Looking me cold in the eye she slowly raised the gun pointing it straight at me. Jesus, was this was how it was going to end?

"Nellie, please calm the fuck down, put the gun on the table."

She just stared at me not moving a muscle and I remained frozen to the spot not daring to speak for fear of antagonising her more. This wasn't how my journey was to finish, my life had a path yet in which direction I was to travel was now very much out of my hands. For about 30 seconds she continued to point the gun straight at me not saying a word or showing any signs of emotion except pure anger. I wasn't sure what to do, then as I raised my hand to speak suddenly she turned the gun and put it in her mouth.

I dropped to the floor in front of her as if I was trying to pay homage at her feet, begging her not to pull the trigger. Pulling the gun from her mouth she directed it to the side of her head while gesturing with an open palm for me not to move or speak.

"Don't you fucking move, if you can't include me in your plans then why should I be part of your life? I thought what we had was special but it's now quite apparent you have a more selfish agenda. I would fucking kill for you and you just don't get it so now I will prove just that and if this is meant to be the end so be it but if I live we hunt and we hunt together."

She shut her eyes and started to squeeze the trigger and I think I must have passed out as when I awoke I found myself on the floor staring at the ceiling. I could hear the TV which was a good sign but couldn't recall if it had been on or off before so chose to just lay while I gathered my thoughts. It was almost as if I was too scared to sit up to face reality but had to say something to at least know if she was still alive.

"Nellie, are you there?"

I held my breath waiting for what I hoped would be her voice then after maybe ten seconds she spoke.

"Yeah, I'm here."

Thank fuck for that, I rolled myself onto my stomach pushing myself up off the floor onto my knees. There she was sitting on the sofa looking straight at me with the gun on her lap.

"Thank fuck you are okay, I don't know what happened?"

She didn't look happy with me at all capped off with a very evil look in her eyes. I went to speak but she stopped then started to speak in a very monotone and direct manner.

"I will tell you what fucking happened, Russian fucking Roulette baby and I am still here to tell the tale. Of course you would have known that ten fucking minutes ago if you hadn't been such a pussy and passed out."

She had played the same game of fate as I had also living to tell the tale which now made two spins with no outs. This had to be a sign that we were tuned to the same wave length, fate had just decided that, dealing her the same cards as me. Happiness filled me as I knew our journey was not yet over and lifting myself off the floor I went to hug her. As I drew close she stopped me with an outstretched arm then raised a finger, pointing straight at me.

"Look fuckface it is simple, no more cheating or I am out of here, we do this together or we end it now?"

I nodded, it seemed shit was about to get real all of a sudden.

33.

The true darkness of any city tends to show itself downtown at the weekend and this end of week's offering was proving no different. As we cut our way through the maddening Saturday crowd we both took a kind of twisted pleasure knowing we had the capability at any moment to turn this jovial playground into a bloodbath. Of course, they wouldn't know that two killers mingled in their midst tooled up and ready for action if the opportunity arose. Nellie's evening had almost started with a bang as she had come close to losing it with a hen party on the train as they passed around a box of chocolate cocks to other passengers. They didn't know how lucky they were really as confrontation was avoided when they'd exited at the next station with Nellie set to explode.

We now found ourselves sat in the main square of what people perceived as "the place to be" at the weekend. In reality it was more the centre of some neon-lit, alcohol-fuelled universe we both struggled to relate to. In all honesty this was the kind of place where if a human cull was necessary it would've surely been at the top of my list.

I can't say these were bad people, it was just this sort of trend-led zombie for me contributed very little to educated society. I have no problem with having fun but following the masses in an almost tribal-like brain-dead manner just disappoints me. The modern human has become an awful creature, self-obsessed with style over substance for which to be fair TV and the media are heavily to blame. I would say that more than 90% of conversations I hear these days are geared around reality TV shows or some series as the media takes control of the general consciousness.

The world is in a sad state yet these people lose themselves in a fake manufactured dream every night just to relive those experiences with others the following day. Undeniably when they aren't doing that they are uploading photos of their "oh so wonderful lives" onto Facebook etc. to show others just how cool

201

or important they actually are. I just hate this, especially the neediness of it all making me wonder if people will ever get back to being real and thinking for themselves.

The night was getting busier as more and more people spilled onto the streets. For all my hatred I always quite enjoyed that you could smell the sex in the air as the courting rituals took place as these soulless, brainless idiots hunted their prey. We too were hunting but in all so different manner albeit in the same arena. We had come prepared to act on our impulses but what we were really doing was a reconnaissance mission. I reached inside of my coat and ran the hand over the gun strapped to my side as a large group of Spanish tourists passed by me.

I hated tourists, not so much the educated couples or families that visit this great city for cultural reasons but the mass groups of teens that wandered around in groups. The Spanish and Italians were the worst in their garish-coloured clothing, little backpacks, loud voices and they always seemed to be smoking. Taking out a large group of these fucks was very tempting but luckily for them I guess my thirst for death had been quenched in this rather eventful of weeks.

I couldn't however say the same for Nellie, who seemed rather agitated by everything. It was nice being able to share my anger, not being completely alone as she was definitely on the same page as me.

"What the fuck happened to the human race, these people make me sick. Look at them with their fucking mobile phones and selfie sticks, all just so self-absorbed, what a bunch of fucking idiots. Why is it that these people feel the need to publicise their mundane lives, when all it really is just a "who's got the bigger cock" competition." Fuck me it's just so fucking boring, look at them, they all look the fucking same in their high street brands and don't even get me started on their fucking haircuts, cunts."

She was correct, this world really was being dumbed down so much so that if we were to execute everyone we saw here for taking a selfie it would be classified more as genocide than murder. Tonight we wouldn't be killing anyone, well not here at least, what we were really doing was fuelling our anger.

Nellie had understood the necessity of self-control as well as the fuelling process but nonetheless seemed on edge. As I turned to look at her my fears were confirmed as she was getting angry but to be fair seemed far from losing control. In fact she was becoming focused and that's what we needed.

"Okay Lee, I've seen enough of this fucking shit, let's leave mass murder to the terrorists but next time there is an attack on an area like this please remind me not to shed a fucking tear."

She stood up pulling her hood over her head as the tones of "Gangnam Style" once again invaded our personal space. It was the third time this hour the bar to our left had played this fucking aural abortion, each time greeted by a large roar of approval. Nellie looked at me shaking her head then turned in the direction of this demonic music.

"You Fucking Cunts!"

Her sweary shouts instantly stopped a few passers-by in their tracks but only for a second as the hypnotic vibe of this vile area drew them back in. She laughed turning her head back in my direction rolling her eyes. We both had pity for these people as yes, they were everything we hated but they were weak. To be fair it really wasn't their faults as they had been tricked into following this manufactured path designed to stop them from thinking for themselves.

"Okay let's go." Something had caught her attention as she took my hand leading me quickly through the crowd sidestepping with disgust those who were gazing into their mobile phones. We hadn't had a target for tonight but now I suspected she may have been acting on an impulse and had changed her mind. I could see the arch of the underground station ahead of us guiding us in its direction but then I saw her target.

The hen party we had come across earlier on the train had gathered outside one of the many fast-food joints in the area where they were currently stuffing their faces. Slipping her hand from mine she made a beeline toward the bride to be who was a grossly overweight woman dressed in stereotypical ill-fitting short skirt, tight top, angel wings, white veil and of course "L" plates. Nellie, now no more than five metres away, decided to make her target aware of her presence.

"Hey Bitch!"

The woman didn't have a chance as Nellie stepped in delivering a perfectly thrown and timed punch right on the button. Her nose seemed to explode as she fell back in what seemed like slow motion. The dramatic event led to a few seconds of confusion as her friends stood frozen watching this large-breasted beast fall, burger and drink going flying as she finally came to rest on her back.

The first reaction was screams and horror then they turned their attention to Nellie, who just stood there Jedi-like, her face hidden in the shadow of her hood. She didn't move and slowly unzipped her jacket then looking up pointed her finger in the direction of the group of girls and started to shout.

"Any of you fucking pricks move, and I'll execute every motherfucking last one of ya!"

Her words were delivered with pure venom as she pulled back her jacket revealing her gun tucked into her belt. Any thought of retaliation from the hen party suddenly disappeared at the sight of the gun as panic and bedlam kicked in. Nellie burst out laughing as people started to flee in all directions with a few of the hen party taking shelter recoiling on the floor behind their fallen friend. Fuck, I had to think quickly as she was creating quite a scene so without another moment to waste I picked her up hoisting her over my shoulder. We made our exit down a side street as she continued to shout in a football type chanting manner as the confused melee disappeared behind us.

"Fucking Cunts, Fucking Cunts, Fucking Cunts, Fucking Cunts."

As soon as we were out of sight her chants turned to laughter but I dared not stop until we were a fair distance away. I must have been running for at least a couple of minutes cutting down as many side streets as I could before coming to a stop out of breath behind a Chinese restaurant. Putting her down she just continued to laugh but we needed to keep moving.

"OK babe, all very funny but come on let's put some distance between us and whatever that just was, no time to fuck around babe, let's move!"

She grabbed my face giving me a huge lustful kiss, she was buzzing but we needed to move. I allowed myself a second to enjoy the moment then taking her by the hand led the way as we disappeared into the night.

34

My bearings were good, meaning we were soon in more familiar surroundings as we now slowly weaved our way in the direction of home. After more than a few years living under its smog and pollution I now knew this city well. On occasion I had chosen to walk home from work across its urban sprawl rather than face the commuter train meaning I'd got to know its network of side streets and alleys. The contrast of the quiet urban suburbs to the madness of downtown was a strange one but one I always found soothing. Not that long ago we had been surrounded by the filth of a Saturday night in full swing yet now here we were in almost complete silence. Apart from the odd car that passed by the world seemed almost deserted from the bench where we now found ourselves sat.

Of course we were surrounded by people but these beings hid behind their garishly coloured front doors, trendy blinds or vile patterned curtains. It was hard to know what worlds lurked behind these walls but no doubt they would be escaping their mundane lives feeding themselves on a diet of fast food and TV.

In many ways these people were an even lower form of pond life than those we had encountered earlier that evening. Although both were living their lives through others´ dreams at least the downtown revellers were making an attempt at living rather than slouching comatose in front of a TV. I despised them all, the dumbing down of this modern world was shocking and was getting worse rather than better and the more it exposed its flaws to me the more I knew I would never quite fit in.

My foot was still yet to fully recover with the pain now more apparent as we'd now stopped yet Nellie was oblivious to my discomfort as she just sat there laughing, reliving the earlier events. She was hyper, still full of energy and if I hadn't stopped to buy us a couple of cans of cider she would have no doubt ably flown all the way home. The can gave out an inviting hiss as I opened it then taking a huge gulp passed it to Nell and just couldn't resist.

"There you go Honey Bunny."

I loved the fact that she had stolen one of Tarantino's most famous lines to cause complete chaos. The sight of the gun would have scared them but when set to such poetry it would have been truly terrifying. I wonder how many of them would have actually seen Pulp Fiction as it seemed more of a Bridget Jones/Bridesmaids type crowd in reality. However, one could take a certain solace that maybe at least one of them may have found it familiar and Googled it.

I looked at Nellie as she drunk from the can her face shinning in the glow of the sodium street lights giving it a yellow shadow. She was out of control maybe more than me and tonight's exercise of self-control hadn't worked. I knew our little adventure was going to end badly, something just told me that but I didn't care anymore. To steal from Guns'n'Roses we both had an "appetite for destruction" and I for one was onboard this ride with no desire to stop until time deemed it to be so. She passed me the can and had that look in her eye I was familiar with.

"Let´s go home and fuck, I feel cold and unsatisfied with tonight's work. I want you to punish me and pleasure me."

She got up straddling me and then not for the first time tonight violently pushed her tongue into my mouth while almost pinning me to the bench. I could feel the frustration in her kisses, in the way her tongue attacked mine and how her teeth clashed. She pulled back taking my head in her two hands and just stared into my eyes. I remember my dad and his "the eyes are the window to the soul" line and maybe he was onto something after all because I saw something I hadn't before.

"Can you feel me and can you hear my calling?"

She continued to stare as if not wanting an answer but it made no difference as I could hear her in the silence her eyes a haze of madness and longing. Just for the moment I did nothing letting myself go sitting there drinking it all in feeling I could live like this forever, it was as if I was living within her. As we once again embraced I reached down the back of her trousers trying to finger her arsehole but found it frustratingly out of reach. Pulling at her knickers instantly drew her closer but the moment was lost as a voice seemed to kick down the door of our party.

"Bloody kids, no respect."

We hadn't heard him approach but no more than ten metres from where we were stood a heavily dressed old man who was out walking his dog. Nellie was far from impressed at the intrusion.

"Why don't you piss off you old cunt."

I could tell the old man wasn't impressed by Nellie's choice of words but he didn't stir or even look in our direction as he took a drag on his cigarette then spat on the floor, looking at his dog.

"As I said Barney, these kids today, no bloody respect."

The dog lifted its head as it recognised its name then started to squat on the pavement. Nellie seemed to forget the old man and turned her attention back to me again whispering in my ear.

"Respect, what a fucking cunt."

I could sense the mischief in her eyes as she didn't say another word rolling herself off me and sitting once again down at my side. We both peered at the old man as its dog continued to do its business on the pavement in front of us. Handing Nellie the can of cider she took a sip before handing it back as the man began to walk away but Nellie wasn't going to let this slip.

"Hey Fuck face, you talk about respect but there you are not cleaning up after your dog you dirty bastard, fucking double standards motherfucker."

This time the old man was startled by Nellie's harsh words, pausing then looking up at us.

"You kiss your mother with that mouth do you?"

You had to give him credit where it was due for standing up for himself but maybe the old man had chosen the wrong fight on the wrong day. Like these things tended to do, it all escalated so quickly and all over a piece of dog shit but in reality, it was about more than that. As Nellie stood she pulled the gun from inside of her coat and pointed it at straight at him.

"My mother is fucking dead you inconsiderate cunt."

She'd certainly got his attention this time as he froze to the spot. However, it wasn't fear I saw but more he seemed to be evaluating the situation, squinting back at Nellie with a look of total contempt before once again spitting on the floor.

"If you think I am scared of you little girl, you are sadly mistaken."

His whole presence grew in that second and I could tell this was not the first time that this man's life had hung in the balance. It began to grate as he spat once more then giving out a small laugh paused before starting to turn away. The whole situation was now on the verge of getting completely out of hand and I knew I had to stop it before it did. Standing I reached across trying to take the gun but Nellie was having none of it and wrestled it from my grip. She was in the zone and refused to be denied taking a few steps forward now pointing the weapon at the old man's back.

"Where the fuck do you think you're going old man? We haven't finished yet, plus you need to clean up this fucking dog shit. You know what, maybe I should teach you a lesson about respect and make you fucking eat, it you dirty bastard."

Rage was pouring from her with every word and this time

the old man felt it as now a look of uncertainty came across his face. He almost stumbled as he turned to find Nellie now standing right in front of him gun in hand. I couldn't let this happen and pulled my own gun taking a step forward pushing it into the back of Nellie's head.

"Don't fucking do it babe, this man doesn't deserve to die, not over dog shit anyhow."

What the fuck was happening? I didn't really know what I was doing but just had to help the old man. My mind skipped back to my encounter with George the war hero in the pub the day I had so dramatically quit my job. Something told me this man was cut from the same cloth and this wasn't how his life was meant to end. He didn't deserve this and I refused to let it happen.

Nellie didn't move as she felt the cold muzzle of my gun rest against the back of her head. I pulled myself closer and reached around this time taking her gun without resistance.

"What the fuck Lee?"

Her voice although calm still contained enough irritation telling me this wasn't the end of it.

"Well do it then, you cocksucker. Let's see if you got the fucking stones."

This time her fury was apparent as all calmness disappeared and she turned to face me head on. I don't know why but I chose not to lower the gun which didn't seem to bother her at all. Looking me straight in the eye she raised her hands cupping the barrel and pushing it into her mouth.

I could see the old man over her shoulder fast escaping into the distance but my concerns were no longer with him. Tears were starting to form in Nellie's eyes as she clasped the gun ever tighter with all her might almost inviting me to end it. I wrenched the gun free, almost falling to the ground as I flew backwards as she just stood there pointing at me ranting.

"You Judas cunt, Judas, Judas, Judas, Judas!!!"

She just repeated the same words over and over again, then slowly allowed herself to slip to the floor bursting into tears. I stepped forward but she wanted none of it slapping my hand away. Pausing for a few seconds I tried again to touch her but like before she once again raised her hand to hit me, this time missing as I stepped back to avoid the blow.

I don't know how close I had come to pulling the trigger but decided the best course of action was to push the two guns into my belt zipping my jacket to hide them from sight. As I crouched down she was now sat with her knees raised and her head in her hands.

"Don't you fucking lay a finger on me!"

Her cries got louder and this time when I rested my hand on her she didn't strike out. Slowly I ran it gently across her back then she finally looked up pulling me close, her voice so full of sadness.

"I'm so sorry; I don't know what's happening to me? I just have so much pain, hate and anger inside of me, it's like since I met you a door has opened, letting it out. I know that should be a good thing but I am not sure if I can fucking control it."

I had been right, she was struggling to keep control and what would happen to the two of us only time would tell. Re-evaluation of our whole project was maybe the best call but in reality, I knew my lack of patience would stifle such a move. A darkness like a murder of crows had been circling around inside of me for a while now but the key was to channel this energy the right way and keep moving forward.

35

Rather than getting up I just rolled onto my side staring up at the ceiling as like every day the morning light cut through the curtains. It had been sitting at the back of the mind for a couple of days since Father Conway and Saturday night but now finally had risen to the surface. I needed to stop, well maybe not stop completely but slow down as my behaviour of late had been quite frankly erratic. The thing was now whatever was inside of me was also seemingly having a similar effect on Nellie.

Up to now she had always been my calming factor yet if she too was coming off the rails it meant serious trouble, which needed addressing before it was too late. I could see the parallel lines our two lives were following, it was just I was more advanced in progression and obviously more evolved.

I had decided to restrict my movements to home in an attempt to understand my mood swings. Of course it could all mean I was bipolar or possibly just going completely mad, anyway I needed answers. My first course of action was to ban myself from both alcohol and drugs then set off on a rigorous daily excise routine.

The gym I had reluctantly used for so long was now out of the question due to my exit from my previous employment and like my working life condemned to the past. This meant an alternative form of exercise needed to be found and consequentially I'd been reading about a criminal called Charles Bronson. Now this guy apart from being quite the character had the most incredible daily workout routine during his incarceration including up to 2000 press ups a day and I was now determined to match this standard.

I had already loaded the cupboards with plenty of healthy food and now intended to eat well as I continued with my new agenda. My body was now back on track but if I was to function at my maximum then it was also essential to find fuel for my mind. I had never been one for the internet and had quite honestly been left behind by the whole thing. Whereas the social media side disgusted me I could see the value of the internet as a source of information, just never had embraced it.

I split my daily eating and exercise routine with internet research with most of my time spent researching the world of violence. Pop culture had already influenced me a lot on this front as my choice of books, cinema and even music at times could testify. However, it now wasn't the Quentin Tarantino, Stagger Lee, American Psycho world I was looking to but more one of reality.

As Nellie passed her days at work I would lose myself in the never-ending river of information the internet provided. I spent a whole day reading up on serial killers such as Ted Bundy, Jeffrey Dahmer and David Berkowitz. It was the American ones I found most interesting but at the same time it was amazing how the drug of killing was now a worldwide phenomenon. From Columbia's "The Beast" to Russia's "Wolf of Moscow" it seemed everywhere had its own Angel of Death.

Although correlations could be made, most killers were from all sorts of backgrounds, with different reasons for their motives. I had little time for those who murdered children or raped their victims as that was just wrong, but others that struck out at the world caught my imagination. The media was too quick to label some as serial killers; doctors, for example, who took matters into their own hands I felt a certain admiration for. To me it all appeared a touch harsh they had been categorised in the same way as some of these obviously very sick people.

Another thing that struck me about all these killings was the reaction to them by society and the media as a whole. I was just as guilty as the next man as I very much enjoyed the stories of violence, killing and death but the way certain countries dealt with such matters was different. You could never say the USA wanted such horrors, which it had plenty to choose from, but it certainly embraced them and defiantly exploited them to make money.

Of course "Natural Born Killers" although not a true story was Tarantino's statement about this very thing. In that movie a young, beautiful couple of serial killers become tabloid-TV darlings as Robert Downey Jr exploits then sensationalises their story. Other successful movies had even been based on true events: "Summer of Sam," "Henry: portrait of a Serial killer," "Zodiac," "Monster" and my personal favourite "Badlands". This all just proved to me that although the world pretended to frown upon such things it still had no problem making money out of them or treating them as a source of entertainment.

My daily study of the internet got more intense as I managed to access actual killings on film. It was amazing that this stuff was so readily available, from clips of beheadings or fatal shark attacks to even suicides. It seemed endless as every search would lead me down a different path, however even I was taken aback by the mindless brutality of "Two guys one hammer."

What the fuck these two morons were trying to achieve was just beyond me. Of course the notoriety was maybe a motive but why kill random people filming the murders on a phone. Two of their clips had somehow ended up being leaked onto the internet, which had led to their arrest but still didn't explain why they had done it. As I read up on the case it seemed rumours circulated that although only two videos existed online these Ukrainian idiots were planning to sell up to forty snuff clips, which they may or may not have already made, to a rich western buyer. This once again confirmed the hypocrisy of this world as the demand for murder and death evolved beyond more standard media outlets.

Let's face it: if you are going to kill, at least do it for a reason and don't strike out at the first random person you come across. I had always felt bad that Nellie had killed Stinky Pete as there was no way he had deserved to die. Of course the unfortunate business of Father Conway had in many ways been far worse than that but at least I was now trying to address those demons. On the other hand I felt all my other kills were justified with a case being made for all of them to die. The way Nellie had pulled her gun on the old man in the street had proved she was coming unravelled and whether or not that was due to my infection was now debatable. Her journey was leading her down the same uncontrollable path I had been on and now it was important to give her focus by finding the two of us a more structured route to follow.

All the internet research had got me thinking and now it had become apparent that I too should document my story. There was no way I was stupid enough to film anything but a work of "so-called fiction" maybe yes. The proof was already there to be seen as I just had to think how many great books had shaped me and maybe this was my chance to aid this lost generation. It wouldn't be looking for absolution or forgiveness as what I wanted was a chance to tell my story, vindicate my actions and to of course most importantly educate.

I have always questioned the classification of fiction as I'm convinced that over half of the so-called "fictional" books I've read are surely based on true events and facts. This method of disguising the truth had given me my blueprint and now with my story almost done and the bare bones already in place all I needed was an ending to bring it home.

36.

Since the unfortunate business of Nellie breaking down in the street I had done my best to keep her happy. It was no surprise really that on the night in question she'd returned home in a mess heading straight to bed only to reappear in the morning as if nothing had happened. On one hand, you had to admire her mental strength to keep things bottled up but the other side of that particular coin was that we both knew her ability to hide emotion was now a fragile one. Eventually she would want to discuss what had transpired but I refused to push her and out of curiosity would wait to see how long it actually took to surface.

It had only taken three nights in the end. Slightly longer than I had anticipated but once again she was now opening up to me. The anticipation of this moment of her offloading had been building within me yet disappointingly now it seemed I no longer felt the same high as before. These outpourings were now leaving me feeling more bored rather than revitalised, still maybe it was a good thing proving my own emotions were now stabilising and I was winning back my own self-control.

"I don't know Lee, everything just seems so right but I can't be sure if it's actually me who controls my actions anymore?"

She was in a bad place, doubting herself as her ability to control the lust for killing was diminishing. I could understand where she was coming from as I too had taken that journey and it was fascinating watching from my ringside seat as someone else walked the same path.

If I was going to be documenting my story I would need to learn to express myself and now a chance was presenting itself. The present situation with Nellie was something I was convinced was a phase as it was one that I had now passed through and the similarities were there for all to see. Now it was important she understood that although our story was far from over there was a light at the end of the tunnel as each further day would prove.

It was now quite clear to me that I was very different and the way I talked to Nellie over the next couple of hours was testament to that. The lessons I had learnt during my transformation into the real me were now bearing fruit. She sat there captivated by my every word which was maybe an insight into how a preacher or politician must feel on a daily basis. Power is a lovely word but an even better one when you actually have it and can use it to manipulate, guide and influence. That night when we fucked it felt almost as if she was worshipping or paying homage to me as she fell under my spell like some little giddy teen might for a pop or rock idol.

The decision was made that we would seek out my ending with a yet-to-be-determined act of closure before heading into a self-imposed exile. Nellie's desire to fuck hadn't given us the chance to discuss what "exile" might mean for the two of us but now as I sat in the bath this morning the whole future ahead appeared so much brighter and clearer.

There would be plenty of time to discuss such things at a later date as my end plan was almost in place. First I would need to convince her to leave her job before selling up all our material belongings. We would draw out our savings closing our bank accounts then cross the sea or ocean to a new country and new start. I had always wanted to live in the mountains or by the sea, which would give me the opportunity, space and time to document my story in the fresh unpolluted air with the sun on my back. We would become self-sufficient living off the land, learning a new language, maybe it would even be time to procreate.

It had to be said I was starting to fall into that age-old trap of hope but this time I had no desire to fight it, so why the devil not believe? For years I had hated the whole idea, labelling it a pointless exercise yet here I was embracing it head on.

I had already calculated that on a disciplined budget I would have enough money to live work-free for over a year even in my expensive surroundings of the big city. Just imagine how far this money could stretch in a cheaper environment and how much more productively it could be put to use. Nellie had earned even more than I, meaning our combined funds could make these dreams a reality.

As my mind drifted it dawned on me that today my murder of Father Conway was now a week old. Of course it still saddened me but I also knew this would be the last time I lost control as his murder had snapped me out of a certain mindset. There was no doubt that I had been losing it but since that dark moment I had found a kind of peace or solace. My dreamless nights had once again returned making me believe that my crazy dream had been no more than a vision my playful and evolving mind had created.

To think now that I had chopped off my own toe seemed the actions of a madman but had also proved how fragile the human mind could be. Nellie of course was fighting her own battles and ones that I now believed I'd already won so triumphantly. If I needed proof I had control it had been confirmed by my prevention of her killing the old man and the stopping of a potentially far bigger incident downtown.

I still wanted to kill but now needed it to be to make a statement and not be in vain. In many ways the lives I had taken had already been statements just not public ones. I kind of regretted that Toby Johnson in particular had got away I mean imagine the media's reaction if they had known a vigilante was on the loose bringing his own brand of justice to the world. Of course in this day and age they would have lapped it up, making any murders we committed newsworthy and, as long as they were justified, creating the debate I craved. It would be easy to find other such low-lives through the internet but it was too late now. I wanted one last show of justice. Something that would make people sit up, ignite thinking and have them re-evaluating their lives.

"What about a group of politicians?"

Since arriving home from work Nellie had been brain

218

storming for a suitable target yet every idea we seemed to come up with had a counter argument. The whole terrorist attack phenomena which had been thrown at the world left few targets a cause couldn't be linked to. As much as politicians, neo-nazis, racists, religious fanatics, paedophiles and even reality TV stars were all worthwhile targets the media would mix those types of attack with a political agenda and that is not what we wanted.

There was the other school of thought. Why not attack the average Joe at a sporting event, pop concert or large public gathering to make a huge statement? Surely if you throw enough shit some will stick, so why not something more conventional? All these scenarios were flawed though, as they still involved too many people to handle, and once again would make it look like terrorism. It just needed to be smaller, something simpler.

Media coverage wasn't my main priority as that was a given and when I eventually put pen to paper the two worlds would come together to make a timeless statement. In the short term I just wanted to stimulate people's minds, to get them thinking so that years later they would be able to relive the events through my so-called work of fiction. What I actually was looking for was a domino effect, yes that was it, a domino effect.

"Nell, what we need is to find a group of people that just won't all die. I mean, in my humble opinion of your everyday Joe's maybe one in three I could deem worthless enough to kill. Now if you take a room of say, sixty people and then execute twenty, imagine the effect that would have on the forty that survived. This is where the domino effect comes in, those forty will spread your word like gospel as they will always be associated with the event thus keeping the story alive and spreading the word."

I wasn't sure she was completely following me but I was right. People always tended to talk more about their bad experiences than they did about the good ones, with death or murder maybe topping that particular list. So if you take a random group of people, killing one in three, the ones who survived would have quite a tale to tell. The important factor would be to use these victims as an example, exposing their flaws as the reasons they died. This is where the domino effect comes in, as the killings are food for thought, leaving those left living with a message and one that would quickly spread.

"I've got it, next Thursday at five o'clock."

She reached across to the other sofa retrieving her work bag then unbuckled it pulling out a paperback book that she passed to me.

"The Happy Buddha"
A book by Chuck Salimos

37

What kind of name was Chuck Salimos? I mean for crying out loud, it sounded completely made up and for me conjured up images of him being some sort of by-product of an illicit rendezvous between a low-class American and a Mexican whore. As funny as all that was I couldn't actually have claimed to have read Chucky's book but knew all about it. Basically it was Paulo Coelho's "The Alchemist" for a simpler generation; one looking for quick fixes and with low attention spans. Of course once a book like this seeps its way into the mainstream's consciousness it tends to infect it. In this case the infection hadn't so much come from the simplicity of the content but from how this book had become a must-have accessory.

This was a most familiar trait of this modern world as mere possessions turned into status symbols. The mobile phone and all the accessories that went with it now seemed to be top of that particular food chain but occasionally still something else would temporarily take its place. This book was doing exactly that, showing the insecurity of the human race as they tried to prove they weren't so superficial like everyone else.

These fucking herds of sheep had now even started laying down their Kindles etc. reverting back to the hard copy as it made them just so such more visible. Of course this bunch of narcissistic cunts had quickly realised that no one could see what you are reading when you're using some electronic device and suddenly the value of the book cover outshone the technology. The hypocrisy of it all as these masses showed off their little tiny books in a quest to look cool and not so shallow amongst their peers! To me the most ironic thing, and maybe what summed up this silly trend was that it was being done with a book that was nothing more than spiritualism for dummies. Saying that it did seem puzzling and slightly troubling that Nellie would have a copy.

"Please, like I would buy this shit, fuck off and don't insult my intelligence."

Nellie's answer soon made perfect sense as it seemed my ex boss was once again inflicting his new-found self onto the staff. The writer was an old school friend of his and little would he have known all those years ago this friendship was now potentially leading to some major homicide. Many copies of Mr Salimos' "The Happy Buddha" had been left in each department with the staff told to read them, which should surely have been classified as bullying in the work place.

"There is even a fucking sheet we have to sign once we've read it to prove we've completed the fucking task."

However much Nellie had complained this book and Mr Dilly's friendship with the writer had given us our opportunity for closure. A selection process had taken place by higher management with a small number of staff hand-picked to spend an evening in the company of Mr Happy Buddha himself. All this was to happen next Thursday in a place called The Vaults Wine Bar and I had a sneaky feeling there may be a couple of gate-crashers.

In many ways I couldn't believe that such a perfect target had fallen into our laps. One of the country's biggest financial firms and my ex employers were now right in our sights. The hypocrisy of the whole situation not only angered me but saddened me at the same time. I mean for fucks sake, how could the writer of this so-called spiritually arousing book sell his soul, meeting with a bunch of financiers and bankers?

What made it worse was that the small number who may actually have deserved to attend such an event would be overlooked as the invitation-only policy collected its select few. It was hard to think of more polar opposites really than the Happy Buddha and a huge financial institution yet it was a sign of the despicable times we were living in that they were coming together. I guess in many ways this showed the fragility of the world and how nothing really separated what was morally right and wrong.

With Nellie still on the inside it soon became apparent

that only thirty or forty would be in attendance, which for me was very manageable. The chosen few would undoubtedly be the more loathsome cocksuckers the office contained and the ones who so perfectly fitted the company profile. It was funny to think how they would be considering themselves so blessed or lucky looking forward to their big day, maybe even indulging in a bit of showing off. How wrong they would be as this stroke of luck was going to be backfiring on them big time turning this casual evening into their worst and bloodiest nightmare.

This whole adventure that started in a lift then had moved on to killing was now coming full circle, threatening to reach its climax. The endgame was going to take us to a new level as we would surely be at least tripling our body count in one sitting. Still this date with destiny was a week away and would require a lot of planning if it was to go smoothly.

Our plan of escape was to be crucial as these days of terrorism meant the police were well drilled and very much on the ball when it came to attacks on the public. Thankfully The Vaults was a small wine bar which I already knew and its lack of size made it very controllable. The place had always been very popular with a lot of my ex fellow work colleagues and no more than a five-minute walk from their office. Of course it would be essential to pay the venue a visit leaving no stone unturned as I established all points of escape and control.

It was regrettable that we had less time to plan than I would have liked but this opportunity was too big to turn down. Since meeting Nellie my life had gone through extremes with it either being everything or nothing. This last week would definitely be classified as a spike but all anticipation needed to be brought down a level as we required focus to complete this final act.

38.

The moment of truth was almost upon us as we sat and waited in the small park no more than a couple of minutes' walk from The Vaults. My mouth felt dry but I was very much in control of my emotions and I squeezed Nellie's hand to share my reassurance. She didn't need it, as over the last few days she had been anticipating the bloodshed and now just glowed with confidence.

Nellie had quit her job on the previous Friday and now seemed to be very much looking forward to a reunion with some ex work colleagues. This morning we had gone through the plan meticulously again and again with both of us stressing the importance of self-control as all the killings we were set to commit had to have purpose. Recklessness was something we just couldn't allow ourselves to be drawn into and all I could do was hope that Nellie was still on the same page as me.

Everything was in place and in only a few hours we would be far from here in another city, another country and about to start a new life. We had our train tickets and what was left of our belongings was waiting for us in a couple of the lockers at the train station. Pulling down my old battered baseball cap to keep out the sun I glanced at my watch, five more minutes and then it would all begin.

Our escape route was planned but after that we would leave it to the open road to decide our fate. Nellie's Heidi-fuelled childhood dreams meant she wanted to head straight towards the mountains and although I wasn't against the idea I felt it best to just go with the flow and see what would happen.

It was strange really but my desire to kill wasn't as lustful as it had once been. The lives I had already taken seemed to have somewhat quenched my thirst for killing, giving tonight's project an almost work-like feel. As I sat there waiting I knew that after today I would not take another life. This phase of my life was almost over having seen me grow through many ups and downs.

At times my emotions had confused me as I struggled to understand my mind as it had taken me down many strange yet wonderful twisting paths. However I now felt my potential was being reached meaning I was confident that I finally knew who I was and understood my purpose. In many ways I had always felt like some kind of angel yet with demons coursing through my veins driving me forward to answer the questions I posed. Well today those questions would be answered in full and this passage of my life completed. A fresh start is what I wanted and to arrive somewhere new where I could reinvent myself under my rules.

Snapping myself out of my daydreaming my mind focused back in on the present and the job at hand. In the scheme of things today was very important as it would be referenced for years, privately by today's survivors and more publicly first by the media and then when I eventually told my story. We would make an impression on this world and wanted people not only to discuss how these chosen few had been killed but also why. It would be an almighty statement against the way people chose to live these days and the modern world would be made to see its shameful side as I made examples of its flaws with every kill, it was time.

Quickly making our way across the park then down a short ally we found ourselves standing at the entrance to The Vaults, the doors were closed but not locked and we were greeted by a large sign:

Closed Until 19.00h for private function
Sorry for any inconvenience

It was now just coming up to five and the train we were due to catch was set to leave at seven-thirty giving us maybe two hours to achieve our goals. As we slipped inside the doors I removed a large chain and padlock from my backpack then proceeded to lock together the front doors from the inside. No-one would be getting in or out unless I said so and once they were secure I paused and looked at Nellie.

"You ready to do this?"

She smiled with the same air of confidence as earlier, which confirmed she was very much made for this moment, so with no more time to waste we made our way down the stairs. I liked omens and The Vaults wine bar as the name suggested was yet another basement bar with this particular theme recurring a lot in my life of late and nearly always in a positive manner.

As we turned around the final corner of the staircase we came together and kissed before stepping into the main bar area guns at the ready. The first impression would be crucial so I addressed my public.

"Good evening Ladies and Gentlemen, now I have your attention, no-one moves and not a fucking word!"

It was essential not to cause panic as the sight of the guns was now no doubt ably doing. The small crowd hadn't been expecting us so the first few seconds of shock temporarily froze them to the spot. Our guns were pointing straight at them and I raised my hand urging them to remain calm then began to speak as we moved menacingly forward towards them.

"It's all very simple, people; everyone just needs to remain fucking calm because any sudden movements and I will turn this place into the fucking Wild West."

It was human nature to surrender when faced with such poor odds and as soon as the first person raised their hands the rest predictably followed suit. Nellie gestured to the bartenders to join the crowd, following them across the room with her gun as they made the short journey from behind the bar to the public area. We were totally on our game and phase one was over but now complete control needed to be established.

"Okay very good people, now everybody needs to kick away their chairs then interlock their fingers placing them on top of their heads, that's everyone except you."

I pointed to one of the bartenders whose face filled with

226

complete horror as he suddenly became centre of attention.

"Please don't kill me sir."

I could feel the fear and desperation in his voice as I gestured for him to move forward but he needn't have worried as I had no beef with this type of worker ant.

"Don't worry Junior, the bartender never dies, just do what I say and then that's the way it stays. So no silent alarms and no wannabe hero moments then you have my word you walk out of here breathing, now what's your name?"

The young man was called Mick and judging by his accent was obviously not from these parts. It was amazing really that the way he spoke now guaranteed his safety, also meaning my domino effect theory would now travel overseas where his part in today's story would have the potential to influence thousands. I instructed him to fetch a bin bag from behind the bar then to collect all handbags and mobile phones. It was funny really watching him filling the black bag as these morons suddenly seemed more relaxed. It seemed they had all misread the situation as they now presumed incorrectly they were part of a robbery. How wrong they were.

My preparation for this moment had been perfect as two days earlier I had stood in this very spot enquiring on making a similar style booking to that of today. The layout had been just as I was expecting and due to the intimate nature of the venue, easy to control. There must have been close to thirty people, some I knew by name but the majority not, which didn't really matter, it was time to set out our stall.

"Okay, I am sure a few of you here today may recognise me and I too see a few familiar faces, so hello to you and all that shit. Anyways, just to clear up any lingering doubts, we are both ex-employees of your present employer and yes, I am the one who did the stabbing with the letter opener."

My words sent a wave of unease through the crowd instantly visible in the expressions that suddenly fell across the majority of their faces. A few gave out whimpers and cries as they now realised that they may be in for a little more trouble than they had originally thought. I had already spotted my ex-boss the minute I'd walked in and of course was always expecting him to be here and now he was cowering at the back trying to remain out of sight, which was fucking typical of the man. He would make an excellent place to start so I deliberately started to stare in his direction until finally catching his eye.

"William, William Dilly is that you?"

He points to himself, which is quite frankly a futile exercise as he desperately hopes I may have mistaken him for someone else. What a fucking idiot, as if after all those fucking months working under his command I would ever forget his ugly face, this was not a man, this was a rodent.

"Come on Billy, don't be shy, come on down, I'm waiting."

I signal for him to join me and slowly he starts to push his way through the crowd to the front. As he makes his way forward a few fellow colleagues pat him on the back obviously trying to reassure our Mr Dilly that everything is going to be just fine, cunts. Finally he reaches me and is almost in tears shaking his head as he mouths the word "Please." Putting my finger to my lips to quiet him I then turn him to face the crowd putting my arm around his large shoulders. As I go to speak I can actually feel him physically shaking with fear.

"The thing I like most of all about this man who is my ex-boss is, let me think......"

I pause before whipping the gun up under his chin and blow his brains out the top of his head. His body instantly goes limp and I allow it to slip from my grasp hitting the floor with a deep thud. Suddenly several people start to scream. Releasing another bullet into the ceiling gets their attention as I turn the gun back in their direction then once again raise my finger to my lips asking for silence, which not surprisingly I get.

"As I was saying, the thing I like most, sorry, that should be past tense now, so, the thing I liked most about my ex-boss was, absolutely nothing, the man was a complete cunt."

The combination of Billy's brains being removed from his head and my kind words were just too much for a few. A realism filled the air as maybe four or five people started to cry and one elderly lady almost fainted only to be hoisted onto a nearby chair. I signalled to the bartender to get her a drink yet not once did we drop our guns keeping everyone very much in our eyeline.

"For fucks sake, why all the crying and screaming? Don't waste your fucking tears and pity on him, for crying out loud. This man was no more than a manipulating fuck, who only ever thought about himself. A daddy's boy, a lazy, useless piece of shit. Anyway, the good news is, now he's dead the odds of you living have just got a whole lot better."

The effect of my words still lingers in the air and they have hardly had a chance to sink in as a voice speaks up.

"Is this all really necessary? Surely there is already enough death and killing in this world. Let us find a solution, my friend, before it truly gets out of hand."

I scan the crowd to work out where these words have come from but don't have to wait long as a scruffy looking man dressed in jeans, a tweed jacket and Happy Buddha T-shirt pushes his way to the front. He stops a metre in front of everyone else with a white handkerchief tucked into one of his raised hands.

"I think it's pretty safe to say you must be Mr Happy Buddha himself, how the devil are you, Chucky?"

As the words leave my mouth Nellie takes five steps forward and punches him hard in the stomach.

"I fucking hate your book; it's a patronizing piece of shit!"

He falls to his knees struggling to keep his hands in the air as she spits on him then presses her gun to the side of his head. A few cries of "no" ring out but soon stop as my eyes scan the crowd looking for any objectors, causing everyone to fall silent again.

"Not him Nellie, I have a job for our little writer friend."

Just seeing him there knelt on the floor made me decide I would be a lot happier if everyone was on their knees. Amazing how persuasive a gun can be as in a matter of seconds I have everyone in three neat lines all kneeling in front of us. It gives the effect of paying homage but in truth they look pathetic with their hands still clamped to the top of their heads. I drag Chuck to his feet and after using him to move the furniture that obscures my view sit him at a table to our left. I had already got him to retrieve his laptop from the top table and it now sits open in front of him, ready for action.

"Okay Chuck, I don't expect today's events to be the plot for the Happy Buddha 2 unless you're thinking of a major change of direction. Anyways, you need to start writing as I want nothing that happens here to slip your mind. You have to remember out of every adversity there are always winners so if you stay alive your fame goes through the roof my friend."

I had no desire to kill this man as to be honest his intentions seemed good if not slightly misguided. Also, it would be a big plus to read about today's show from another perspective, in fact I was already looking forward to it. However, the clock was already ticking and I needed to get this show on the road.

"OK people, this is how it is going to work. I will keep it simple, basically some of you are going to live and some of you are going to die."

39.

By my estimations we still had around seventeen bullets between us and although I didn't intend to use them all, the ones we would needed to be deemed worthwhile. Every kill would be punctuated with a reason giving the victims martyr-like status and Chucky something positive and creative to write about.

The selection process was almost going to be God-like and it was a powerful feeling deciding people's destinies. I firmly believed that one in every three people was worthy of execution so with that rule in mind at least 10 more people in this room today would die. Still these decisions needed to be made carefully and not in haste so I turned to the bartender.

"Mick, go fetch me a bottle of Irish whiskey from behind the bar, Bushmills if you've got it. Nell, you want a drink?"

As I looked over to her for an answer that recent familiar feeling of dread once again raised its ugly head; Nellie was really pissed it seemed and had what could only be described as a general air of displeasure about her.

"For fucks sake Lee, let's get a fucking move on. This is just such fucking bullshit! I know you love your dramatic pauses all about pop culture seven deadly sins shit, but come on! Forget this making fucking statements bollocks, all these cunts are guilty, look, I will fucking show you."

I wasn't going to stop her as she needed to vent and maybe killing someone would allow her to settle down again. In many ways she'd been right as my desire to draw upon the seven deadly sins was more Hollywood's Se7en than Dante, still I wanted to make statements. I watched as she moved swiftly between the lines of people kneeling in front of me before stopping at a blonde middle-aged lady wearing a flowery dress. Grabbing her hair from behind she pulled back her head before resting the gun in the centre of her forehead.

"This evil bitch wears white stilettos to work."

She pulls the trigger, which sends a shot ringing out, instantly killing her chosen victim. Then in an almost callous manner which seems ridiculous in the context of the moment she allows the body quite deliberately to fall to the floor face first. I don't say a thing and watch as now she looks down in horror at her shoes, which are now covered in blood.

"Fuck!"

Her shouting was almost as ear-splitting as the gunshot but then composing herself she quite causally wiped her dirty shoes across the dead woman's back. I needed to say something.

"Come on Nellie, we're meant to be making an example of these people and fashion disaster isn't really a reason to die."

As I spoke people were now starting to cry as an atmosphere of panic once again filled the room. She looked at me and then turning from side to side started to walk back in my direction stopping just before she reached the front line of our captives.

"Okay, you want fucking reasons, I will give you fucking reasons, what about one of your personal favourites and ticking one of your silly little seven deadly sins boxes. Ladies and gentlemen, I give you gluttony!"

She doesn't even give me half a chance to answer before once again raising the gun, this time to the back of a fat woman's head letting a shot off leaving her face a bloody mess. As the body topples forward I can see the damage the exit wound has left, as where there once had been her right eye there is now a bloody hole.

"Come on please, these people are innocent they don't deserve to die."

For all of Chuck's obvious faults you had to commend him for his bravery but speaking up may not have been the wisest of moves at that particular moment. As the wailing intensified Nellie turned her attention back to him raising the gun and pointing it in his direction. Fuck this was spinning out of control.

"Come on Nellie, fucking chill will you, we talked about this, now come on, let's have a drink, stop just for a second please!"

She didn't lower her gun but instead stepped over the dead body that lay in front of her positioning herself perfectly for a clear shot at Chuck.

"How come he gets a fucking pass? He's the worst of the lot, making money from spiritualism and giving Zen-style talks to this bunch of cunts. Come on Lee, this fucking hypocrite deserves to die, maybe more than anyone else."

She had a point and I glanced at Chuck, who was still sat behind his laptop now with his hands raised, looking quite concerned.

"But I don't make money from my books, all profits go to Tibet, we are trying to build a school for the poor children, didn't you read the foreword of my book? And as for today I was doing a favour for William, we went to school together, that's all, and he put up the original investment to get me started so this was meant to be a thank you."

Nellie took a deep breath trying to take in Chuck's rather rushed and nervous attempt at self-preservation. She smiled lowering her gun but before we had a chance to speak turned on the spot shooting a bald man square in the face. This time hysteria did break out as people started to scream at the sight of yet another dead body. One man whose face was now coated with blood went to stand in what was an obvious moment of panic only for Nellie to take two steps to her right and smash him in the face with the butt of her gun. She stood and watched him as first he stumbled then fell but she wasn't finished there. Walking to the front she now took centre stage, standing at my side and again raising her gun at the now cowering crowd then shouting.

"SHUT. THE FUCK. UP!"

It was more the tone than the level of her voice that had the required affect as a silence fell over the room. A fair few were still crying, which was understandable seeing that in the space of less than five minutes three people had been murdered in front of them. The man Nellie had hit was now back upright, kneeling again after a younger man next to him had helped him back into position. I caught his eye, giving him a reassuring smile trying to convey that his good deed would save him from my wrath, however from Nellie's I couldn't be so sure. She just stood there scanning the faces no doubt trying to decide who would be next as she casually reloaded her gun.

"How about that drink now Lee?"

I nodded to the Mick, who quickly headed behind the bar no doubt in need of a drink himself. I was pretty sure he would do nothing silly especially after Nellie's demonstration of power. She clicked her gun shut again then turned to me and smiled.

"OK, the first one wasn't just her shoes although that still was a good enough reason. She is or was the head of the payroll department and I know for a fact that dead fuck screwed one of my ex workmates over his holidays. The second one was what it was, gluttony, that one was for you babe and your seven little deadly sins shit. As for the third, I could hear him praying! Why pray when there is nobody listening, what a thick cunt, you know how it is? I fucking hate religion."

With a shrug of the shoulders she was done and I couldn't imagine how her little explanation was making those who still survived feel. I needed to restore some order and to move the dead bodies quickly as pools of blood were already starting to form and flow across the floor. I turned to Mick's barman colleague who was kneeling at his side with the large black bin bag full of phones and bags sat in front of him.

"What's your name?"

He looked away pretending he thought I was addressing someone else then after a slight tension-filled pause looked up in my direction.

I was pleased to find that like Mick he too was from overseas, the story of our work today was indeed set to travel far and wide. Warren was his name and a big lad he was too with a funny little beard which made him look older than he probably was. With the help of Chuck the two men cleared the dead bodies to one side of the room, each one leaving its own snail-like blood trail as they were dragged across the floor.

While all this was going on Mick had returned with a bottle of Bushmills pouring a shot for Nellie and then one for me. We knocked our glasses together downing them in one then not allowing the whiskey time to settle in my system I poured myself another. Downing that I once again looked across at the three lines of people on their knees in front of me. Some were still quite shaken up while others were now still and it seemed just lost in thought. A pick-me-up was needed and I turned to Warren, who was wiping his bloody hands on his trousers as he and Mick both returned to their spots kneeling.

"What's the most expensive liquor you got here Warren?"

Of course it was brandy, it always fucking is which I could never understand as brandy always tastes like shit to me, poor man's whiskey. It felt cold drinking in front of these poor souls and I wasn't a complete monster. These people at least deserved a drink if they were going to die or have to watch others do so. Undeniably it would make little difference in saving lives but at least the alcohol would relax them, maybe take the edge off, also bringing Nellie down a notch.

"Okay boys, crack open that expensive shit, one shot for

everyone, on the house of course."

As the two bartenders stood and made their way to the bar I felt the urge to kill returning. Maybe it was the whiskey or Nellie's little show but something had sparked up my system again. The catalyst was irrelevant and I pointed to a middle-aged man with a beard wearing a suit but more importantly a Mickey Mouse tie.

"You with the Disney tie get up and come here."

The temporary air of peace my ordering of the drinks may have brought to the room was lost again as he slowly made his way forward, head bowed, finally coming to a stop a couple of metres in front of me. Killing against crimes of fashion seemed pretty fair in this case but Nellie had already covered that base. Anyway, after her random killing spree I needed to give these people some hope, yes I would give this man a chance to save his life, Mickey Mouse tie or not.

"Well to be honest, with you just wearing that fucking God-awful tie means you should really die. But no, I am going to give you a chance to save your worthless life, now get on your fucking knees!"

As Nellie covered me I reached for our backpack pulling out the sawn-off shotgun and breaking it open to make sure it was loaded. The two cartridges smiled up at me as I clicked the gun shut, the noise making the man kneeling in front of me look up in pure terror.

"Please, no, I don't want....."

I raise the sawn-off and point it straight at him to quiet him, which of course it does. At this range this gun would surely have the power and capability to blow his head clean off of his shoulders, well a part of it anyhow, I guess time would tell how much.

"Sshh, no one here wants to hear you beg, it's just so

236

undignified, plus I am throwing you a fucking bone champ, so at least try to be a little bit fucking grateful."

He starts to cry as the rest of the room either cover their eyes or look away. Once again I hear a few cries and whimpers so turn my attention away from the stricken man in front of me and back to the main room.

"Come on people it's show time, let's get ready to rumble and all that bollocks, so if anyone looks away they will be next to share a bit of one on one with my double-barrelled friend. Chucky, I hope you're getting this baby as there could be a big scene in act two."

Everyone looks front and centre as I raise my weapon giving them a wink as I do so before turning my attention back to Mr Mickey Mouse tie.

"Pop quiz motherfucker, and it's simple, you get the question right you live, you don't you die, can't really say fairer than that, right?"

Everyone is now staring at me and I can feel the tension building. I don't really like this guy to be honest and would love to decapitate him but that would hardly be a statement. Fuck, I guess Nellie's bloody start is rubbing off on me, fuck this, it´s question time.

"Ok motherfucker, today's chosen subject is music and what I want to know is: which famous rock star´s name is an anagram of oral sex?"

Unless he's a wiz at anagrams he has no chance of knowing this as he strikes me as the Genesis, Coldplay-listening type. And we're not talking Peter Gabriel. Right I will give him ten seconds then we'll see what this bad boy can really do. One, two...

"Axl Rose, he's not one of my favourite singers, I'm more of a Bowie man really.

Fuck me, where the fuck were you sitting when I was working? I knew I should have gone with the Tupelo question and as he looks up at me I have no choice but to lower my gun and address the room.

"Never judge a book by its cover ladies and gentlemen, our badly dressed friend here has just saved his own life, now get the fuck back in line before I change my mind and never, I repeat never wear that tie in public again."

Holding my hand out I help him to his feet and as he scampers his way back across the floor a few people start to clap. Nellie and I simultaneously raise our weapons pointing them again in their direction, which puts an end to their little celebration. I feel a strange mixture of both anger and shock but fair play to him; he got the question right so I had to let him go.

My little pop quiz has distracted me so now no more let off's; I need to weed out the evil ones and make my statements then get the fuck out of here. The bartenders momentarily distract me as they return with two large trays of brandy and I give them a nod as a sign of permission to hand them out.

It was interesting watching the body language as the shots were delivered; some sipping at their drinks while others downed them in one. Enough of this bollocks.

"Okay motherfuckers, no more of this shit! Drink them or lose them. Mick, Warren collect the fucking glasses and leave them over there, then back to your fucking knees, it's time to crank this up a bit!"

Thirty seconds of what can be best described as desperation passed as everyone in front of me rushed to finish their drinks. Nellie would be getting the urge to strike again so I needed to select someone quickly. Fuck it, I poured myself another whiskey and looked at her.

"You do it, fucking pick anyone you want but bring them here."

She smiled as I picked up my shot and downed it then watched her once again stroll between the lines as the bartenders returned to their places. The theatre was great; I always loved the drama real human life could bring to an occasion with its lovely jagged edge. She continued to slowly parade between what were all now potential victims then stopped behind everyone at the back of the room before stepping forward and kicking a very nondescript Asian man in the back causing him to fall forward.

"This motherfucker."

I gestured for him to come out front and like the man before him he slowly made his way to me with his head bowed.

"Please no music questions for me."

I had no intentions of doing so, the pop quiz time was over and now it was questions of how he had lived his life that would save him or not.

"Don't worry no more pop quizzes, this is all about morals from here on in, now you got ten seconds to tell me why I shouldn't kill you, go."

He had a panicked look on his face as his breath suddenly quickened dramatically. I raised my gun again making sure he was looking straight down one of the barrels.

"Please I am a father with four young children, please don't take away their daddy."

Four fucking kids, what the fuck was up with this guy? Was he for real?

"Why the fuck would you have four fucking children? Isn't the planet overpopulated enough for you? What is it, are you a fucking catholic, silly question, obviously not, okay you're just a lazy fucker then. Better start saying your prayers because I am about to rebalance your disgusting reckless procreation."

239

For some reason I didn't want to waste the sawn-off on this guy so handed it to Nellie then pulled my handgun from my belt, he had three seconds then I would blow a hole in this over-populating motherfucker's head.

"Please, I only ever wanted two but the second time my wife was pregnant she had triplets, I'm sorry, please I promise I'm a good father and a good man."

What the fuck, at this rate I wasn't killing anyone, wait, if he wants to live someone else has to die, nice. I pull him to his feet and face him to the crowd.

"Okay champ, you get to fucking live but now you pick someone to die."

Without hesitation he points to a young woman, who at once starts screaming as Nellie walks across the room and grabs her from behind covering her mouth with her hand. I turn back to my new-found Asian friend and pose the obvious question.

"I think we are all a bit curious, so why the fuck this bitch?"

He looks across the room where Nellie still has her hand over the woman's mouth but also now her gun resting at the side of her head. Pausing he looks straight at her with a look of pure hatred then goes into a rant.

"She is a harlot and a tart, this woman stole my job because she fucks the bosses, that also is ironically the reason she is here today as she was fucking Mr Dilly. Fuck you Anita, you are nasty a woman and a slag."

His thick what I guess was an Indian accent along with his choice words gave his whole little tirade a comedy feel. Anyway his choice was made and any right of reply the little harlot Anita had was lost as Nellie pulled the trigger leaving her brains plastered on the nearby wall. Looks like my seven deadly sins were being covered now as this would come under wrath and greed I guess, who gives a shit, that was some great theatre there.

I go to laugh out loud but stop as the phone behind the bar starts to ring making me want to shoot it for ruining my moment.

40.

It was quite surreal as the rings of the phone filled the room acting as a momentary distraction and creating an eerie silence amongst all present. Taking a deep breath to calm myself I filled our shot glasses and passed one to Nellie with us downing their contents in one in perfect synchronization. Returning my glass to the table Nellie caught my eye as she looked so radiant, majestic even as if, like me in the past, the whole taking of lives had revitalised her. The phone continued to ring but it wasn't that on my mind as suddenly I had the urge to fuck Nellie. She detected it too stepping in close, her hand finding my hard penis trapped oh so frustratingly inside my trousers. I wanted to take her here and now bending her over the table, knowing I would have no problem performing in front of this captive audience. After all it was our animal instinct to fuck, but that fucking telephone was starting to drive me nuts. I pointed my gun in its direction, pretending to shoot it before redirecting it back onto the main room. Maybe I would fuck her and kill someone at the same time, what a rush that would be.

"Do you want me to answer that phone?"

I look across at Warren, who now had the look of someone who instantly regretted opening his mouth. Nellie however appeared a little more upset that our intimate moment has been interrupted, beating me to the punch.

"No, I think we are quite capable of dealing with the fucking phone ourselves, because we're not fucking morons!"

Nellie released my cock from her grip then kissing me tenderly on the lips grabbed the sawn-off shotgun and headed behind the bar. She quickly reached the phone picking it up and holding it to her mouth before starting to shout down the line.

"WILL YOU JUST FUCK OFF!"

Angrily she replaced the handset onto its wall mounting then taking a backward step swung the shotgun at the phone smashing it with all her might.

Suddenly the room was no longer filled with hypnotic telephone rings but with music and bizarrely Hot Chocolate's "You Sexy Thing."

She had obviously hit or triggered something to set off the sound system with this bizarre turn of events obviously tickling her as she now burst into laughter. It was hardly Tarantino but still created a strange sort of tension as Nellie now climbed onto the bar top and began dancing in a deliberately over-the-top manner, gun in hand.

To be fair she seemed to be enjoying herself and proving the personal point to me that those who can dance always know how to fuck. A good thirty seconds of gyrating hips suddenly came to a halt as she jumped off the bar pointing her gun at the two bartenders.

"Will one of you fucking cunts please turn this shit off as its quite frankly repulsive."

Warren was the first to react heading behind the bar hitting a button that instantly cut the music, sending us back to a thankfully shit-music -free zone. As he made his way back from behind the bar Nellie flipped out, grabbing him by the throat and jamming the sawn-off into his stomach.

"Who the fuck did you nod to? I fucking saw you."

She doesn't even give him a chance to answer before smashing him in the face with the gun; she was getting good at that. He remains standing but blood is now streaming from his nose as Nellie turns and looks across the room and starts to yell.

"Fuck!!!!!! The fucking toilets!! There must be someone in there."

I instantly wished the ground would suck me up as on our arrival I had neglected to check the toilets, what a fucking idiot! My aura of control left me as it dawned on me that I had been so careless. The adrenaline of the moment had swept me up and how much that was now going to cost us would depend on who may or may not be in the toilets.

Nellie was already on it, moving across the room handing off the sawn-off before drawing her handgun and coming to rest against the wall slightly to the right of the toilet door. Pausing for a second she carefully peered through the glass of the door, obviously seeing something as she readied herself for action.

"Don't you take your gun off these fucking people Lee, there is someone in there, but I can't make out who, so I'm going in."

She disappeared from view then what seemed like a couple of screams were followed by a gunshot. There was a moment of silence as nothing happened then suddenly Nellie burst back into the room holding a large-breasted lady by the hair, her gun resting under her chin, fuck, it was Annie.

"There were fucking two of them, the other one tried to be a heroine so I shot her in the face, so she's dead and I think you already know who this bitch is."

Nellie forced Annie down onto the floor then pressed the gun hard into the back of her head, causing her to wince in pain. It was Annie alright and she was even wearing that white trouser suit which I could now see was coated with blood. Fuck, this was turning into a fucking disaster.

"Nellie, check her for a phone."

Annie was now on all fours with Nellie who was still holding the gun to the back of her head. Clicking her fingers Nellie held out her hand.

"You heard the man bitch, give me your fucking mobile."

244

Annie pushed herself up onto her knees then reached into her inside pocket pulling out her mobile and handing it over her shoulder to Nellie.

"Check her recent calls."

I was frantic as I watched from close by, carefully trying not to let this unfortunate business distract me from those captives that still knelt before me. Taking a step back Nellie starts to go through the phone then froze looking up at me before throwing it across the room.

"Fuck! She called the police, fifteen minutes ago."

Our dreams were in tatters as I already knew it was too late, the phone behind the bar must have been them trying to make contact. I picked up the bottle of whiskey off the table next to me pulling the stopper out with my teeth then took a long drink before throwing it across the room. As it smashed against the side of the bar I stepped forward letting off my gun.

"FUCK! FUCK! FUCK!"

I didn't even know who I'd killed but with every "fuck!" I'd pulled the trigger and now three bodies lay at my feet. The screams were deafening as people tried to take cover behind each other, hoping they weren't next. Chuck was now under a table and the bartenders were crawling towards the bar as everyone tried to find shelter from the onslaught. It didn't matter anymore as it was over and I turned to Nellie, who was now crying but still pointing the gun at Annie.

"Don't cry babe, it isn't over yet."

Of course I knew that wasn't true as the police would surely be waiting for us outside if not already on their way in. I walked over to Nellie and kissed her but it seemed Annie was making her last stand.

245

"Don't kiss him bitch, kill this motherfucker, he feels nothing for you and fucked me when you were together."

I can tell Nellie is confused as she pushes me away then slowly raises her gun, pointing it this time in my direction.

"Is it true Lee, you fucked her when were together?"

Annie starts to laugh but soon stops as Nellie punches her hard in the face splitting her lip as she slumps down onto her front. She is still conscious but only just and now rolling onto her side starts to spit blood onto the floor. Nellie still doesn't lower the gun.

"Don't be so fucking silly Nell; she is trying to play you, save her own sorry ass. Now come on, kill this bitch and let's get the fuck out of here as we may still have time."

My answer was so cool and collected that she had no choice than to believe me and as she lowered her gun gestured for me to pass her the sawn-off. I knew what she wanted to do and smiled as I handed it over as Annie once again spoke up, this time struggling to get her words out.

"Don't believe him, he's fucking crazy, kill him!"

Using her foot Nellie pins Annie down onto her back but quite commendably she still hasn't given up and tries to reach out, holding up her hand as Nellie points the sawn-off down at her.

"Fuck you, you jealous cunt, relationships are built on trust and this is my man, go to hell bitch!"

The powerful blast blows straight through Annie's outstretched hand then destroys maybe ninety percent of her head, showering the two of us in blood. Reaching out I take Nellie's hand and then dropping her weapon she throws her arms around me.

"I love you Lee Shelton."

I held her tightly looking over her shoulder and across the room. Everyone was still there as they had nowhere to go and were trapped as we still stood between them and their escape route to the so-called safety of the outside world. Some had managed to hide behind upturned tables but all still cowered with fear, waiting to see what would happen next.

As I looked over them I felt a kind of guilt that I had lied to Nellie when Annie had exposed the truth. Maybe I had deserved to die at this point and Annie would have been justified in condemning and sentencing me to my death. Life wasn't like that though and anyway it was all too late now as my lying would ensure my life would be extended at least for the short-term future.

It was time to make a move and I pushed Nellie gently off me kissing her and turned to face the crowd for the last time. There would be no more killing today, I needed these people to tell my story and although events hadn't gone as planned I still felt we had managed to get my point across reasonably well.

"That's all folks, you're the lucky fuckers, but just remember God didn't save you I did, adios."

I throw a salute in their direction then leading Nellie by the hand grab our backpack and head towards the stairs. I stop as I see Chuck still hiding under the table where his laptop sits and making my fingers into the shape of gun pretend to shoot him.

"Just remember that death is not the end, it's only the beginning. and don't forget to wear that T-shirt when you're on CNN."
He smiles, which is a kind of odd but then I guess he knows today will be a major publicity coup for him maybe meaning they would get to build that school after all.

As we make our way up the stairs I already know that the

end is close and stop just before we turn the final corner to give Nellie a long kiss. She takes my head in her hands looking me in the eyes with a kind of sadness and I smile to comfort her then we turn the final corner.

The moment we enter the foyer I instantly catch a glimpse of the police set-up outside, waiting for our exit. We both react quickly taking cover one on each side of the front doors and more importantly out of sight of the police. I look across to Nellie, who looks broken and a million miles away from the shining, radiant beast of earlier.

There was a hopelessness about the moment as we stood there looking at each other for maybe the last time knowing we had failed. There would be no trip to the sea or the mountains nor a new life and any hope of raising a family were now all but over. Maybe meeting her had been the best thing to have ever happened to me but I still had a will to live.

"Promise me you will never lie to me Lee."

She was starting to well-up again no doubt thinking about Annie's words and maybe questioning me for the final time.

"I promise."

There is no point in upsetting her now and just one thing left to do which will prove to her we are in this together until the end. I pull my gun out of my belt and point it to the side of my head.

"I don't want to go to prison Nell, I just can't live without you so come on, let's end this now looking into each other's eyes, let us die together as martyrs."

Her weeping now turns to full-on crying as she pulls her gun out, and mimicking me, rests the muzzle against her temple.

"That is the most romantic thing anyone has ever said to me. I love you Lee, you're the best thing that ever happened to me, you complete me."

She smiles, giving me a nod.

"I love you Nellie and you complete me too. Goodbye my love, after three: one, two, three."

I watch as she pulls the trigger blowing a hole straight through her head leaving blood running down the glass of the front door. There's nothing romantic about the moment as her body falls ungracefully landing in a crude heap propped up only by the wall. I wasn't going to die like this and lower my gun for the last time, once again I'd lied but she'd had to go, at least happily knowing I had finally told her that I loved her. My story would have a better ending now that she'd taken her own life as people would feel sorry for me losing my soulmate with the media just drinking that shit right up.

Holding my gun out I drop it in full view of the police outside then slowly step out from the corner with my hands raised, sinking to my knees. As soon as I'm in their eyeline I can see them with their guns trained on me still keeping a safe distance. This wasn't to be the end but more a fresh start as now I had a generation to inspire and a story to tell, they would have their leader and I would be their king.

THE END

Note from the author

I will never be the most talented writer and really have little desire to be famous. The reasons I chose to write are because I enjoy it and find the whole process very therapeutic. At school I suffered from mild dyslexia and always had a problem with both reading and writing but this should never be a deterrent.

Every English essay I wrote as a student was always failed for bad spelling, missing words and awful grammar but this all changed at fifteen. I sat my English O level with little hope of passing but as always wrote the story with my normal vigour and enjoyment. I can't remember exactly what I wrote about that day although I think it may have been a story revolving around village cricket for some reason. A few months later the result came through and to my great surprise I ended up with a pass, a C grade. This was the first time I had ever got anything other than a fail at English and still shocks me even now as I write this.

In hindsight, I have always had the ability to tell a good story and I actually think that day it counted for something. I have no doubt that my spelling, grammar and mistakes were the same as always, as they still are today but something happened. I am convinced *whoever* read that paper enjoyed it and looked beyond my flaws to mark me on its content. Whoever you are, thank you because that pass has always stayed with me giving me the self-belief that one day I would write something which I now have.

Of course writing this book wouldn't have been possible without the help, inspiration and support of several people so I would like to thank in no particular order and for a variety of different reasons Steve, Bob, Claudia, John, Fiachra, Chris, Claus, Ian, Carolina, Lily, Mazy and of course my parents.

23294709R00143

Printed in Great Britain
by Amazon